FINDING
HOME

FINDING HOME

A Timber Creek Novel

HUNTER LYNN

FINDING HOME
A TIMBER CREEK NOVEL

This is a work of fiction. All of the characters, names, incidents, organizations, and dialogue in this novel are either the products of the author's imagination or are used fictitiously.

iUniverse books may be ordered through booksellers or by contacting:

iUniverse
1663 Liberty Drive
Bloomington, IN 47403
www.iuniverse.com
844-349-9409

Because of the dynamic nature of the Internet, any web addresses or links contained in this book may have changed since publication and may no longer be valid. The views expressed in this work are solely those of the author and do not necessarily reflect the views of the publisher, and the publisher hereby disclaims any responsibility for them.

FINDING HOME
Editing by Amber Koontz
Cover Design by Kelly Matz

ISBN: 978-1-6632-2625-9 (sc)
ISBN: 978-1-6632-2624-2 (e)

Library of Congress Control Number: 2021914807

Print information available on the last page.

iUniverse rev. date: 10/14/2021

To Aaron,
My love, my light, my home.

To Stacy,
My shining star in the universe.

PROLOGUE

Gavin Taylor stepped off the mound and walked its perimeter. It was his ritual. He circled the mound, scuffed his cleats against the dirt, and knelt down to let it run through the fingers of his left hand. This rite helped him focus on the task at hand and not the fifty-five thousand fans, prime time television cameras, and a season on the line.

"You got this," he muttered to himself. The stadium music had stopped, but the fans were riled-up, eager to watch him fail.

The umpire tossed Gavin the ball, and he took his mark as Anthony Johnson, the Dodger's cleanup hitter, stepped up to the plate. Gavin bent down, locking his gaze on his catcher's fingers. The catcher pointed his index finger at the ground beneath him, signaling a fastball, and crouched inside.

After winding up to throw, Gavin released what he felt was a solid pitch. The ball smacked inside Xavier's glove.

"Ball."

Gavin shook his head in disbelief and directed a caustic smile in the umpire's direction. Xavier Hernandez, his catcher and close friend, threw the ball back to him and settled back into his crouch. Johnson took his position in the box. The sign from Xavier was for a slider on the outside corner of the plate. Gavin checked first base, anticipating a potential double steal, set, and delivered the next pitch.

"Ball two," the umpire barked.

The fans were rabid, taunting him with merciless abandon. A 2-0 count to the home team's second-best hitter. No outs. He needed to shift the momentum with this pitch.

Xavier locked eyes with Gavin and signaled for him to calm down. Gavin took a deep, centering breath, and Xavier called for another slider.

No, Gavin thought, *I need a fast ball*. He shook his head, and Xavier flashed the sign again. He shook it off once more. Xavier signaled for a fastball, and Gavin nodded. Adrenaline pumping, Gavin wound up and threw the ball with everything he had.

CRACK! The crowd was on their feet, willing the ball to keep traveling. Gavin watched as it soared down the line with his hands clasped behind his head.

At the last second, the ball hooked to the left, just foul. The fans groaned in unison, and Gavin breathed a sigh of relief.

"Time!"

"Dammit," Gavin said under his breath as Xavier jogged to the mound.

"Carly here tonight?" the veteran catcher asked.

Gavin motioned behind the third base dugout, where his wife, Carly, was seated. She was wearing her Padres cap backwards, as she always did, and her long, raven-colored hair was pulled over one shoulder. Carly's bright blue eyes and huge smile radiated pride for her man. She'd been in the stands cheering him on since high school. His wife was his foundation, the rock from which he drew his strength.

"Do it for her," Xavier said. He smacked the ball into Gavin's glove. "Pendejo, don't shake off another sign. This is what I do. You just make sure the ball finds my glove." He jogged back behind home plate to a chorus of boos from displeased fans.

Gavin settled in. His fingers rotated around the ball hidden in his glove. He wound up and hurled the ball towards home plate.

Foul. It was now a 2-2 count. Xavier signaled for another sinker, and Gavin delivered. Inexplicably, the batter froze in place and watched the pitch sail by.

"Strike three!"

The next hitter was worth every penny the Dodgers had invested in him. Xavier called for a slider and Gavin delivered. "Strike one!" The second pitch was a sinker called for the strike zone. Gavin felt good when he released it, but his trajectory was too low. The ball skipped against the dirt at home plate and bounced off Xavier's glove, rolling to the backstop. The runners on first and second advanced to their next bases.

Gavin ran towards home plate, ready to receive a throw from Xavier if the runner sprinted home. Xavier ripped the mask off his face, retrieved the ball, and threw it to the third baseman. It was too late; the runners were safe.

"Son of a bitch!" the veteran exclaimed. He glanced at Gavin. "That one's on me, rook."

The fans' hopes were restored, and flashes of light danced across the stadium. Gavin's eyes found Carly, and she blew him a kiss. *This one's for the game baby.*

Xavier called another slider and set up on the outside corner. Gavin wound up and delivered a slider quickly to the outside. The batter swung at air. Xavier threw the ball to third, holding the runner. He then laid one finger between his crouched legs, surprising the hell out of Gavin. The batter was well known for crushing fast balls.

Let Xavy do his job, Gavin reminded himself. He set, glanced at the runner on third, and broke into his windup. His muscles stretched and expanded as he hurled his body forward. "Yer out!" the umpire shouted.

The home team fans fell quiet as realization dawned.

Gavin walked around the mound and surveyed his surroundings. A steady calm settled over him. He was laser focused, completely in the zone.

Xavier threw him the ball and got back in his crouch, calling for an inside fastball. "Strike one!"

His second pitch was another two-seamer to the outside corner. The batter gamely swung, but the pitch tailed outside. Two men on, two outs, and two strikes, Gavin calculated. His cleat dug into the rubber, his eyes closed, he exhaled softly through his nose. Xavier called for an inside sinker. The batter swung wildly and missed. "Strike three!"

Gavin threw his head back and howled. The Padres had clinched the pennant and were going to the playoffs. Xavier was the first one to the mound, lifting him and spinning him around.

When Gavin swaggered into the clubhouse after the celebration on the field and his post-game interview, the entire team roared their approval.

"There's our closer!"

"No fear!"

Massey came to greet him with a huge smile and a head lock. "Thanks for bailing me out, kid."

"I got your back, Mass. No worries. I almost gave it away myself."

Everyone doused each other with champagne, and the music was cranked up. The team's owner doled out cigars and expensive bottles of tequila. Gavin wasn't a drinker, so he gave his bottle to Xavier, who didn't complain.

After he and Xavier showered and were cleared to leave, they headed to the family area where Carly and the other wives, including Xavier's wife, Anna, were waiting. When Gavin arrived at the big-league club, Anna had taken Carly under her wing and taught her the ins and outs of being a baseball wife. Both Xavier and Anna had proven to be trusted advisers, as well as friends, helping Gavin navigate the media and fans.

"Hey there." Gavin smiled from ear to ear as he approached his wife. His eyes roamed over her body, every luscious curve accentuated in her fitted Padres t-shirt and skinny jeans.

She squealed and jumped into his arms, hitching her legs around his waist. "Baby, you were amazing out there!" She drew her head back to look at him. "I'm so damn proud of you. You stayed so calm!"

He pressed his forehead against hers and breathed her in. "It helped me so much seeing your gorgeous face in the stands."

Her mouth spread into a slow grin. "My romantic cheeseball. This was all you, baby. You did it!" He captured her mouth and kissed her roughly.

"Get a room!" one of the players yelled.

Carly giggled, and Gavin reluctantly released her, kissing her on the cheek before her feet hit the ground.

"So, what's the plan?" she asked, wiping the lipstick from Gavin's mouth with her thumb.

He rolled his neck and rubbed a knot of tension from his shoulder. "Go home and rest, then pack for St. Louis. I fly out in three days."

Carly waggled her eyebrows. "Well then, let's not waste any more time here. I need to get my man to bed!" she yelled, reaching around to grab his ass.

Anna and a few of the other happily married wives saw the humor in it, but some of the women leered at her with open envy.

"Seriously, babe?" Gavin said under his breath, red faced with embarrassment.

"What?" She looked up at him from beneath her lashes with mock innocence. "There are a lot of hungry eyes in this room, and you're on the menu. I need to mark my territory from time to time."

They said their goodbyes to Anna and Xavier as Carly pulled Gavin by the hand toward the exit.

When they were settled inside of their slate grey BMW, Carly reached for her seat belt and paused, looking over at Gavin. "Need me to drive? Your shoulder must be sore. That was a long inning."

"Nah. Surprisingly, it isn't too bad. I'll ice it when we get home."

"Good." She was quiet for a long moment, scrolling through her phone. Gavin eyed her curiously as they pulled out of the parking garage and headed toward the 5-South. He rubbed the pad of his index finger under her chin. "Hey. What's going on in that beautiful head of yours?"

She looked up at him, shrugging a casual shoulder. "Nothing... why do you ask?"

"Because I know you," he said, glancing over at her. "Quiet means something's brewing."

Carly cracked a smile. "You don't know anything about me," she replied playfully.

"I'm waiting..."

"I was just curious if you've given any more thought to living in Tennessee during the off season?"

Gavin groaned. "Car, what the hell are we gonna do on a ranch?"

"We've lived in San Diego all our lives! I love the idea of a ranch." She leaned into him, curling her fingers through the hair at the nape of his neck. "Think about how cute we'd be with a couple of horses, some steer, and a ranch hand named Jed." She giggled. "You would look hella good in a cowboy hat, baby."

"Pfft," he replied. "I don't think so."

"You know I used to love visiting my nana in Tennessee when I was a kid. It's actually a really beautiful state."

"Not to mention Hicksville."

She kissed his cheek and rested her head on his shoulder. "Maddie would have a ball. She's turning four soon, and I want her and her brother or sister to have fresh air and lots of room to run and explore. Horses to ride, a pond to feed ducks..."

Gavin's eyes grew wide. "Wait. What did you just say about a brother or sister?"

Carly moved to sit caddy corner in her seat, facing him. His eyes darted back and forth between her and the road. "Okay, before you freak out, I'm not one hundred percent sure." She rested her hand on her flat stomach. "But I'm a week late and my boobs hurt like hell."

"Woo-hoo! Dear God, please let it be a boy!"

Carly tipped her head back and laughed. "While I do love your enthusiasm, let's not get ahead of ourselves." She raked her pink nails down his stubbled jawline and tilted her head. "But you'd be happy?"

"Are you kidding me? Of course I'd be happy."

Gavin's cell phone chirped from the console. It was his agent, Jamie Mack.

"Woo! Dollar signs baby!" Carly squealed.

He grinned and pushed the button for speaker phone. "Jamie Mack! What's the business?"

"Gavvy-Gav, my favorite client! I've got some news."

Gavin pressed the mute button. "I'm his favorite because I struck out his favorite tonight. Postseason bonus!"

"Woot, woot!"

"I just got off the phone with the Padres GM. I reminded him that you've got a rookie deal and you're at the end of it. It was total fate that they called you up at the break," Jamie said.

Carly took him off mute. "What's he offering?" It was always about dollars and cents with his wife. Having come from one of the richest land development families in La Jolla, California, it was bred in her. Gavin focused on baseball while Carly took care of their finances.

"Oh… hey, Carly," Mack said with an edge to his voice, knowing firsthand that she could smell his bullshit from miles away. "The GM is offering a four-year deal at four million a year."

"Holy shit!" Gavin exclaimed.

Carly held up her hand to stop Gavin from continuing. "Umm… that's a good start, Mack, but I feel like Gavin's worth a lot more than four."

Mack cleared his throat. "Carly, he's 22 years old and has only pitched in twenty-five major league games."

"Closers across the league are being paid more than ever before, Mack," Carly replied. "Gavin has been rated a top-five prospect in the Padres farm system since he was eighteen, and his ERA was the best compared to other closers that are getting ten a year. Oh, did I mention he's never been on the injured list and just saved his team's season? I'm thinking the magic number here is seven, Mack. I know Houston's looking for a closer, and so is New York. The Yankees might even pay more."

Gavin pressed the mute button. "Baby, I don't want to go to New York or Houston."

Carly waved him off. "Shhh. I'm just trying to work him." She took Mack off mute.

"Jesus Christ, Carly. Why can't you be like the other baseball wives and focus on shopping and Botox," Jamie replied. "I'm Gavin's agent, but it feels like you're his GM! Gav, what do you think?"

Carly rolled her eyes and pushed mute. "Misogynistic mother fucker."

Gavin looked at her pointedly, dropped his chin, and arched a brow. "This guy's got our future in his hands, Car. Be firm, but play nice. I commend you on knowing the market, though. Maybe you should ditch commercial real estate and become a sports agent. You're a tenacious negotiator."

Gavin checked his blind spot as he merged onto the freeway and took his agent off mute again. "She's right, Mack. New York might even double it. I'd be giving San Diego a hometown discount at seven million."

He could sense Mack's irritation. "Fine," his agent groaned. "I'll tell him seven, but you better pitch your balls off against St. Louis. No pun intended."

"You know I will. We really appreciate you, Mack. Don't we, Carly?"

Carly planted on a fake smile and raised her middle finger. "Oh yes, so much. Couldn't do any of this without you."

Thank God for the mute button, because it took Gavin a full thirty seconds to stop laughing. His wife's intelligence, confidence, and wit were just a few of the reasons why she had him wrapped around her little finger.

"Hey, Mack," Gavin said, unmuting the call. "Can you look into ranches for sale in South Western Tennessee?"

Carly gasped, squealed, and clapped her hands in quick succession.

"Tennessee? Last time I checked there wasn't a major league ball club in that state."

"This is personal." Gavin flashed her a grin. "Carly wants an off-season ranch for our potentially growing family."

"Congratulations you two! My cousin lives in Nashville, I'll have him look into it. With a recession looming, there are bound to be options."

"You're the best, Mack!" Carly yelled, ending the call. She looped her arm through Gavin's and snuggled in. "You really do love me."

He kissed her on the head. "More than anything in the world."

"I'm so happy, Gav. Maddie is gonna make such an amazing big sister, don't you think? She's such a little caregiver already. Ugh, I'll have to work off the baby weight again, which was not an easy feat after Madison, but well worth it."

"I think it makes you even sexier. The mother of my children. That's hot action right there."

"Oh yeah?" she whispered, sliding her hand up his thigh. "You should be rewarded for saying such sweet things."

"Baby, while I love where your mind's going, we're on the freeway going seventy. Not the best timing." His post-game adrenaline mixed with thoughts of Carly lying underneath him in bed nearly made him swerve off the road. "We're only an hour away from home, patience please."

"Fine, party pooper."

The freeway lights flashed across her face. "I know I say this all the time, but I'm so damn proud of you, baby."

He reached over and squeezed her thigh, his eyes flitting between her gorgeous ocean blue eyes and the road. "You're the reason I am who I am today, you know that don't you?"

When they reached their exit, Gavin pressed down on the break as he approached the red light at the end of the off-ramp. Before he stopped completely, the light turned green and he continued into the intersection.

"Gavin!" Carly screamed.

A car horn shrieked, there was the vicious crunching of steel and the shattering of glass. The car violently rolled over twice, slamming Gavin's head against the driver's side window. Everything went black.

ONE

Gavin

Seven years later

The car horn sounded its raucous blast, unremitting, as Gavin Taylor woke up in a cold sweat, gasping for air and taking in his surroundings with unfocused eyes. For a moment he was confused as hell. Then, the perpetually smug face of Declan Reynolds came into focus, directly in front of him. Gavin's eyes dropped to the air horn in Declan's hand, and he cursed under his breath.

"You can't pass out in my bar, man."

Gavin grunted and ran a hand through his matted hair. "Fucking hell, you trying to make me go deaf?" Wiping the drool from his beard, he looked around the clean, dimly-lit space. "There's no one here, who the hell cares?" He nodded to his empty lowball glass. "Another whiskey, neat."

Declan set the air horn down underneath the bar and grabbed a bottle of Maker's Mark. "It's Tuesday afternoon. Everyone's busy being productive, working for a living." He eyed Gavin reprovingly before pouring a small amount of bourbon into the glass. "You look like shit, friend. Everything okay?"

Gavin's jaw ticked. Every day for the past seven years had been a struggle for him on some level, but when September rolled around, that

1

day in particular, all he wanted to do was drown his all-consuming pain in whiskey and not feel a damn thing. "I work hard for a living, I'm not your friend, and that's no business of yours," he grumbled. "Your job is to serve me drinks, not inquire about my life." He had the kind of face Gavin wanted to punch–frat house, pretty boy looks, the corners of his mouth pulled up into a subtle smile like he was sharing a joke with himself, and you were the butt of it.

Declan threw a dish towel over his shoulder and held up his hands in surrender. "Hey, sorry if I crossed a line. You're just so damn strange. Makes people around here uncomfortable."

Prick, Gavin thought, as he pried his wallet from the pocket of his jeans and smacked a hundred-dollar bill down on the bar. Declan's eyes grew wide. "It's not my job to make people feel comfortable, but does this help ease your level of concern, *friend*?" Gavin knew he shouldn't have come here. He preferred to do his drinking at home in private, but when he woke up this morning and visualized himself drowned at the bottom of his pond with a bottle of booze in his system, he knew he needed to break away. He picked up the glass and knocked back the whiskey.

The door to the bar creaked open and Stan Reynolds, the owner of the establishment, hobbled inside. He'd done business with Stan in the past and knew he was a good man, but there was something about him that made Gavin uneasy. Maybe it was the way Stan looked at him, like he could sense his level of pain. A fellow soldier in the hard knocks of life, forever broken in some way. Having served two terms in Iraq, Stan had lost a leg and suffered from PTSD–something Gavin was all too familiar with. He never spoke with him about it, though. A man's past was his own, and certainly none of Gavin's business, just as his was none of Stan's.

Stan made his way behind the bar, his brows pulled low. Empathy radiated from his deeply set eyes, which were framed in dark, puffy circles, like badges of honor. "You okay, boy?" Even after five years, Gavin couldn't stomach the level of hick talk in this town. *Someone calls me boy one more time,* he thought.

Gavin knew he looked rough. He'd been due for a haircut and beard trim weeks ago, and his eyes were most likely bloodshot and swollen from lack of sleep.

"I was just on my way out." He stood up, too fast for his drunken brain's liking, and the room spun like a tilt-o-whirl ride at a state fair. Squeezing his eyes shut, he inhaled a deep breath and pressed his hands on the bar to get his bearings.

Stan rounded the bar, concern etched in his senescent features. "You have someone who can drive you home?"

"I'm good," Gavin murmured, as he staggered to the door.

"Well, I hope your day gets better, boy. Tell Prater I said 'hi.'"

Gavin gritted his teeth and stumbled into the blindingly bright afternoon. His eyes ached as they attempted to adjust to the gleam of the intense Tennessee sun. It was a beautiful day; the azure-colored sky unclouded as far as the eye could see. Birds chirped cheerful, whimsical songs. The lush, towering oaks that surrounded the town square rustled lazily on a balmy breeze. Portions of their leaves had already begun to turn vibrant shades of yellow, red, and rusted orange. The beauty of this region depressed him. He often thought about relocating to the desert, where it was barren and ugly, to match what had become of his heart.

It had been Carly's dream to own a ranch. Once Gavin knew his ball career was over, he didn't think twice about buying the old Miller Farm for a steal and relocating to the small Tennessee town of Timber Creek. But living here without her had never felt right. He only stayed because it was what she would have wanted for their daughter. He came to enjoy working on the ranch. It gave him a small amount of purpose, kept him moving from one day to the next. But he could do without everything else that went along with residing in the annoyingly picturesque town.

It was only three o-clock, and he'd just about consumed his weight in whiskey. His plan for the rest of the day was to do the kind of drinking that would make Ben Sanderson from *Leaving Las Vegas* proud. Having already finished off his last bottle earlier that day, he rounded the corner and headed for the liquor store, which also served as the town's general store. The prying eyes of store workers and volunteers preparing for the town's annual Harvest Festival followed him as he sluggishly made his way down Main Street. It wasn't even October yet, and the place already looked like one of those cheesy Hallmark movies Carly used to force him to watch. One of the many downfalls of living in a small, rural town were the gossiping busybodies who stared at him with naked curiosity, leery of him, just because he was a private man. Their heightened reaction to him now, turned down mouths and self-righteous judgment radiating from their eyes, proved just how disconnected he was from this town, even after five years.

A block ahead his daughter Madison appeared in his hazy line of vision, dressed in vibrant, multi-colored leggings and white ankle high combat boots. She crossed Main Street, moving like a storm, even with the weighted down backpack hitched over her small shoulders. A wave of nausea rippled through him as he picked up the pace toward the liquor store on unsteady legs. When she made a beeline for the candy shop, he sighed with relief, wiping the sweat off his forehead with the back of his hand. Even on his good days, when he was a functioning alcoholic, keeping busy on the ranch, he could see the trace of disdain in her eyes when she studied him. It was a gutting kind of pain to look into her bright blue eyes, so similar to her mother's, and see just how much he'd failed her.

Thank God for his foreman's wife, June Prater, who was like a mother to Madison. She had a soft, caring spirit and wasn't intrusive or judgmental. Although he knew he was a colossal fuck up, Gavin wasn't particularly open to receiving sanctimonious advice on how to properly raise his daughter.

Madison was an old soul, strong and curious, vivacious, and full of life–albeit a bit too sassy at times for his liking. Even at the young age of eleven, Gavin felt she had surpassed him in so many ways. She wasn't quite old enough to remember her mother, but she was old enough now to know that her dad wasn't like the other dads in town. He didn't attend school functions or help with the local fair and innumerable holiday festivities. He'd closed himself off from the world a long time ago, living as a ghost, incapable of giving her the life she deserved.

They'd been so young when they had her; Carly was 17 and he was 18, but Carly had been a natural from the start, maternal beyond her years. He swallowed around the fist-sized knot that formed in his throat every time he thought about the strong bond she and Madison had had, and would have had now. Gavin loved Madison fiercely, but he knew nothing about real parenting–the kind that was substantial and impactful. His own childhood had been a lonely one. There hadn't been a parental role model in his life to prepare him for rearing a child of his own by himself. Despite their young age, Madison had been a happy surprise, but he'd never envisioned a world where he'd be raising her without his wife. An image of Carly with her hand pressed to her flat stomach, beaming as she told him he was going to be a father again, made his heart ache hard enough to get his foggy brain's attention. There would be no deep self-analysis for him today, only the thick glaze of alcohol induced numbness. A protective layer against the heart wrenching nostalgia.

A new shop was opening next door to the general store. He had heard in passing that the space had been leased but hadn't cared enough to make inquiries. The banner that stretched across the storefront window read *Country Chic Boutique Grand Opening*. Pastel colored balloons and floral print lanterns floated leisurely on a breeze. Strands of twinkle lights framed the giant pane of glass that started at the sidewalk and went all the way up to the eves of the roof. His reflection in the window caused him to do a double take. He looked like yesterday's trash, nearly unrecognizable with his long beard and chin length hair. It was a bit much, even for him. "I should probably get a beard trim tomorrow," he mumbled to himself, sniffing his shirt. "And a bath." A couple holding hands gave him a wide berth as they walked past, whispering to each other while giving him the side eye. *Good*, he thought. If his increasingly homeless appearance contributed to the people of this town leaving him the hell alone, he would embrace it.

Pressing his face to the window, he cupped his hands around his eyes and took in the racks of stylish women's clothing. Hicksville, Tennessee had never seen the likes of a store such as this. Around here, basic western wear was the clothing of choice. His gaze landed on a dress that reminded him so much of his wife. He squeezed his eyes closed and let himself picture her in it. Carly's long black hair falling in a lustrous sheet over layers of pink lace as she strolled through an open field with a baby on her hip while a four-year-old Maddie chased butterflies. His eyes watered and burned. It felt like someone had punched him in the throat while they ripped their hand through his chest and squeezed his heart as it begged to be returned to safer ground. He needed a fucking drink.

A door at the back of the store opened, and a woman appeared, her arms piled high with clothing. He turned away quickly and stumbled next door.

"Hey stranger, I haven't seen you here in a while!" The cashier's tone was thick with boisterous sarcasm and several decibels louder than the average human. Gavin flinched, rejecting the volume of the man's voice, and spread his arms to his sides. "What can I say? I'm helping out the local economy."

"While I love taking your money, I do worry about you sometimes." The cashier paused, head tilted, as he gave Gavin the once over. "You look worse than when I saw you two days ago. In fact, I don't think I've ever seen you lookin' so rough, and that's saying a lot. People see you walking in here looking like this?"

"I don't give a shit what people think of me, Ibrahim. I keep telling you this," Gavin replied. He grabbed three bottles of whiskey from the shelf, placed them clumsily on the counter, and fumbled in his pocket for his wallet. It slipped from his fingers. "Goddammit," he mumbled, grunting as he bent down to pick it up.

"Can I interest you in a bottle of water, Gavin?" Ibrahim asked.

"I drink a glass of cranberry juice every morning. It restores my liver." Gavin threw some money on the counter and secured the heavy bag around his wrist.

Ibrahim chucked. "I don't think that's how it works."

Gavin waggled a finger in the cashier's face with heavy-lidded eyes. "I like you, Ibrahim. You're not judgmental like most everyone else in this godforsaken town, and I'd love it if we could keep it that way."

Ibrahim pressed his lips together and nodded. "Tell you what," Gavin said, turning toward the door. "If it makes you feel better, I'll splash a little water in it."

"Take care, Mr. Taylor."

Gavin crossed the street to his pickup and sat on the edge of the brick lined sidewalk, setting the bag of bottles down next to him. He pulled one from the bag, unscrewed the lid, and took a long swig. The urge to relieve himself came upon him suddenly and fiercely. He stood, unzipped his fly, and proceeded to take a leak on one of his truck's tires. His free hand gripped the jagged edge of the bed and he moaned, dropping his chin to his chest.

"You're pissing on the wrong truck, son." Gavin turned his head languidly in the direction of an older man clad in a plaid button up, dark denim jeans, cowboy boots, and a ten-gallon hat. The man leaned against the cab of the truck, arms crossed in front of him, frustration and sympathy at war with each other on his weathered face. "I'd like to think we've got the kind of relationship that deters us from taking a leak on one another's property."

"Prater, this is my truck," Gavin mumbled. He watched as the orange, foul-smelling urine splashed against his work boots, just coherent enough to register the moment as a low point.

"You dumb son of a bitch, you came in that truck." He jerked a thumb over his shoulder to another blue truck, darker in color, parked four spaces away. "This one's mine."

The flatbed in front of Gavin came into focus. Unlike his own truck, it was rusted along its edges and filled with long planks of wood. "Shit." He fumbled with his fly and turned in the direction of his truck.

Prater moved to stand in his way. "Don't even think about it. I'm driving you home."

"Did Stan call you?" Gavin slurred, scowling at his foreman. "That guy needs to mind his own damn business."

"He's a good man and was only trying to help. Now, I strongly suggest you get in the truck, son."

Jim Prater was sixty-five years old and tougher than an over cooked steak. He had little patience for senseless chatter and idiocy and didn't shy away from letting you know when you pissed him off. Years ago, Gavin had made the mistake of giving him shit and got knocked on his ass for it. Now he knew better than to talk back to the man. Prater may have been rough around the edges, but he had a good heart. He was extremely loyal, discreet, and the hardest working man in town. On top of structural upkeep, caring for the horses, and herding steer, Jim also dealt with the clients. Gavin appreciated that most of all.

Although Prater didn't own the ranch, everyone in town assumed he did. Gavin liked it that way, as privacy was of the utmost importance to him. His employees were the only people in town who knew about his failed pitching career, but Jim was the only one Gavin had really opened up to about the details of the accident that had led to Carly's death.

Gavin begrudgingly tossed the keys to his truck in the direction of Prater's outstretched hand, missing it by a mile. "What's all this wood for?" he muttered.

Prater pursed his lips and bent down to grab the keys. "Need it to mend the stables, thanks to Zeus. He got spooked and kicked out his door today. Tried to make a getaway." Eager to get home and continue saturating his liver with amber-colored poison, Gavin didn't process a word of what Prater was saying. Today he didn't want to think about the ranch or responsibility in general. He grabbed hold of the truck's passenger side door handle. "Well, it's getting late, and I've got a shit ton more drinking to do."

"Don't you think you've had enough, boss?" His two ranch hands, Miguel Rodriguez and Alejandro Cortez, were walking toward them with large sacks of feed slung over their shoulders.

Gavin groaned. "Why the hell did you bring them?"

Prater raised a shoulder in nonchalance. "Figured if I was coming into town to pick your drunk ass up, I might as well bring them with me to pick up some supplies."

Miguel and Alejandro spoke Spanish to each other in long, fast strings as they threw the sacks of feed into the truck bed. The jocular pair had come to work for Gavin a few years back. They were trustworthy, discreet, hard working, and good family men—but big-time banterers, and they never tired of busting his balls.

"He's hammered again," Miguel said with a smirk as he walked around the truck to stand next to Gavin. "We should put him on a horse when we get home."

Alejandro laughed and mimicked a drunk man trying to ride a horse.

Miguel looked at Gavin, shook his head, and sighed. "Cada Septiembre." *Every September.* Gavin glared at them. "Would you two assholes like to be unemployed? Because I can arrange it." He picked up the open bottle and took another swig of whiskey, pushing him from lubricated to disoriented.

9

His body swayed forward. Miguel and Alejandro caught him right before he hit the ground.

Prater sighed. "Alright boys, that'll be enough of that. Get him into my truck and head back to the ranch. Maybe get him some water and a cup of coffee along the way." He motioned to Gavin's truck. "I'll be right behind you."

The door to the bar swung open and Declan stepped outside to survey the scene. "What the hell's going on out here, boys?" His gaze landed on Gavin, and he made no attempt to hide the disgust in his eyes. "Prater, how long are you going to employ this alky piece of shit?"

Prater's stance remained casual, but his heavy grey brow pulled down low. "Declan, I don't remember asking for your advice. I don't tell you how to run your bar, so don't tell me how to manage my men."

Miguel helped Gavin into the truck and buckled him in. "I hate this guy," Miguel muttered, eyeing Declan.

"Pinche pendejo," Alejandro agreed.

"You got a problem, amigos?" Declan bowed up as he strode toward them.

"I reckon their problem is you," Prater replied flatly, pulling a pack of cigarettes from his shirt pocket. "That's their friend you're talking about."

Declan took two steps back from Prater. As cocksure as he was, it seemed even he knew the old man was highly capable of kicking his ass. "Oh yeah? I don't speak Mexican, so will you pass on a message for me? Tell them they should show this town some respect and speak English."

Gavin's eyes rolled open. "I'm gonna bust this dipshit's jaw," he grumbled as he fumbled with his seatbelt.

"He's not worth it, boss," Miguel said, urging Gavin to stay in the truck.

Declan snorted out a laugh. "No, if he wants to fight me, let him go. I've been wanting to take a swing at his scruffy drunken mug for years." An amused smile spread across his face. "This should be fun."

"Declan, if you want your balls to stay attached to your body, I suggest you stop talking and go about your business," Prater warned, lighting his cigarette. "Just because your daddy and I go way back doesn't mean I won't teach you a lesson right here and now."

A squad car pulled up behind the truck and an officer stuck his head out the window. "Everything alright here, Prater?"

Prater drew on his cigarette and blew out a long stream of smoke, tipping his hat at the officer. "Everything's fine, Officer Marbury. We were just leaving."

When the officer was out of sight, Alejandro and Miguel turned to Declan and grabbed their balls in unison. Declan stabbed an angry finger in their direction. "You wetbacks better watch your backs." He turned and walked back into the bar.

"Grab my booze," Gavin grumbled.

"Lord Jesus, give me strength," Prater said, clearly tired of the whole scene. "Let's head home."

The one-hundred-acre ranch was located on the outskirts of town, tucked away and isolated. Two barns sat on opposite sides of the farmhouse; one used as a stable and the other as storage for various farming equipment. The sprawling five-bedroom rancher was well-kept and tidy.

Gavin groaned as Prater helped him up the porch steps and he registered the multitude of fall décor items including pumpkins, smiling scarecrows, and garland made of brightly colored leaves. He hated all things festive but tolerated it for the sake of his daughter. The front door swung open, and they were greeted by the kind face of June Prater. His senses were assaulted by the smell of pumpkin pie, and he nearly vomited on the *It's Fall Y'all* doormat. The mere thought of food made his stomach turn.

"Hello there! You're just in time to try my latest creation."

Gavin cleared his throat and planted on a smile as he and Prater made their way inside. He set the bag of whiskey bottles down on the kitchen counter and tamped down the urge to pour himself a glass right then and there. "You're gonna win this year June—I can smell it."

June's gaze lingered on him for a moment before she smiled and turned to the stove. Gavin was always amazed at how she treated him with care and compassion, knowing he was a horrible father and an all-around mess. There weren't many people like her in the world, and he appreciated her more than he was able to express. He knew Madison was a big reason why she and Prater were so loyal to him. They loved his daughter like their own.

"That darn Ann Davis has won five years in a row, just because she's the mayor's mama," June tutted with an exaggerated roll of her eyes. "Everyone knows she uses ready-made crust, it's shameful! This year, I'm going to win that trophy and mount it in my pie shop. If I don't, I'm filing an official complaint with the town counsel." She walked toward Gavin with a full pie balanced in her hand and stabbed a fork into the middle of it, lifting out a generous bite. "Here you go, try it."

He held his hands out in front of him, positive his stomach wouldn't be able to hold it down. "Oh, no thank you," he protested as she shoved the bite into his mouth anyway. She cut a full slice for her husband who immediately dug in. "Mmmm… June, you've outdone yourself with this one," Prater said around the bite. "Is the bottom layer cheesecake?"

Nodding her head, June beamed with pride. "Spiced cheesecake. I thought I'd experiment with some recipes that put a little twist on tradition to ensure victory." She looked at Gavin expectantly. "Well?"

Spots danced in his vision, and he could feel the bile rising in his throat. He ran out the front door and stumbled to the porch railing, vomiting on the grass below. A guttural moan escaped him as he wiped his beard with the back of his hand and trudged back inside.

"That was delicious, June."

She pursed her lips. "I'd feel more confident if you hadn't just thrown it up on the lawn."

Madison walked into the kitchen. "Nana June, is the pie done?" Her fluorescent tie-dye-socked feet stopped in their tracks when she saw Gavin leaning against the counter in a cold sweat. "Oh… hey, dad," she said, her icy gaze flicking over him. He ran a shaky hand through his hair and attempted a smile. "Hey, Mads."

June dished Madison out a huge piece of pie and topped it with fresh whipped cream. She was rewarded with a smile and a hug from Madison, who sat down at the kitchen table next to Prater and devoured the slice. Although Gavin was grateful for June, he couldn't help but feel a pang of jealousy, something he knew he had no right to feel.

"I saw you at the candy store," he said. Cringing inwardly at the awkwardness of his pathetic attempt to make conversation, he turned to wash his hands at the sink. The throbbing pain behind his eyes intensified.

"I saw you leaving the bar," came her quick-witted reply. "And the liquor store."

Shit, he thought, *she saw me*. Gavin squeezed his eyes closed and inhaled a shaky breath as he reached for the bag of whiskey. "Remember to lock up, June." He could hear Madison's barbs as he made his way down the hall to his room.

"He's worse than ever. I can't stand being around him."

"Maddie, your father is going through a lot right now," June replied.

"Yeah, but he never freaking talks to anyone about it."

"Now, Madison, it's not respectful to speak that way about your father," Prater scolded.

"Sorry, Papa Jim." Her voice was small, despondent.

Gavin slammed his bedroom door closed and sat on the edge of the bed, curling his hair into his fists. They say time heals all wounds, but his experience had been the opposite. The pain and emptiness had grown increasingly prominent in the years since Carly's passing, holding him

13

captive. Even his nightmares were more vivid and intense. The more he hurt, the more he drank. The more he drank, the worse it got. It was a vicious and incredibly lonely cycle.

Still fully clothed, he fell into a restless sleep until his eyes popped open at 2 a.m. The urge to urinate pulled him from his bed, and he shuffled down the hallway to the bathroom. When he was finished, his feet moved of their own accord toward Madison's room. Heavy snoring, reminiscent of a chainsaw cutting through a log, sounded over whirling white noise. June had stayed the night in his guest bedroom, as she often did when Gavin was having an especially bad day. It was never spoken of, so he wasn't sure what she knew, but he was fairly confident Prater had told her the reason why Gavin was at his worst when September rolled around–why he shifted from a standoffish yet functioning man to a valueless drunk.

When he reached Madison's room, he creaked open the door and peered inside. The soft glow of her mermaid night light lit the room just enough for him to make out her form, curled up in bed, wrapped in a blanket Carly had knitted. An image of Carly sitting in his recliner, hands knitting nimbly over her pregnant belly, filtered through his numbness. He hadn't seen the blanket in years, had forgotten it even existed. Did Madison know the significance of today? There was a time, a few years back, when Maddie would inquire about her mother often, with hopeful eyes that faded when he had brushed the topic aside. Eventually, she'd given up, as Gavin had never been able to muster the strength to speak with Madison about her mother. It had been quite a while since she last inquired, her faith in him now nonexistent. A sudden and sharp realization of how selfish he'd been almost brought him to his knees. He should be keeping Carly's spirit alive, sharing stories with Madison about how beautiful, free spirited, and full of life her mother had been. Maybe he could try to open up, be a better man... for her. He made his way back to bed, his heart in his throat, and bawled like a baby into his pillow. After a quarter bottle of whiskey, everything went black.

TWO

Hayley

Hayley Jackson stood outside her Country Chic Boutique storefront and beamed with pride. Grand opening day had finally arrived. All she had left to do was power up the Square register and wait for her best friend and co-manager, Kinsley Hart, to arrive. Then, they would officially be open for business. The heavy glass door unlocked with a click, and she pushed it open, inhaling a lungful of citrus and honey scented magnolia.

She slipped out of her blush-colored, cropped leather jacket and unwound the ruffled scarf from her neck as she walked to the back room, humming *Snapback* by Old Dominion with a skip in her step. A telltale ding sounded from inside her purse, signaling a notification from Plenty of Fish, the dating app Kinsley had signed her up for. Hayley groaned. Even if she were to come across someone on the app who appeared to be date worthy, she had little time for men right now. Most of the contenders lived in Nashville, which was an inconvenient, hour-long drive from Timber Creek. Close enough to be doable, but far enough away to be a justifiable deterrent. She knew Kinsley meant well; it had been a year since Hayley had slept with a man or even been on a date. Her last break up had been far from amicable, which had prompted her to put romance on the back burner and focus solely on her career.

Messy break up aside, Hayley's years in New York City had been an invaluable experience. Studying fashion and marketing at the Fashion Institute of Technology had turned her from a country girl with raw talent and massive potential to a legitimate clothing designer and business owner. The City had modernized her, made her more well-rounded. She soon caught the attention of executives in the industry who had played an integral role in helping her launch her clothing line and online store. At first, she had kept her pieces in line with the trends of the City, but she soon felt stuck and uninspired. She started sketching a boho-modern take on women's country clothing and spent a year designing her line and obtaining the funding and resources needed to launch an online store. Four years later, she'd had enough of city life. She had really missed her family and felt a visceral tug on her heart to venture back to her roots. Suddenly, she'd found herself making plans to open a brick-and-mortar novelty store in her hometown. It surprised her how much Timber Creek still felt like home. The City had been good to her, but when it came down to it, Hayley Jackson would always be a country girl at heart.

She was standing behind the checkout counter, scrolling through *Country Chic's* Instagram page, when Kinsley breezed through the door in four-inch heeled boots, two cups of liquid mana wrapped in her dainty hands.

Hayley abandoned her phone and reached out her hand. "Oh my gawd, you are the *best.*"

"I know," Kinsley sing-songed as she passed her the to-go cup with PS written on the side of it. Hayley took a long pull of her favorite festive beverage and moaned. "Mmmm… pumpkin spiced lattes are my *everything.*"

Kinsley snorted. "Damn, you really do need to get laid, you're practically climaxing over one sip of an overhyped seasonal latte."

Hayley held out the drink to her friend. "Try it, and you'll see why!"

Kinsley shook her head decisively, the ends of her hair skimming over her cashmere covered shoulders. "Nope. I am a no frills, non-conformist when it comes to my coffee."

Hayley met Kinsley Hart on the first day of classes at FIT, and they'd been inseparable ever since. Although she was born into a rich and pretentious Rhode Island family, Kinsley had managed to come out the other side of her childhood relatively unscathed and down to earth. Hayley wouldn't classify her bestie as drop dead gorgeous, but she was exceptionally adorable with her shoulder-length, blunt bob and bangs, huge bright green eyes, and a smattering of freckles sprinkled across the bridge of her button nose. She was a tiny but mighty young woman, with an excellent eye for fashion, a feisty attitude, and personality in spades. They made a fantastic team; Hayley had been beyond thrilled when Kinsley had agreed to co-manage the store. She wasn't sure if her Big-City-spoiled bestie would be able to handle living in a small town, but it helped that she was a trust fund baby and could eventually live part time in NYC, if she wanted to.

Kinsley looked around the store and squealed, clapping her hands in quick succession. "This is so exciting! It looks amazing in here!"

Hayley followed the direction of Kinsley's gaze to the massive, hand-painted mural along the back wall, which depicted a field full of wishing dandelions, their white floaties blowing on a swirly breeze. Hayley's dad had helped them out enormously over the past few months, hiring painters and overseeing construction workers, plumbers, and electricians while Hayley and Kinsley tied up loose ends in New York.

"It really does, doesn't it?" Hayley's contented smile turned into a frown when her phone dinged with yet another dating prospect.

"I know that sound!" Kinsley snatched Hayley's phone from the counter and waggled her hidden-by-bangs but no doubt perfectly-sculpted eyebrows. "Ooohhh this one's cute! Let's see. His name is Tom, and he loves the rodeo, long walks around his parent's farm, and his tabby cat, Shelby."

Closing her eyes, Hayley mimicked snoring.

"Okay, okay, he does sound like a boring-ass mama's boy, but all that really matters is that he is *hawt*." She held out the phone to an unenthusiastic Hayley.

"Meh."

Kinsley deadpanned. "Tell me, Hales, has the vaginal atrophy set in yet?"

Hayley took a sip of her latte and rolled her eyes. "It hasn't been *that* long."

"It's been long enough," Kinsley said, setting her cup down on the glass countertop. "And look at you! You are drop dead gorgeous with an ass that won't quit." She motioned to Hayley's body and shook her head mournfully. "Such a shame all of *that* is going to waste."

"Would you stop?"

"I totally understand why you wouldn't want anything serious right now, but you need to get laid every now and again. You're a busy woman. Sex releases stress and tension." Kinsley pressed her palms together with her eyes closed and inhaled a yoga-esque breath.

Hayley couldn't help but laugh. "Kinz, you know me. I'm not a one-night stand kind of gal, and I don't have time to drive to Nashville every weekend for dates."

"Well, no offense, but the options in this town are fairly slim." Kinsley walked to straighten a rack of jeans. "From what I've seen, you've got married men, old men, jailbait, and some homeless looking dude who stumbles around town. Although, that bartender from the other night was a snack, and his three friends weren't half bad."

Although she and Kinsley had been in Timber Creek for four weeks, they'd been too busy getting the store ready to enjoy any kind of nightlife. Two nights ago, Kinsley had finally dragged her to the town's only nightlife option, The Republic. Unfortunately, the owner's son, Declan Reynolds, was Hayley's least favorite person on the planet and had been tending bar that night. She'd only offered him and his loser friends a clipped hello before pulling Kinsley to a table at the back of the bar, much to Declan's chagrin.

"Declan Reynolds?" Hayley scoffed. "Not a chance in hell."

Her caustic response only served to peak Kinsley's interest. "Ooohhh… I knew there was a story there. Do tell!"

Hayley shrugged, fiddling with an arrangement of silk magnolias. "He's an asshole of epic proportions. A mistake from my past."

Kinsley's entire body deflated. "That's all you're gonna give me?"

"It's not worth talking about."

"Hales," Kinsley said softly. "Can you just go on one date? Please?" She clasped her hands together pleadingly.

Dropping her hands from the arrangement, Hayley turned to Kinsley with narrowed eyes. "Why are you pushing so hard for this?"

"I love you, and I want you to be happy," she replied, picking a nonexistent piece of fuzz off her sweater.

"And…?"

"And… things with James have gotten a little stale, so I need you to start paving the way for our new and exciting Tennessee dating lives while I figure out how to let him down easy."

"Really? Aww, I like James. I thought things were going well between you two." Hayley pouted her bottom lip.

Kinsley ran her fingers down the sides of a long, floral print dress with a series of crisscross straps at the back. Hayley was proud of the piece and thought it looked amazing with the lace-back denim jacket she had designed. Matched with a pair of camel suede booties, it was the perfect fall outfit. "I love this dress. You are so fucking talented." Her best friend had a propensity to get legitimately distracted, even in the middle of important discussions.

"Kinz, focus!"

"Sorry! Anyway, I can tell this whole long-distance thing is not gonna work for me. I thought the old *absence makes the heart grow fonder* adage would start to kick in, but so far it hasn't. And I'm not a video call sex kind of gal. I need actual man hands touching all of this." She motioned her hands over her body. "Even my vibrator is starting to bore me. I'm seriously tempted to dump him and sign up for the app myself." She sighed longingly with a far-off look in her eyes. "Maybe *I* need a cowboy from Nashville with a massive cock who loves cats and the rodeo."

"Kinz, the cowboy could have a micro penis for all you know. You loved *James's* massive cock. I feel so bad that I tore you away from him."

She waved away Hayley's concern with a manicured hand. "Are you kidding? This is going to be so much fun. And you didn't tear me away from anything, I chose this. Honestly, things with James were starting to fizzle out before I left." Kinsley pointed a stern finger at Hayley. "I'm warning you now, once I officially break things off with him and we hire some more bodies, I will be dragging you to Nashville on the regular. You aren't as busy as you think. The website is running like clockwork."

Hayley knew she had a point. The online portion of their business was running quite smoothly, thanks to a slew of savvy work from home assistants on the East Coast. Granted, it kept her busy, but maybe she *was* making excuses because she feared getting hurt again.

Kinsley walked to the front window and gasped. "Look!" A long line had formed outside the store. Hayley's heart raced with excitement. She had expected there to be a good turnout, but it seemed every woman in town had shown up for the Grand Opening. She felt truly touched and appreciative. Hayley knew her line would bring joy to the women of Timber Creek, who had scant options as far as local clothing stores were concerned. While she loved a well-placed plaid now and again, it was overkill in this town. If that crowd were an indication of things to come, they'd definitely need to hire extra help, especially with the Holidays right around the corner.

Hayley spent the next two hours meeting new people and reminiscing with familiar faces. After the crowd had thinned, a darling girl, dressed in a black and white polka-dot skater-skirt and fuzzy, cropped sweater, zipped through the door. Glittery black socks were pulled up to her knobby knees, and her feet were clad in white Doc Martens. She looked around the store, wide-eyed with wonder, and gravitated toward one of Hayley's bolder pieces: a colorful, patterned mini-maxi dress, which would probably land at the girl's shins. She was a small, willowy thing, with the most gorgeous blue eyes Hayley had ever seen. Her dark hair was pulled back into a long fishtail braid.

"Well, hi there. Can I help you find something?"

The girl pursed her lips and put a hand on her hip. "Well, I was hoping to find a dress for the Fall Festival, but, as you can see, I'm a long way off from fitting into anything you have in here. Have you considered adding a tween line?"

Hayley bit down on her smile. This firecracker of a girl was a Timber Creek anomaly. "How old are you?"

She jutted out her narrow chin. "A very mature eleven."

"You do seem quite mature for your age." Hayley tilted her head and crossed her arms. "I think a tween line is a great idea, maybe I should put you in charge of marketing."

"Yeah. You definitely need me." Her expressive eyes scanned the store as she spoke. She turned to another rack of dresses and held one up to her petite frame. The look of dejection on the girl's face made Hayley's heart sink. And were those tears in her eyes? She turned to hang up the dress before Hayley could confirm.

"I'm so sorry I don't have anything that will work for you."

The girl turned back around and shrugged off the apology, but the intensity behind her eyes spoke differently to Hayley.

"Your hair is beautiful, did your mama do that?"

The girl shook her head. "My mom's dead. Nana June did it." The way she said it surprised Hayley. It was so matter of fact, like she wasn't bothered by it in the slightest. "I want to dye it purple, but my dad won't let me." She rolled her eyes and Hayley cracked a smile.

"What's your name?"

"Madison Taylor."

Hayley didn't recognize the last name, but she had been gone almost six years.

She held out her hand to the girl. "Nice to meet you, Madison Taylor. I'm Hayley Jackson. I have a close friend in New York named Madison."

Madison's glittery lip-glossed mouth fell open. "You lived in New York?"

"I did."

"That's pretty cool." She scrunched up her face. "Why did you come here?"

"Well, I'm from here. I grew up in Timber Creek."

"You're joking." The girl made no attempt at hiding her disdain for their town. "I don't believe it. You don't sound like you're from around here."

Hayley laughed. "Give me another month and my country girl twang will be back, I promise. I'll prove it. What do you call a happy cowboy?"

"Ummm… I don't know. What?"

"A jolly rancher."

Madison curled her lip, looking deeply unimpressed. "OMG, you really did grow up here."

Hayley giggled. "Timber Creek is a great place! My favorite childhood memories were made in this town. Fishing at the creek and going off-roading in the hollers with my dad. I will admit that Timber Creek has never been known for its style, but you certainly have a wonderful sense of fashion."

Madison looked down at her outfit and frowned. "I know, but no one around here seems to think so. I get picked on a lot. The kids around here are all so *basic*. I am who I am, and they need to deal."

Bless her heart, Hayley thought. "What does your daddy do about that?"

"He tells me to buy boots and flannels."

Hayley gave a hearty laugh, earning curious looks from nearby shoppers. She liked this girl. She reminded her of herself at a young age, sassy with a side of defiance.

"Well, I'm so happy you haven't taken his advice. You are fabulous, trust me. Very on trend. You must go into Nashville quite a bit. Or do you shop online?"

"I mostly shop online. Sometimes Nana June takes me to Nashville."

The girl was quiet for a moment, assessing Hayley with inquisitive eyes. "You're really pretty." Hayley felt legitimately flattered. She could tell this child was no nonsense and only said something if she truly meant it.

"Why thank you, that's so sweet of you to say."

Madison checked the time on her large-faced hot pink watch. "I better go." She held out one of her small hands to Hayley. "It was nice meeting you. Think about the tween line."

Hayley had an idea. "You know what, Madison, let me take down your measurements really quick, just in case inspiration strikes."

Madison appeared thrilled by the idea, and Hayley motioned for her to come to the back room. She found her tape and began scribbling down her measurements.

"I feel like a real fashion model."

"I could totally see you as a fashion model."

When Hayley was finished, she gave the young girl a quick hug. Fast-paced and decisive, Madison left the boutique, crossed the street, and hopped into a waiting sedan.

The rest of the day overwhelmed Hayley, but in a good way. She had the most fun she had had in a long time, and it made her heart happy to see Kinsley in her element, laughing and joking with the women of the town. She'd even convinced some of the older women to buy dresses for their granddaughters, nieces, or daughters. Her best friend could definitely charm customers when she wanted to.

Hayley answered what felt like a million questions about her time in New York and whether she'd consider dating one of their nephews or grandsons, most of whom she'd gone to high school with and had skipped town the second the diploma hit their hands. Each of her responses was a polite but firm no and an empty promise to reconsider should things become desperate.

The boutique photographers Hayley had hired to take professional shots of the store had paid off, as several of her customers were from out of town. Photo fashion journalists from New York and Nashville showed up to snap photos for feature stories they were writing on Hayley's impressive level of success at such a young age.

Who needs a man, she thought as she slung an arm around her best friend and flashed the camera a confident smile.

THREE

Gavin

Carly's panicked screams intermingled with the high-pitched screeching of tires. Gavin had zero time to react before their car's midsection was struck by another vehicle and flipped. The airbag deployed and smacked against his shoulder. Shards of glass flew into Gavin's face, and he instinctively covered it with his arms to protect his eyes. His head jerked sideways and slammed into the window, rendering him unconscious.

Cringing against the unrelenting blast of a car horn, his eyes flicked open, revealing a scene too nightmarish to comprehend. They were upside down. His eyes rolled back to see the blood pooling beneath him. His shoulder throbbed. He grabbed it instinctively, thinking he might be bleeding out, but his hand showed no blood.

"Carly!" She hung beside him, her body limp and unresponsive. "Carly, baby, can you hear me? Answer me!"

She stirred, turning her head, just enough for him to see the giant gash on the right side of her forehead. Blood poured from the open wound.

"Carly, I need you to wake up now, okay? Wake up!" Her eyes were slits, opened slightly, but not enough to reassure him. He ripped off a piece of his shirt and put it in her limp hand. "Carly, I need you to press this to the wound on your head while I call for help." He fumbled for his cell phone and dialed 911 into the keypad.

"Hello? We've been in an accident! My wife. She's bleeding. A lot. We just exited the 5 onto Encinitas Boulevard. Please, send someone, fast!"

Carly coughed and wheezed. "Gavin. Help me."

"She's having trouble breathing. And her head...there's so much fucking blood."

Her eyes rolled shut. "Stay awake, baby. Don't leave me." He abandoned the phone, his hands trembling as he fumbled with his seatbelt. Freeing himself, he fell onto the bloody shards of glass. His neck was bent, body contorted, and his shoulder was on fire, but he managed to open the door and roll out of the car. He stumbled over to Carly's side and tried the handle, but the smashed-in door was jammed. "Fuck!" Lying flat on the pavement, he reached for her through the shattered window and saw that her right arm was badly broken. "I'm here baby," he assured her, stroking her hair and kissing her face. "I'm going to get you out."

"I can't move...can't feel my legs," she muttered.

Gavin ripped off his shirt and held it to the gash on her head. "Where the hell are they? Where the hell are they?" Minutes felt like hours until, finally, he heard sirens in the distance. "Carly. Carly, listen to me. The paramedics are here. They're going to take you to the hospital and fix you. Please, hang on. Please, please, hang on baby."

"Gavin," her voice was barely audible over the piercing sound of the sirens. "Hold my hand." Tears rolled backwards down her face. "I'm dying. Don't let me die."

He was consumed with helplessness and fear, knowing that all he could do was whisper empty promises into her blood covered ear. The ambulance pulled up, and the paramedics rushed toward them with supplies and a gurney. But he knew it was too late.

Carly's once exuberant face was pale and lifeless, her body already growing cold.

"Gavin," she whispered, "Maddie... tell her I love her. Take care of her... I love you... so much."

Her beautiful blue eyes went still, lifeless, yet open, staring straight at him.

"Sir, we need you to move!"

He fell back onto the asphalt, sobbing. "She's gone, she's gone! Not my Carly... please... not my Carly."

Gavin woke up in a cold sweat with Carly's name on his parched lips. Tears soaked his face and pillow as his mind once again reeled with images from that horrible night. Carly's back had broken, and her lungs had collapsed from the impact of the airbag. She was pronounced DOA at the hospital, and Gavin was left with mental snapshots of the love of his life's suffering as she left the world, well before her time.

For Gavin, months of rehab followed. Shoulder surgery was followed by physical therapy and mental health therapy, which was followed by thoughts of a potential comeback. But to say Gavin didn't have it in him anymore would have been an understatement. The accident had left him a mere shadow of his former self. Although that had still been good enough to keep him on a team's roster, he would rather not play at all than play mediocrely. Once he had made the decision to leave baseball behind for good, Mack helped him find the ranch. Although Timber Creek irked him in many ways, it was the perfect place to disappear in anonymity, hide behind a beard, and be nobody, while still providing a semblance of a life for his daughter.

The alarm clock on his bedside table read 10 a.m. He had overslept and, once again, shirked his morning chores. *No matter*, he thought. His employees had come to expect extraordinarily little from him that time of year.

It was a bad sign that he didn't feel like total shit after the kind of drinking he'd done yesterday, which meant he was still drunk. *Best to keep the train rolling.* He took a swig from the bottle on his nightstand. *I'll sip slower today. Maybe cut it in half tomorrow...*

The smell of pumpkin pie seeped in through the crack under his bedroom door, and his empty stomach growled. June was at it again. A pang of guilt hit him like a punch in the gut as he shuffled into the kitchen and looked around the immaculate space. Lately she'd been here more than her own home, solely out of the kindness of her heart. She went above and beyond: making Maddie breakfast, seeing her off to school every morning, cleaning, and cooking dinner for them most nights. He should be paying her; he had tried many times, but she'd refused. Her sisters helped manage the pie shop she owned on Main Street, which gave her the flexibility to help Gavin out. She seemed to love baking in his kitchen. Beyond experimenting with recipes for the festival, she often used it to bake pies for the shop in the wee hours of the morning. "There's something about your oven," she'd told him. "Bakes extra TLC into my pies." Gavin's house smelled like a bakery 24/7.

"Good morning!" June trilled, wiping her hands on a dish towel. "Sit, I need your opinion! This one has a smidge of cocoa in it."

He sat down in front of the slice of other worldly smelling pie and dipped a forkful of it into a bowl of fresh whipping cream. The sweet, spicy flavors danced on his tongue, and he closed his eyes, basking in the pleasure of it. It was rare when he allowed himself to genuinely enjoy something. "Mmmm… Damn, that's good pie."

June beamed from the stove. "Well, you're holding it down this time, so that's a good sign."

He gave a hint of a smile. "June, if you don't win this year, I will literally beat the shit out of those judges."

She giggled. "Gavin Taylor, you will do no such thing. But thank you for saying so."

After scarfing down the remainder of the piece, he stood to set his plate in the sink, pausing there to collect his thoughts. It was so difficult for him to show emotion, to let his feelings out. But he knew he owed her this. "June," he began, turning to face her. "I want to apologize for last night. I know… I was incredibly rude. And it wasn't a first-time offense. I just want you to know… I hope you know… how much I appreciate everything you do and have done for me and for Madison."

She walked toward him with her plump arms open wide and enveloped him in a hug. He couldn't remember the last time he'd been hugged, and the foreign human contact nearly broke him. "Oh, I do dear. Don't you worry." She pulled him back at arm's length, rested her hand on his bearded cheek, and pinned her kind, grey-blue eyes to his. "You're a hard nut to crack, Gavin Taylor. I don't know the ins and outs of what you're dealing with, but I know enough to know that you've been in pain for a long time. I care about you and Madison very much, and I'm always going to be here." Her eyes welled up with tears. "I'm happy to help. It brings me joy."

The woman is an honest to goodness saint, Gavin thought. He didn't know what she'd seen in him over the years to allow him so much grace.

June cleared her throat and pulled away from him, plucking a tissue from a box on the counter to wipe under her eyes. "Speaking of Madison…" The shift in her tone and overall body language didn't leave Gavin with the warm and fuzzies.

"Yeah?" His voice dropped an octave.

"Seems she left school again. Apparently, there was a bit of an altercation; some of the kids were teasing her again. The principal wants to set up a meeting with you."

Gavin scrubbed his hands over his face and groaned. He was miles outside his comfort zone when it came to his daughter and horrible at navigating these types of situations. Last time she got caught ditching he was too shit faced to respond parentally beyond "Don't do it again". "Okay, thanks June. I'll talk to her." He pretended not to notice the flash of worry and skepticism in her eyes. "The boys already leave?"

"Yes, they sent the cattle out to graze and are checking the fences for repairs," she replied. Gavin nodded. "Thanks again, June." He went to his room to change his clothes, grabbed the bottle of whiskey, and headed out the back door.

From the outside, the old pole barn behind his house was nothing special. The oak planks were slightly dilapidated, the hinges rusted, and the sliding doors often stuck. What was inside made it special to him. It housed a variety of exercise equipment: a weight bench and free weights, adjustable dip station, a treadmill, and his most prized possession: a pitching cage, complete with a mound, a pitching rubber, a metal strike zone, and a radar gun to record his speeds. After flicking on the lights, he walked to the cage. He hadn't used it in a couple weeks, and it was time he got back to it.

Although he'd never play again professionally, baseball would always be a part of him. It called to him like an ocean summoned a surfer, and this cage was a way to set himself right. For some reason, this anniversary had been particularly hard on him. He was naturally a very structured man who enjoyed working around the ranch, but it felt like he was trudging through tar to come out the other side of this godforsaken month. Maybe it was the fact that Madison was getting older and more aware of what a fuck up he was. He took a swig from the bottle, promising himself it would be the last of the morning, and grabbed a couple baseballs. He paused on the mound to let the whiskey settle before beginning his routine. Soft throws to warm up. Fastballs when he was loose. Then, the nasty stuff.

Nothing had changed in the years since he'd been out of the game. His fastball lacked speed, and his slider lacked command. But on the mound, he felt focused. Almost normal. As close to normal as he could feel anyway.

After a couple of grueling hours throwing and lifting weights, his cell phone alerted him of a text message. It was from Xavier Hernandez, one of the few people from his past who still reached out to him. He had an update. St. Louis had fired its manager, and Xavier had just been promoted from bench coach. His first game managing the team would be this evening.

As always, there are two tickets waiting for you at Will Call.

Xavier knew Gavin would never come, even if he could work out the logistics and travel to games on occasion. Still, he always sent texts his way.

Gavin picked up the bottle of whiskey. "Screw it." He downed another swig before replying to Xavier with nothing but a thumbs up and clapping emoji. He maxed the weight on his leg press to three-sixty and regulated his breathing in time with the repetitions. After ten reps, his thighs were on fire. His current semi-inebriated condition was not conducive to that type of workout, but Xavier's text had irked him, and he needed to do something other than dwell on the fact that his friends were succeeding without him.

"I don't believe it's wise to mix alcohol and weights." Prater took a seat beside him and replaced the bottle of whiskey with bottled water. He took a long sip of the amber liquid and grimaced. "This isn't Tennessee whiskey. If you're gonna drink, do it right." Gavin wiped his brow with a towel and downed the bottle of water.

"I'll keep that in mind, Jim." Still coming down from his workout, his breath came out in heavy pants as he gave Prater the side-eye. "I'll also keep it quiet from June that you're sipping when you shouldn't."

The two men chuckled. They kept each other's secrets well.

"How's the arm?"

Gavin shrugged. "The same. Feels good, but still not up to snuff."

Prater took another sip of whiskey. "Maybe the issue isn't physical. The amount you drink certainly isn't going to help you get to where you want to be."

Dropping his chin to his chest, Gavin sighed. Beads of sweat dripped from his forehead onto his clasped hands. "How long have you known me, Prater? My drinking isn't news. I know I've been a mess, but I'm gonna get better."

"Right, right, it's the end of the month. Time to get back to normal. But, Gavin, your normal is exactly what I'm referring to. The days you call 'good', you're still downing several drinks a day. I reckon you'd never thought of doing that in your hay day. Maybe if you put down the bottle, even for just a couple months to really see what you could do, you'd find yourself whole again."

Gavin reflected for a quiet moment before he walked to a bookshelf in the corner of the barn where a dusty shoe box full of old photos and memorabilia sat. The box served as a time capsule of his past life, and he shared its contents with no one, not even Madison. He wasn't sure what prompted him to open the lid and pull out a picture of him and Carly together. Maybe it was because he'd come to know Prater as a friend and felt compelled to share a little more of himself with the trustworthy man.

He offered the photo to Prater who examined it with a gentle smile. "She was beautiful. You two made a mighty handsome couple." A chuckle escaped him. "Ah, and look at you. That baby-face. Who knew you were so handsome underneath all that scruff?"

"This was my first day in the majors. Everything was falling into place. We were building the life we'd dreamt of and had so much ahead of us. And then, poof. Gone in an instant. Not a day goes by that I don't think or dream about that night. It plays in a loop, over and over and over again in my mind. It's so damn exhausting." Gavin looked around the barn. "You want to know the real reason why I do this, knowing I'm never gonna be what I was? I do it for a few moments of peace, not because I want to make a comeback or believe there's a chance in hell that it could happen." Gavin took the picture from Prater and placed it back into the box. "That ship has long since sailed."

Prater stood and picked up a couple of baseballs. He flicked them to Gavin, who caught and then tossed them into a nearby bucket.

"What would you do, if you were me?"

Prater sat down again, quiet for a long moment. "I'd get over it and move on."

"Get over the fact that my wife died? Wow, that's some sage advice." Gavin fumed, sitting down beside him on the weight bench. "Your wife is still alive, Jim. You've been blessed with a long, happy marriage. So, forgive me when I say that I don't think it's your place to lend advice on the matter. You will never understand the level of hell I go through every single day."

Prater's demeanor hardened. "I buried my son six years ago, after he was killed in Afghanistan. And I'm old enough now that I've buried quite a few friends. So, I can assure you, Gavin, I've grieved plenty in my time." Prater reached into his empty front pocket for a cigarette and sighed. "I mourn the loss of my son every damn day. I know what a helpless, powerless, gut wrenching feeling it is to not be able to go back and change what happened. No one should have to bury their child, and I'd have given anything to trade places with him. Daniel made a choice to join the Marines, and I respected that. He's a hero in my eyes, and I miss him all the time. But I'm still here, and life must go on. I have people who count on me every day. I don't have the luxury to fall apart, and even if I did..." he looked over at Gavin with glassy eyes, "who would take care of you?"

Prater leaned on his forearms, fingers entwined loosely in front of him. "There's a little girl in there who needs you to be a father to her. It breaks my heart that the two of you have drifted so far apart." The old foreman's mouth turned down, and he let out a breath through his nose. "I've got just enough pride not to say this to another soul outside this barn, but there are so many times that I've looked back on my time with Daniel and wished I had done more for him and with him." Prater shook his head. "I'm not telling you to forget about Carly. I'm saying you have to find a way to move on from it, while still keeping her memory alive. Do you ever talk to Madison about her?" Gavin knew he already knew the answer to that question. "'Cause I'm sure she'd love to hear stories about her mama; see some of those pictures you've got hidden away in that box framed on the mantle." He rested a hand on Gavin's shoulder. "Son, you can't keep wandering around life like misery is your middle name."

A hard lump built in Gavin's throat. "What if not doing that feels like an insurmountable task?" He wiped his eyes and let out a long shaky breath. "I'm sorry. I should have been more sensitive; I didn't know about your son." *After five years, how did you not know?* He admonished himself. "If it makes you feel better, I'm well aware of the fact that I'm a selfish bastard."

Prater cracked a smile and patted Gavin's shoulder. "I know it's hard. We honor the dead by remembering them, but also by living out the rest of our lives honorably, as they would have wanted us to." A beat of silence passed between them, then Prater grunted, hesitating another moment before he spoke.

"Guess now's as good a time as any to tell you we're in the red this year. Lucy ran the numbers a couple weeks back."

Gavin deadpanned. "We're losing money? Shit! Jim, you're just now telling me this?"

"Well, with all due respect, you haven't exactly been available for these types of conversations. Figured it was best not to burden you with it."

"Like, how much are we talking about?"

"Around ten thousand dollars."

Gavin scoffed at the amount. "That's pocket change, you know that. Where are we losing money?"

"You pay us, the boys, and Lucy a fair sum. Stable repairs. The price of beef fell."

"Jim, I could lose that much for ten years and we'd still be fine. We'll pull from my savings if we need to."

"With all due respect, you hired me to be your foreman. If you're losing money, I'm losing money. It means that in ten years' time, there won't be any money for our families. You'll have nothing left to leave Madison. Miller had the same problem, you know. He didn't take advantage of the money-making potential this ranch has to offer. He depended on the cows to cover all of his expenses, and eventually that stopped being enough. He reverse mortgaged and refinanced until there wasn't a bank in the entire state that would lend to him. Do you want that to be Madison's legacy? A ranch that's hemorrhaging money?"

Gavin stood and motioned for Prater to follow. He locked the barn door behind them and let out an exasperated sigh. "What do you suggest?" He already knew he wouldn't like his foreman's answer.

"Do I really need to say it? Open to the community. We have plenty of empty horse stalls we can rent out for boarding. We have an arena, so why not offer riding lessons and guided tours of the ranch? We can also convert our abandoned structures into vacation rentals. Hell, let's put a saloon on the property so you can keep your drinking in house and stay out of trouble."

Gavin stopped walking, and Prater turned to face him. "Jim, the appeal of living here and the beauty of our arrangement is that I don't have to be around other people, let alone interact with them on the level you're talking about."

Prater ran a hand through his thinning hair and pinched the bridge of his nose. "Son, you are frustrating the hell out of me. You put your faith in me to run this place. If you don't trust my advice, I might as well resign. Or you can run it yourself, since you clearly have a better plan. Oh, wait, you don't, other than finding the bottom of another bottle."

Gavin worked his jaw. The old man was pissing him off, but he did have a point. "Look, I don't appreciate you using my daughter to try and guilt me into this… but you're probably right."

"The fall festival is in two weeks," Prater said. "Let's rent a booth and ask if we can set up horse rides next to it. We can pass out business cards; get our name out there. I'll put in a couple calls to contractors; get some quotes on restoring the old cabins."

Gavin groaned.

Prater snickered.

"Good. I'll start making arrangements."

They walked through the back door and into the kitchen. Madison was seated at the table, her schoolbooks laid out in front of her. She looked up at Gavin, her face twisted in confusion.

"Why are you here? These days you're usually at the bar when I get home."

"Why are you wearing that?" Gavin retorted.

Prater cleared his throat, looking about as comfortable as an atheist in church. "Gav, I think a storm's coming through. I'm gonna go help the boys wrap up for the day." He gave him a look that said *remember what we talked about* as he left the room.

Gavin nodded once before turning his attention back to his obstinate daughter.

"Maybe I decided you need help picking out outfits for school. Seriously, Madison, if you tried to blend in a little more you wouldn't get picked on. I'm telling you, these wild outfits of yours are to blame for this mess. I've let you have free reign on the clothes you order, but now that it's affecting your schooling, I may have to take my credit card back from June and cut you off."

"You wouldn't dare!"

"Watch me." He could hear how unreasonable he sounded. Prater's words of advice were there in his mind, and he had taken them to heart, but he couldn't help it. Although he knew it was immature and foolish to engage in yet another war of wits with his preteen daughter, she knew exactly how to push his buttons.

She threw the pencil she was using for her homework onto the hardwood floor with a smack and glared at him. Her breaths came in rapid succession through flared nostrils. "Thanks for having my back, dad. At least there's one person in this stupid town who appreciates me, besides Nana June and Papa Jim."

"And who might that be?"

"Her name is Hayley Jackson, and she opened up the new store in town, *Country Chic Boutique*. She said she likes my style. She encouraged me to be myself, unlike my own father!"

"Well, she sounds horrible." *Stop being such a prick to her, Gavin.* He closed eyes and took a deep, calming breath, wishing to God he had a drink. "Is that where you went after you left school yesterday?" he asked evenly.

Madison pursed her lips and stayed quiet.

"Answer me," he said firmly.

"No," she said, just as solidly.

"You're lying!"

"I'm not. I left school yesterday to go fishing. I left school today to visit her store." Madison folded her arms in front of her defiantly, with a smug smile, indicating she had won.

Gavin gritted his teeth and pointed a finger in her face. "You leave school one more time and you're grounded for a month. That means no fall festival, understand? And I'm done with your disrespectful attitude."

Madison pushed back her chair to stand and picked up her schoolbooks. "Whatever you say, *dad*." She spit out the word, like it was sour on her tongue. "I'm sorry to be such an inconvenience. I'll try not to bother you anymore; feel free to go back to the bar now."

She stomped out of the room, leaving Gavin filled with shame and regret. He felt like even more of an asshole when he realized he'd yelled at her in front of June, who was quietly making them dinner. She set Madison's hot chicken sandwich and fries aside and pulled a plate from the cabinet.

"That didn't go too well, now did it?" The sound of raindrops pelting the roof echoed through the kitchen. "I know raising a girl her age can be tough. She really is a sweetheart, but also quite fiery." June laughed softly.

Gavin growled. "She's her mother's daughter. Carly used to bust balls with the best of them. There was no winning with her either. Madison's her mini me."

"That's the first time I've ever heard you talk about Carly, but I gather that you loved her dearly. Obstinance and all." June set a plate of casserole and green beans with biscuits on the table. "Sit. Eat. I can't remember the last time I've seen you eat an actual meal."

Gavin scraped back the chair and plopped down, heaving a heavy sigh. "It's different with Madison. She's a child, and I'm no good…I'm not good with her." June pursed her lips but remained quiet, letting him speak. "I know I went about that the wrong way, and I didn't mean half the shit I said. I don't know what to do… how to make things better with her."

June took the seat across from him with a cup of tea. "Well, it's not really any of my business, and, from what I gather, you won't approve, but she's been talking about Hayley Jackson nonstop. Hayley grew up here, was a fiery thing herself when she was small. Grew into quite a looker," she said with a wink.

A woman, tall and curvy, with arms full of clothing, flashed through his mind.

"She's Shea Jackson's girl. You know, the Shea Jackson who owns half the town?" Gavin had obviously seen the name around town: Shea Hardware, Shea Appliance, Shea Real Estate. Beyond that, he knew nothing about the family.

He shrugged. "Whatever you say."

June shook her head at him and tsked, stirring her tea. "Apparently, our hometown golden girl has made a real name for herself. Everything she sells is from her own personal line, and from what I hear, it's all quite nice. It surprises me, the ladies of this town aren't really open to change. If Hayley weren't a Jackson girl, I don't think her reception would be as warm. Anyway, enough of my blabbing." June must have noticed how Gavin's eyes had glazed over. "I said all that to say Madison keeps talking about wanting a special dress for the fall festival, and it seems Hayley might be willing to help out. I reckon if you go to the boutique yourself and talk to her about making Maddie something, your daughter might be more open to listen."

"To my dipshit advice, telling her not to be herself? God, I'm an asshole. But dammit, June, I don't want Maddie to keep getting picked on."

"Hayley may just change things around here. Styles and opinions," June said. "Your daughter loves fashion, Gavin, it's her thing. I've sat with her many times, scrolling through websites for clothing, watching her little face light up. Look at this as an olive branch of sorts, a way to tell her that you see her."

"Thanks, June." Gavin stood up and headed to his room to change.

Gavin drove his blue Dodge Ram into town, past the swarm of ladies milling in and around the clothing store, despite the steady rainfall. He contemplated popping into the bar for a quick drink while he waited for the crowd of nosy women to dissipate, but the bar looked crowded too, and Declan was the last person he wanted to see. Maybe it was his day off and Stan was working the bar, he thought. Did he want to risk it? *Probably.* He'd left his flask at home and needed a refresher before talking to that Hayley woman about things pertaining to his daughter. He swung into the last open parking space in front of the bar.

Gavin felt every eye in the place pegged on him when he walked through the door, shaking the rain from his hair and wiping his hands down the sleeves of his jacket. When he approached the bar, he was relieved to see Stan, welcoming him with warm eyes and a smile. "Mr. Taylor, it's nice to see you!"

"Whiskey, neat."

"Comin' right up. Need a menu? I just got the kitchen remodeled, so we're serving food now. We have some pretty mean chicken wings."

The door leading to the kitchen swung open, and a waitress carrying a tray of food appeared. Declan was fast on her heels, dish towel slung over his shoulder, trademark cocky smirk planted on his face. *Shit.* Gavin immediately regretted his decision. Declan did a double take when he saw him.

"What makes you think you're welcome back in here?" he groused, shooting daggers with his eyes.

Gavin mirrored his hostile expression. "Don't need the douche-tude today, man."

"What did you just say to me?"

"Declan." Stan's stern voice caused his son to stand down, but there was something in Declan's lingering gaze that Gavin didn't like. A threat… a warning.

"Everything okay, Deck? Need us to help you set this guy straight?" shouted one of the four men playing pool in the corner of the bar, wearing a camo ball cap and two-sizes-too-small, patriotic t-shirt.

"You'll do no such thing," Stan intervened, sliding Gavin's drink in front of him. "Go back about your business, boys."

An unfamiliar face occupied the seat beside him. The man was focused on the television above the bar, seemingly unaware of the drama that surrounded him. A baseball game was on, and Gavin's interest was instantly piqued. *Xavier's first game.* Shit, he'd completely forgotten.

"St. Louis is up by two over New York," the man said, his eyes still fixed on the screen.

"Hmm," Gavin grunted, sipping his drink as he settled in to watch the end of the game.

When the game cut to commercial, the man turned to him. "Are you new in town? I don't think we've met."

Gavin grew tense, annoyed by the feeling. "I work at the ranch."

The man chuckled. "The mysterious Miller Farm. Y'all sure keep to yourselves up there, don't ya?" He looked at Gavin more intently. "Ah yes.

I think I've seen you around, but we've never officially met. My name is Pastor Bradley Wilkes." He extended his arm, and Gavin gave him a reluctant handshake. "Gavin."

"You're a man of few words, aren't you, Gavin?"

"And you're a Pastor in a bar. What do your parishioners think about that?"

The man chuckled. He was a rotund, clean cut guy with rosy cheeks and a kind smile. Gavin surmised they were around the same age. "I don't own a TV, but I do love baseball. I frequent this place on game days. I quit drinking a few years back."

Gavin nodded at the man's drink. "A vodka cranberry?"

"Nah, just cranberry. Taste it for yourself if you don't believe me. Oh, the game's back on. St. Louis promoted a new manager, and he's about to get his first win."

Gavin turned his attention to the game and watched two consecutive relievers give up a walk and a hit. He polished off his drink. "I hate to say this, but they're about to blow it. St. Louis has the worst bullpen in baseball. That's why they fired their manager. I doubt even Hernandez can help them this late in the season."

"Those are strong words, Gavin. Xavier Hernandez is a first ballot Hall-of-Famer. I have faith that he'll do some good. Watch, he'll put a closer in now who will shut the door."

Gavin shook his head and laughed through his nose. "Sorry, Preacher man, your closer sucks. If the talent's not there, it doesn't matter who's in charge. I'll bet you fifty dollars cash the closer blows the save."

The young preacher's cheeks reddened. "I'd take that bet if I had fifty dollars on me."

"No matter, I don't need your money." Gavin lifted a shoulder. "Just letting you know I'm right." The men sat quietly and watched as the closer gave up the winning runs. The camera panned to Xavier's livid face, and

Gavin laughed softly. "Oh man, he is pissed at these jokers." He reached for his phone to text Xavier.

Tough luck, bro. Keep UR head up.

"How are you so good at this?" the Pastor asked with incredulous eyes. "I can banter about baseball all day long, but you sound like an analyst. Did you ever play?"

Gavin ran his finger around the rim of his empty glass while his heart pounded against his ribcage. "Grew up playing. Got injured, so I didn't make it too far. Ended up here." He'd become a pro at giving vague answers, giving people just enough to stop them from probing any further.

"Maybe we can watch another game together one of these days. Or you could come on down to the Main Street Baptist Church sometime. Sunday services are at nine and eleven; we'd love to have you."

"Maybe," Gavin placated, standing. "Thanks for the company." He tossed a twenty-dollar bill on the bar and grabbed his jacket, glancing out the window at the boutique.

"Later, Gavin," Stan yelled as Gavin pushed open the door and stepped outside. The rain had stopped, leaving behind the scent of earth and a biting chill in the air.

The crowd outside the boutique was gone, and the store looked relatively empty. He slung his jacket over his shoulders and crossed the street, curious to see for himself why his daughter–and apparently the whole town–was so smitten with Hayley Jackson.

FOUR

Hayley

Hayley winced against the burn that went along with having your cheeks squeezed by an overzealous elderly woman. She gently removed the woman's hands and grasped them between her own.

"You are so kind to come out and support me, Miss Ann," Hayley said graciously, smiling though her cheeks were on fire.

"I wish I could buy your dresses; they are all so pretty. But where would I wear them?" She looked around the boutique, her sparse grey brows drawn low, her head covered in tiny, spring-like curls, which permeated the air with a skunk-esque, fresh-from-the-beauty-shop perm odor.

"Well, I don't think you need an excuse to wear a pretty dress," Hayley replied. "Feels good to get a little dolled up, even if you're just grocery shopping. I've got plenty of casual looks as well."

Miss Ann beamed. "Oh Hayley, your mama must be so proud of you. Finally, a Jackson daughter has found success! I always had a feeling it would be you."

Hayley gave her a tight smile, resting a hand on the old woman's arm. "Now, Miss Ann, she's proud of all her daughters, and they are happy with the lives they've chosen. It's their business if they want to stay home and raise their babies. One of the most important jobs out there, if you ask me. And the hardest."

Having kids was the furthest thing from Hayley's mind, but she adored her nieces and nephews. It had been so nice for her to finally connect with them in person, instead of through Skype. All three of her sisters were frazzled but happy.

"Humph. Well, yes. I suppose." Miss Ann hadn't changed much since Hayley had her as a teacher two out of her four years at Timber Creek High. She could be sweet at times, in her own way, but she was generally prickly, prideful, and the queen of backhanded compliments.

"Speaking of babies, we need to find you a good man," she prodded, with a twinkle in her eye.

Kinsley was perched on a stool behind the counter, choking on the sip of La Croix she had just taken. "I'm sorry," she coughed out. "I am in total agreement, ma'am. Hayley needs to start having babies soon or it will just pass her right on by." She flicked her wrist for added theatrics.

Hayley had to look away from Kinsley and bite down on her smile to keep from laughing. "Anyway, Miss Ann, are you ready for the fall festival pie bake-off? Mama tells me you're going for your sixth win in a row. That's impressive." Hayley's mama had also told her that the multiple wins were courtesy of Timber Creek's mayor, who also happened to be Ann Davis's son. She knew June Prater could make a mean pie. As a kid, she'd often stopped by her quaint little shop after school for a slice of cherry with vanilla bean ice cream.

Miss Ann's eyes lit up, and she clasped her boney hands together. "It's in the bag. I hear June Prater is trying out all sorts of new recipes, but I say it's best to stick with tradition. Don't misread me, I think she's a wonderful baker. I just don't think she's got what it takes to win." She shook her head mournfully. "Heavens me, I should have rethought becoming a teacher and opened up a pie shop of my own…"

Everyone who had you for a teacher would have been grateful for that, Hayley thought, teeth clenched behind her fake smile.

"Well, I must be going. The cats won't feed themselves!"

Hayley took a step back, just in case she decided to go for her cheeks again. "It was so nice to see you again, Miss Ann. Have a wonderful evening." She breathed a sigh of relief when the woman was finally out the door and away from view. A few more minutes and day one would officially be in the books.

"Damn, and you thought I was bad." Kinsley popped a stick of gum in her mouth. "Half the women in town are trying to push you down the aisle. Didn't one of them even try to hook you up with her married son?"

"Sweet baby Jesus. Yes," Hayley muttered, shaking her head. "Mrs. Jenkins' son, Leroy. He was pretty cute but only had eyes for Lindsey Clark. Mrs. J couldn't stand her, and apparently that hasn't changed."

"I heard one woman going on and on about her nephew Sam from the hardware store."

Hayley curled her lip. "Sam Stevens? Not a chance. He follows Declan around like a little puppy, always has. Trust me, Kinz, the available men in this town aren't worth your time. I punched most of them back in the day." She straightened a rack of dresses and put misplaced items back where they belonged.

"My plan is to take one of these small-town boys for a test drive, after I officially end things with James."

Hayley refolded a stack of lace trimmed camisoles. "To Declan's boys you are fresh deer, my friend. One date and you'll be running back to poor, sweet James. There's a reason why that group of losers are still single."

"Wait, what? Did you say deer? Do you think they'd take me out hunting?" Kinsley replied with an *I just ate something rancid* look on her face. "Oh *hell no.*"

The twinkle lights that lined the ceiling were Hayley's favorite decorative feature in the store. She looked up at them and smiled before powering them down for the night. "Calm down, Kinz, it was just an expression. Can you wipe down the counter and close the register?"

Kinsley pressed a few buttons on the screen and grabbed a bottle of Windex and paper towels from underneath the counter. "I can't stand the sight of blood, and you know I'm a vegetarian."

"No one's gonna force you to go hunting, weirdo. But yeah, most of the men around here do. They also eat plenty of meat. You don't have to join in, but if you legitimately want to hook up with a guy in this town you can't lecture them about it. It's their world. They ain't gonna take kindly to a newcomer telling them what they can and can't do."

"Is it weird that I just got a little turned on by that accent?"

Hayley batted her long lashes. "Not at all, sugar."

"Oh, yay! It stopped raining! *Shit*." Kinsley set down the bottle of glass cleaner and stared out the window, concern etched in her delicate features.

"What is it?" Adrenaline shot through Hayley at her friend's sudden change in tone. She followed Kinsley's gaze out the window.

"That drunk homeless guy I was telling you about is headed this way. Should I call the police?"

A man Hayley had never seen before was shuffling his way across the lamp lit street. He had a long, unkempt beard and hair that fell just below his shoulders. He was tall, almost imposingly so.

"Huh. I don't think he's homeless," Hayley murmured as he pushed open the door and stepped inside the boutique. She examined him curiously. Although he was scraggly looking, his clothes fit him well and looked expensive.

"Good evening, sir," Kinsley spoke up. Hayley heard the subtle hint of nervousness in her friend's voice and nearly rolled her eyes. She had lived in a major metropolitan city for years, and she was leery of this guy? "Just so you know, we close in five minutes."

"Then I guess I have five minutes to look," the man replied curtly, scraping through the rack of dresses Hayley had just straightened. *The customer always comes first*, she reminded herself.

It had been such an amazing first day, but Hayley was exhausted and ready to go home to a bottle of wine, a meal, and a bath. "Are you looking for a dress for your wife? Girlfriend?"

"No."

"I don't think we've met before." Hayley extended her arm to shake his hand. "I'm Hayley Jackson, the owner."

The man ignored her introduction and continued combing through dresses, seemingly frustrated. "I'm looking for a dress for my daughter. Heard you might be able to help."

"Oh... okay." Even behind all that scruff, Hayley thought he couldn't have been more than thirty, far too young to have a daughter old enough to fit into any of her dresses. "How old is your daughter, and what's her size?"

"She's eleven, and the size of an eleven-year-old."

Kinsley snorted out a laugh from behind the register, eliciting a glare from Hayley. *Sorry*, she mouthed.

Turning her attention back to the man, Hayley planted on a smile. "I'm so sorry, but I only make clothing for women. A girl was here earlier today looking for a dress. Madison, I believe her name is? Sweet little thing. Is she your daughter?"

"Yes." The man reached into his back pocket and pulled out his wallet. He examined the price tag on the dress nearest to him, one of her more expensive pieces.

"This dress is one-hundred-and-thirty dollars." He opened his wallet, exposing a fat stack of bills. Hayley tilted her head to the side and pursed her lips, curious as to where he was going with this. He pulled out three of them and held them up between his index and middle fingers.

"I'll give you three hundred dollars to make a custom dress for my daughter."

Hayley was at a loss for words, in limbo between feeling intrigued and annoyed. "Ummm..."

"Four hundred," he added, drawing another bill from his wallet.

Kinsley came to stand by Hayley's side and gasped softly at the four bills in his hand, which was comical considering how wealthy she was.

"*Well?*"

Hayley didn't appreciate the man's pushy attitude or being put on the spot. "As I told your daughter today, with all of the craziness surrounding our launch, I can't work on a line for younger girls just yet. Maybe in the spring, once things have settled down. Please understand, these things take time."

The man deadpanned. Hayley found him to be so odd. Disheveled, yet arrogant and well-dressed. It didn't add up. "I'm not talking about a whole damn clothing line. I'm talking about one dress for my daughter. The Fall Festival is still two weeks away, surely you can take time out of your oh-so-busy schedule for that."

She took a calming breath and tamped down her irritation. One of the most important rules of customer service was to keep a professional demeanor, no matter how difficult. Her former self would have ripped this asshole a new one. He was clearly an outsider, flashing his money.

"Sir, I understand that your daughter wants a dress, but I'm afraid it won't be possible for me to design one for her at this time. There are plenty of online options for a girl her age. When I spoke with her, she mentioned that she already purchases most of her clothing online?"

His expression darkened. "Don't talk about my daughter like you know anything about her." There was fire behind his deep brown eyes, the only thing Hayley found appealing about his face. He pointed a long finger at her. "Because you *don't.*"

She felt a rush of adrenaline. The need to put this man in his place broke through her *always stay professional* creed. "You better get your goddamn finger out of my face before you lose it. I've tried my best to be patient, but your five minutes are up, and I'm gonna need you to leave my store." She pointed a decisive finger at the door. "*Now.*"

He took two steps back and swayed slightly, hands up in an act of contrition and surrender. "Look... I'm sorry. I didn't mean to offend you."

But Hayley was too fired up to listen to his attempt at backpedaling. She squared her shoulders. "I suggest you leave."

After he left the boutique, his tail between his legs, Kinsley clicked the door locked, turned the open sign to closed, and looked at Hayley with wide eyes.

"*Wow.*"

Hayley marched to the back room for her jacket and purse. "I don't know what that guy's deal was, thinking he could just throw his money around and we'd jump? Asshole."

Kinsley was more pragmatic in her thoughts. "Agreed..." she said, shouldering into her own jacket. "But, on the other hand, it's what we do. It would take no time at all, and you were smitten with her. Oh, and did you see all of that effing cash?"

Hayley rested her hands on her hips. "It's the damn principle!"

Kinsley drew her head back. "Wow, he really got to you. I've never seen this irrational, hot-headed side of Hayley Jackson. If this is how you were with all the boys in Timber Creek, I feel genuinely sorry for them."

"I don't know who the hell he is, but he's no Timber Creek boy; I can tell you that."

"You are such a hometown snob and not even a fan of Timber Creek boys!"

"You're the one who was scared and thought he was homeless!"

The two friends looked at each other and giggled.

Hayley sighed, slinging her purse over her shoulder. "God, I'm exhausted. Let's go home."

With the exception of the asshole and her bruised cheeks, the day had been as close to perfect as she could have hoped for. Hayley felt an extreme sense of gratefulness and satisfaction. The women of Timber Creek had shown up for their town's favorite daughter. Generations of her family had lived and prospered there. She felt proud that she would now officially be a part of her family's legacy.

The storm clouds had cleared, and the sky was dotted with stars, lighting up the sky like snowflakes in the night. Hayley lifted her head and closed her eyes, breathing in deeply. The air smelled of rain and sweet maple. It was cold in her lungs, but she didn't mind it. Pulling the collar of her jacket up around her face, she looped her arm through Kinsley's as they made their way across the street on tired feet.

Hayley was thrilled Kinsley had agreed to live with her in the remodeled craftsman style bungalow, two streets down from the boutique, which she'd fallen in love with and purchased on the spot. They hadn't lived together in New York, so she was a little nervous that it would be too much living and working together, but the past month had been a blast.

Their plan was to share a celebratory bottle of wine over some homemade fried green tomatoes; Hayley's favorite southern delicacy growing up. Her mom had taught her how to make them when she was a teenager, and she couldn't wait to make them for Kinsley. She stopped in her tracks when she saw Declan Reynolds ahead of them, sweeping the sidewalk in front of The Republic.

His boy next door looks and charm were dangerously deceiving. Underneath that layer of superficial appeal, he was nothing but trouble. She knew that firsthand. He greeted Hayley with a bright smile as they approached him. When they were in high school, a smile like that from Declan would have made her weak in the knees. Now, her response came in the form of gritted teeth and narrowed eyes. His gaze flicked over Kinsley, dismissing her immediately. Hayley wanted to kick him in the balls.

"Hey there, Jackson. Looks like you gals had a great first day. Line went halfway around the block."

"Yes," Hayley said tersely. "It was a phenomenally successful day."

Declan whistled through his teeth. "Well, look at you," he scoffed, shaking his head. "Never thought I'd see Hayley Jackson acting all prim and proper. It's a shame what big cities do to hometown girls. Makes them pretentious as hell."

"Excuse me?" Hayley's voice went up an entire octave.

Kinsley's eyes ping ponged back and forth between the hostile pair with curiosity and fascination, like she was watching an episode of Jerry Springer.

"Relax, Jackson. I'm only teasing," he said, a planted-on smile stretched across his annoyingly handsome face. "What are you ladies up to this evening?

"None of your business. Goodbye, Declan." Hayley tugged on Kinsley's arm.

Declan dropped his broom and followed fast on their heels. "Come in for a celebratory drink, on the house. I'll call up one of my boys to join us," he offered, finally acknowledging Kinsley's existence.

"Ooohhh that could be…"

Hayley put her hand up to stop Kinsley from continuing and swung around to face him. "No, thank you, Declan. We have plans."

Declan perused her body with greedy eyes and a wolfish grin. "That's a real shame, Jackson. Some other time?"

"Don't call me Jackson, Deck. We're not teenagers anymore. Grow up."

As they walked away, a thought popped into Hayley's head, and she turned around. "Say, Declan!"

"Yes, *Hayley?*" God how she wished she could smack that smirk off his face.

"A man came into the boutique tonight. Tall guy, scruffy hair. Has money. You know him?"

Declan abandoned his broom again and walked toward them with purpose. "Oh, I know him alright. Works out at the old Miller Farm for

Jim Prater. Used to only see him around every once in a while, but he's been comin' around more lately, throwing down a shit ton of cash on drinks."

"How long has he lived here?" Hayley asked, growing more curious.

Declan shrugged. "Maybe five years? They pretty much stay on their side of the fence. Come into town to get supplies every now and then. You remember Prater? He's kind of a badass. It's a shame what happened to his son Daniel. He was a decent guy. But that Gavin dipshit and his two amigos are real prizes, don't know what he sees in those jack wagons. Gavin's always drinking, neglects his kid, pawns her off on the Praters. A real winner." Declan paused. "Why? Did he do something to you? You want me and my boys to fuck him up a little?"

"No," Hayley replied firmly. "I can fend for myself, thank you very much." She motioned to Kinsley that it was time to keep walking.

"Ummm… I'm gonna need the backstory on this Declan guy, ASAP," Kinsley said as they continued home."

"Like I said before, Kinz, not worth talking about." Technically, that was the furthest thing from the truth, given that Declan was responsible for the most embarrassing ordeal of her life, something she vowed to put behind her and never speak of again. Even after seven years, it still made her blood boil when she thought about what he'd done; how maliciously he'd used her. She was hoping he'd left town by now, but no such luck. Riding on daddy's coattails was a hell of a lot easier than making something of yourself.

"Hmmm." Kinsley's look said she clearly wasn't buying it.

Hayley's scowl turned into a smile as they neared their home. The front porch was an explosion of pumpkins in all shapes, colors, and sizes. Bright yellow and purple mums lined the porch steps. Dried corn stalks tied with curled burlap ribbon stood on either side of the front door. It looked like fall had thrown up on their porch, but she loved it. Life was good, and even the likes of Declan Reynolds and the town drunk couldn't ruin that.

FIVE

Gavin

Gavin kept to himself for the remainder of the evening. Once the house was quiet and settled, he grabbed a bottle of bourbon from the liquor cabinet, threw on his work boots and coat, and made his way to the horse barn. Prater had a point, he thought. Only five horses occupied the stables, including his horse, Zeus, and that left five stalls open for boarding. Madison's mare, Pegasus, whinnied from the next stall over. He had stopped teaching his daughter how to ride years ago. Nowadays, she went to Prater for guidance when she took Pegasus out for a trail ride.

He rubbed Zeus's neck and ears and patted his side, admired the meticulous work the boys had done repairing the door, and made his way up the hayloft ladder. Piles of hay and bags of horse feed covered the large, open space. He crawled to the loft window and sat with his long legs hung over the edge. It was a clear and cold night, a smattering of stars glimmered and gleamed in the onyx sky. Finneas, the barn cat, appeared and rubbed against his arm with a soft purr before darting away, most likely in search of a mouse. Relishing in the quiet time alone, Gavin took a drink of bourbon and surveyed his property.

Miguel and Alejandro lived with their wives and young children—four between them—in small, well-kept homes, a few acres from the main house, one acre apart from each other. Jim and June lived in a cozy cabin on the opposite side of the ranch, small in stature, but large enough to suit their lifestyle. Gavin saw the brake lights of June's sedan in the distance as she turned down the long dirt road that led to the cabin. He'd insisted she go home tonight.

He could hear the faint gurgling of Timber Creek, which ran through his land, convenient for watering livestock. During their first couple years on the ranch, he had taken Madison there to fish quite often. They would sit on the riverbank for hours, waiting patiently to catch their dinner. He remembered the way her tiny hands had gripped the pole so tight, the look of unadulterated joy on her face whenever the line tugged.

"I have to stop," he mumbled to himself. Grief, anger, and frustration had come to a head, and he was taking all of it out on his daughter. He took another swig of bourbon and made his way back to the house.

The house was dimly lit and quiet, aside from the steady ticking of the wall clock and gentle hum of the refrigerator. Heat pumped through the vents, heightening the lingering scent of pie. He paused at his bedroom door, looking down the bare walled hallway at Madison's. Numbing himself with booze was no longer working. He was at a crossroads with his daughter and needed to make a choice. Was he going to put in the work and learn how to be a proper father, or would he continue to wallow in self-pity and push her away even more? Prater had been right. He should talk to Madison about her mother, no matter how painful it might be. He must keep Carly's memory alive, instead of storing her away in a dusty box. He imagined her peeking down through the clouds, broken hearted by the state of things. If he wasn't willing to try, he might as well sign Maddie off to the Prater's and drink himself to death. What would he have left to live for?

He went to the bathroom mirror and raked his fingers through his coarse, straw-colored beard. "You are one ugly mother fucker."

The interaction with the shop owner had shaken him. Although she had tried to be polite and professional, he'd noticed the flicker of disgust in her eyes. He wasn't used to interacting with women and had immediately felt foolish and insecure. His own inadequacies had caused him lash out for no damn reason.

He had spent years not caring what anyone thought of him, but that woman had made him feel zero-to-sixty self-conscious. A wave of embarrassment washed over him as he pictured the look of disdain on her appealing face. The way she chastised him for pointing his finger at her, like some out-of-control douchebag.

Hayley Jackson was a beautiful woman; he couldn't deny it. He privately admitted that it played a role in the cringe worthy embarrassment of their encounter.

And then, he had an epiphany.

Squatting down, he rooted through the vanity cabinet and found his old grooming kit. He plugged in the electric razor and began shaving his beard, revealing the strong jaw, chin, and upper lip he hadn't seen in years. He gathered his hair in a ponytail and sliced through it with scissors. Using a trimmer, he buzzed up the sides of his head, and used the scissors to trim the top. Although he would need a barber to polish the look, scraped back with a little bit of pomade, his DIY cut didn't look half bad. He tossed the remains of his hair into the trash and admired his work. "Damn, if I don't look human," he mumbled. Rubbing his jaw, he moved his head from side to side in awe of seeing his face again.

Feeling a hundred pounds lighter, Gavin clicked off the bathroom light and went to bed. For the first time in seven years, he had a decent, dreamless night sleep.

Bright and early the next morning, he rolled out of bed to take a leak and did a double take in the bathroom mirror, having forgotten all about his impromptu makeover. After taking a moment to appreciate the change, he threw on his work clothes and went outside to meet the boys.

"Holy shit, where's your beard?" Miguel asked.

"Where did the squirrel on your face go?" Alejandro chimed in.

Miguel furrowed his brow in confusion. "Why are you awake?"

"Have we all died, and is this heaven?" Alejandro added.

Alejandro and Miguel's Australian Shepherd herding dogs, Bart and Remy, greeted Gavin with happy barks and tail wags. He ruffled the fur on each of their heads.

"I just felt like working today, guys. Don't need to make a big deal about it."

A smile formed on Prater's lips. "Nice to see that good-looking face in person." Gavin couldn't recall the last time his foreman had looked at him with anything other than concern or exasperation. He pulled on his work gloves.

"All right, boys; let's do some work."

His hands shook, and his head throbbed as he spent the day working on irrigation lines, but, oddly enough, he didn't crave alcohol. It felt good to get back to work, to be useful again—a tactile purpose in an otherwise purposeless life. On more than one occasion he had to excuse himself to vomit, but he refused to rest or quit.

"Best to have a little sip here and there," Prater advised when they were headed back to Gavin's house for lunch, bottles of water in hand. "The amount you were drinking, going cold turkey can be dangerous."

The end of the workday found them each with a bottle of beer in their hand on Miguel's front porch.

Miguel perked up. "Hey, what are we still doing here? It's Saturday night, amigos, let's get some tequila and have some fun."

Prater reached into his shirt pocket for a cigarette and eyed Gavin. "Let's head home, wake up early, and do some fishing. From what I remember, your last encounter with Declan wasn't exactly cordial," Prater pointed out, lighting his cigarette and taking a deep drag. "I'm getting too old to play referee in a bar fight."

"Pfft. We're not gonna let that pendejo keep us from enjoying ourselves. Come on, Jim," prodded Alejandro. "When was last time we had fun on a Saturday night?"

"Never," Miguel agreed.

"Why not share a drink and a laugh," Gavin said. He leveled his gaze at Prater who looked genuinely surprised, most likely at the prospect of Gavin laughing. "I promise I'll keep my wits about me. Sip slowly and only have a couple."

"I've never heard Gavin laugh; do not deny me this one thing." Miguel clasped his hands together, mimicking a prayer.

Prater held up his hands in surrender, cigarette dangling from his lips. "For the chance to hear this pretty boy laugh, we will have some drinks."

"Tequila!" Alejandro shouted enthusiastically.

"Fuck no, tequila es no bien!" Gavin fired back, wagging his finger in Alejandro's direction.

***

When the men arrived, The Republic was hopping. The four men wove their way through the bar, past tables filled with patrons who eyed them curiously, and chose a table tucked away in the back. A curvy young waitress with a mass of red hair and heavy-handed makeup approached them, holding a pad and pen.

"Do y'all know what you want, or do you need a minute?"

Alejandro held up four fingers. "Four Don Julio's, por favor." Prater and Gavin groaned. Tequila was not their thing, but they conceded, nodding their heads in agreement. His distaste for the drink meant that Gavin wouldn't be tempted to drink as much.

"Who's your daddy, young lady?" Prater asked the waitress, much to the chagrin of his friends. They busted out laughing while Prater gave them a blank look, seemingly confused.

"What? I just want to know who her daddy is!"

The woman did not look amused. "My daddy is John James, owns James Brother's mechanics over on Elm. Big guy, six-eight, 250 pounds." She motioned around the table with her pen, clearly growing impatient. "Is this gonna be on one tab?"

"This is on me," Gavin spoke up. "And tack on some chicken wings and alligator bites."

"Talia?" Prater's eyes lit up with recognition. "I thought you were off making it big in Nashville. John told me you had a baby? A little girl?"

"Yes," she replied in a clipped tone.

He shook his head in disbelief. "By God, that makes an old man feel even older. I remember when you were knee high, and now you've got a little one of your own."

Talia smiled curtly. "I'll go put your orders in."

When she walked away, Gavin cracked a smile. "Jim, for future reference, we don't ask women who their daddy is."

"I don't understand why the hell that is so funny," Prater replied.

"You're asking her what man owns her. Like sexually." Alejandro shook his head. "Ay de Dios jefe, daddy does not mean what you think it does."

"At least not outside Stan's Bar," Miguel chimed in.

Prater's face turned as red as a tomato, and he leaned back in his chair. "You've got to be shitting me."

Ten minutes later, Talia dropped off their shots along with a bowl of limes and walked away without saying a word.

"You old charmer," Gavin teased, holding up his shot glass. "Here's to Prater never making that mistake again."

"And here's to you assholes learning how to get your damn minds out of the gutter," Prater replied.

They laughed, clinked their glasses together, and threw back the shots in unison. An ugly burn made its way down Gavin's throat and he winced. "If I start crying, it's your fucking fault, Alejandro."

"Maybe we can find *your* daddy later," Miguel teased, fist bumping Alejandro.

"Yes, you're quite the comedian Miguel."

"I'm here all week."

"Ba dum chhh." Alejandro mimicked playing drums.

For the next half hour, the men joked, bantered, and discussed matters concerning the ranch. Gavin had missed a lot in the last month and was glad for the opportunity to catch up. He appreciated his men. They took care of business when he was down, and were loyal to him, faults and all.

Prater talked to the boys about the potential growth opportunities he and Gavin had discussed. They were surprised and appeared genuinely pleased. Having still not fully committed to the idea of opening the ranch up to the public, Gavin stayed quiet during that portion of the conversation. The mere thought of it made him feel like he was breaking out in hives.

Prater's cell phone rang, and he excused himself to take the call outside.

"Gavin, we need more shots!" Alejandro hitched a thumb toward the bar. "And we ain't talking to that racist prick, Dicklan."

Miguel snickered. "He said Dicklan."

The place was packed, and Talia hadn't come over to check on them in a while. Gavin spotted her a second later with a huge tray of food and an overwhelmed look on her flushed face.

"You think I want to talk to the racist prick?" he scoffed, popping the last alligator bite into his mouth. When they stuck out their bottom lips, Gavin rolled his eyes and pushed himself up from his chair. "Son of a bitch, you guys are pussies. One more round, then we need to go. It's getting way too crowded in here."

Gavin spotted an empty stool and sat down, relieved to see that Declan was preoccupied with a group of women at the other end of the bar. A bartender he'd never seen before was talking to a woman seated on the next stool over. She handed him her phone and he typed something into it before handing it back to her. "I'll be in touch," the woman said seductively.

He looked at Gavin with a shit eating grin, like he was the first guy to ever score a women's number in a bar. "What can I get for you?"

"Four shots of Don Julio."

"You got it." He winked at the woman before turning around to grab the bottle of tequila.

Gavin grabbed a raw peanut from the bowl in front of him and cracked it open, sweeping its remains onto the shell riddled floor.

"Jake, I got this."

Gavin cursed under his breath as his eyes connected with Declan's incredulous gaze.

"You can't take a hint, can you?"

He slid a frilly looking drink in front of the woman. She didn't look up from her phone as her pink polished fingers flew over the screen.

"Four shots of Don Julio or I'm telling *daddy*," Gavin shot back.

Declan glared at him. "Four shots for the lush and his *amigos*, coming right up." When he turned around to grab the bottle of tequila Gavin lifted a middle finger in his direction.

"Thanks, Dicklan."

The woman barked out a laugh and swung around to face him. She crossed her petite legs, leaned a casual elbow on the bar, and propped her head up with the tips of her fingers. "Wow. I take it you two aren't besties. I haven't seen an exchange of testosterone fueled rage like that in years, and I lived in New York." He immediately recognized her as the other woman from the boutique and looked away.

"Understatement." He grabbed another peanut from the bowl, twirled it round and around with his fingers, and wished the ground would open up and swallow him.

A loud crash sounded from the kitchen. "Dammit, Talia!" Declan abandoned the empty shot glasses and stomped into the kitchen. Jake was serving someone else. Gavin was tempted to reach for the bottle and pour the tequila himself.

"Have we met? You look kinda familiar."

Gavin shifted his gaze back to her and shook his head. "Don't think so."

She scrunched up her freckled nose and examined him. "I know I've seen you before. I'm Kinsley Hart. What's your name?"

"I can assure you we haven't met."

"Hayley!" Gavin froze as Kinsley craned her neck to look at the group of raucous women Declan had been pestering earlier. "Get your hot ass over here!" She had to yell over Florida Georgia Line blaring from the jukebox.

Shit. Gavin thought as his heart rate picked up speed. He tapped his thumbs together, nervous as hell. A few seconds later, Hayley Jackson was standing between them, drink in hand.

"Who's your friend?" Gavin could tell by the lazy cadence of her voice that she was drunk.

Kinsley took a sip of her drink. "Not sure yet, I was gonna ask you how I know him. He's being rather mysterious."

Hayley poked Gavin's shoulder three times. *Hard.* "Excuse me, sir, can you turn around?" He squeezed his eyes closed, scratched his jaw, and turned to face her, praying his lack of beard meant she wouldn't recognize him.

Last night her hair had been pulled over one shoulder in a thick braid. Now, it fell in soft waves well past the swell of her breasts, which were accentuated nicely in the low-cut dress she wore. His eyes traveled down to her cowboy boots and then back up her body, taking in the floral-patterned dress, long and fitted with a slit that stopped mid-thigh. She flashed him a naughty smile that left Gavin feeling a lot of things at once–confusion being one of them. The woman in front of him now was the antithesis of the prim and professional woman he had encountered last night, up until he'd pissed her off anyway.

"He's very handsome." Hayley's fingertips slid down Gavin's smooth cheek. His eyes fluttered closed for a split second, skin blanketed in goose bumps under his long-sleeved shirt as the sensation from her touch traveled all the way up his spine. He realized then just how much he'd missed a woman's touch.

"I would have remembered this face." A tiny crease appeared between her brows, and she tilted her head as if trying to place how she knew him. She drew in a sharp breath. "Wait a minute. This guy? Really, Kinz?" The volume of her voice was high enough for the back of the bar to hear. If the situation weren't so damn humiliating, he'd find it fascinating, being the sober one for once and witnessing this level of intoxication. But Gavin was a quiet, brooding drunk. This woman was *loud.* "He's the asshole from last night! The finger pointer!" Hayley lifted an index finger and spun it in front of Gavin's face. "He shaved and cut his hair, but I know it's him!"

Her friend's mouth formed a round O shape. "Well, this is awkward."

Gavin's humiliation morphed into irritation. He wasn't about to sit back and let this woman, who knew nothing about him, publicly berate him. "Look, I'm sorry about last night. I was having an… off day. As soon as I get my shots, I'll be out of your hair."

He said a prayer of thanks when Prater appeared a second later. "The boys are getting mighty restless, what's the hold up? Declan refusing to serve you?"

Gavin looked over to find Declan back with the group of ladies. Jake was behind him, preparing drinks. "Yup. Looks that way."

Hayley put her hand on Jim's arm. "Mr. Prater?'

His eyes widened and a smile stretched across his wrinkled face. "Hayley Jackson?"

Gavin watched as they embraced with warmth and affection. If June's arms felt good around him, he couldn't imagine what this woman's would feel like. That thought, mixed with an unexpected twinge of unwarranted jealousy, told him he needed to get the hell out of there. Too bad they had him boxed in.

A portion of Hayley's martini sloshed over the side of the wide rimmed glass and onto Prater's shirt as she let go of him and pulled away. "I was soooo sorry to hear about Daniel," she shouted. A song about drinking beers in the back of a pickup truck ended abruptly, and an awkward silence settled over the bar. Gavin felt every eye in the place on them. Thankfully, *Friends in Low Places* started up, eliciting an eruption of cheers. "You and June are always in my prayers!"

Prater cleared his throat and scratched the back of his neck, clearly uncomfortable.

Gavin was hit with pangs of guilt and shame. He'd been too wrapped up in his own grief to realize that the Prater's had been dealing with a shit ton of their own.

"Thank you, Hayley. We're getting by. Busy keeping these boys in line nowadays." Jim patted Gavin on the back. "Declan! I believe we ordered some shots."

"Soon as your boy here learns some manners, I'll get right on that," Declan yelled from the other end of the bar.

"I suggest you hop to it."

"Jim, you got this?" Gavin asked. "I'm gonna head back over to the boys."

Declan sauntered over to them, poured the tequila haphazardly into the shot glasses, and slid them in front of Gavin.

"Where's mine?" Kinsley whined.

"Oh, they're not for you, darlin'. They're for the town lushes."

"Watch it, Deck," Prater warned.

"Hey!" Hayley yelled, poking Gavin on the shoulder again. Unused to this level of social interaction, he was starting to feel claustrophobic. He downed one of the shots before turning to face her. She raised a brow at him, and he noticed the color of her eyes then, honey colored and luminous in the dim lighting of the bar. "You don't buy local girls drinks, outsider?"

He needed a drink. A *real* drink.

Reluctantly, he turned back to Declan. "Can I get one more for the lady? And a whiskey, neat."

"How about five?" Declan suggested with a villainous grin. "Hayley's sisters look thirsty, and Kinsley here sure seems excited about the prospect."

Kinsley looked up from her phone and raised her hand. "Yes, please!"

Declan shrugged while Gavin made a mental list of all the ways he wanted to mess up his pretty boy face. "It'd be such a shame to let all of your hundred-dollar-bills go unspent."

Gavin patted his pockets for his wallet. Realizing that he must have left it at the ranch, he glanced guiltily at Prater.

"This is on me. I'll take the shots to the guys," Prater said, eyeing Declan as he collected the glasses. "Gavin, come back and join us when you're ready to escape all of… this."

Hayley hiccupped. "Jim Prater, how dare you suggest that he would want to escape *me*."

"I was talking about these two knuckleheads; they need to learn how to play nice. It was wonderful seeing you, Hayley Jackson. Welcome home."

Declan delivered three shots to Hayley's sisters, who cheered their approval, then set another three in front of Gavin. "Can't you count? I didn't order six. And I'm still waiting on my whiskey."

"Oh, one's for me. Thanks, Gav." Declan held up the shot to Hayley who had squeezed herself further between Kinsley and Gavin and set her martini glass on the bar. "Cheers, Jackson."

She curled her lip. "Still not interested in being cordial, ass wipe." An uninhibited laugh burst out of Gavin.

Declan looked as mad as a bull seeing red. "What the actual fuck, Hayley?" He pinned Gavin with a hostile glare. "What are you doing with this ass clown, anyway? A haircut doesn't make him any less of a drunk; this side of a week ago he was passed out right where you're sitting."

Hayley rested a hand on Gavin's back and shrugged. "He doesn't look drunk to me. In fact, he looks pretty damn delectable."

"Okay." Kinsley stood up. "Sweetie, I think maybe it's time to head back over to your sisters."

"No! Why?" Hayley protested. "I'm enjoying my time with... what's your name again?"

"I think you should listen to your friend, Jackson."

"I think you should mind your own damn business, *Reynolds!*"

Kinsley sighed. "Well, this has become a real shit-show buzzkill. I'm going back to the gals; you three have fun."

She guided Hayley to sit on the barstool and whispered something into her ear before turning to a highly amused Gavin. "Okay, so my friend here has obviously had one or five too many. She probably needs to go home, but I'm gonna let her stay a little longer, because she seems to be having fun, and fun is not something she does very often. Also, I'm not nearly drunk enough yet." She pointed to the group of women. "I'll be right over there, keeping my eye on you."

Gavin held his hands up in front of him, legitimately confused. "You don't have to worry about me, I'm not interested in the least. Heading back to my friends now."

She looked at him like he had two heads. "Yeah, right. Like you'd say no to *that.*"

"Shut up and buy me a drink!" Hayley shouted.

Gavin quirked a brow at Kinsley.

"Okay, well, to her credit, she's not usually like this." Her smile was saccharine sweet as she wiggled her fingers at Gavin. "Bye, bye now."

He pointed at Hayley's martini and wondered how in the hell he had roped himself into becoming this women's babysitter. "You already have a drink. And a shot."

Her glazed over eyes scanned his face. "You look *sooo* different." Knowing how bad he looked last night, Gavin tried not to be offended by the shock in her tone. "Did you make yourself over to impress me?" She took a long sip of her drink, eyeing him over the rim of her glass.

Gavin frowned. While she *had* played a part in his decision to groom, he certainly didn't do it to impress her. "Little presumptuous of you, don't you think?"

"You look like a young Prad Bitt. She shook her head and snorted. Brad Pitt. Unfortunately, you're a liar." She poked a finger at his chest. "And I don't do liars."

"Excuse me?" he bristled, glancing behind the bar for Declan. *Where is that fucker with my drink?* "We only just met last night. Yeah, I behaved like an asshole, but I don't recall lying to you."

Hayley downed the last of her martini. "So, you're a ranch hand, huh? Work for Jim Prater?"

"Yeah…" *Where the hell is she going with this,* he wondered as he eyed the bottle of Maker's Mark.

She shook her head in disappointment and draped her left arm across the bar, diverting his attention from the booze. "Last night you walked into my store and offered me four-hundred-dollars to make your daughter a dress." Her head dropped to her arm, eyes rolled up to look at him. "You wear top of the line clothing. Outsider, fashion is my forte. There's no way in hell you're a lowly ranch hand."

Gavin stayed quiet, wondering how in the world this woman had figured him out after meeting him once and why she was so interested in the first place. *She's not interested, dickwad, she's drunk.*

They said nothing for a long moment as her heated drunken gaze landed on his mouth, her own glossy lips parted slightly. The warm, full-throated timbre of a seductive country ballad swelled and waned. She pulled herself up and swayed into him, so close he could smell her perfume, heady and warm like spiced vanilla, even over the pungent smell of fried food wafting in from the kitchen. His eyes were drawn to the cleavage spilling out of her dress, revealing the scalloped edge of a black, lacy bra. Gavin felt dizzy, and, for the first time in a long time, it had nothing to do with alcohol. Hayley reached in front of him for a shot of tequila, downed it, and smacked the shot glass down on the bar. "Okay, outsider. Buy me another, and tell me something about you that's true, or we'll call it a night."

Conflicting thoughts swirled around in his brain. She was an incredibly beautiful woman; he couldn't deny it. Any single, red-blooded man would be crazy not to pursue her. But he wouldn't, and she wasn't genuinely interested. She was off her ass drunk. Tomorrow she would listen in horror as her friend gave a play by play of her flirtatious encounter with the dress-demanding asshole.

A strange sort of sadness washed over him. He had tamped down the sexual side of himself for so long, but the way this woman was looking at him, like she'd screw him in the bathroom stall right now if he were willing, awakened something inside of him that he'd purposely left dormant. Sure, he took care of himself on the regular to memories of Carly, but she was the last woman he'd slept with. He didn't want to dishonor what they'd had together with tawdry one-night stands, and he had no desire to be in a relationship of any kind—now or ever. But now he felt an unwelcome stirring, a pang of longing, when he thought about what it would be like to be with this beautiful, hot mess of a woman in front of him.

"Oh my God. I'm making a total idiot of myself. I'm… I'm gonna go." She stood up to leave, but his long legs had her caged in. "Thanks for the drinks," she said, pushing his leg aside.

He lifted his hand and slipped his fingers around her slender wrist. "Wait."

She looked down at it with a sharp intake of breath. "Why should I?"

You shouldn't, he thought. *You should walk away right now.* He let go of her wrist. "My name is Gavin. Gavin Taylor." His brain and his mouth were working in opposite directions.

She plopped back down on the stool, and a slow smile spread across her pretty face. The apples of her cheeks were flushed, which only added to her appeal. He let out a breath he hadn't known he was holding. "Alright, Gavin, Gavin Taylor. You just bought yourself a drink with me. Deck! Martini, now."

"I'm cutting you off Jackson!" Declan yelled from the other end of the bar.

Gavin couldn't help but laugh. He'd laughed more tonight than he had in seven years.

"My name's Hayley Jackson, by the way." *Well, no fucking duh*, Gavin thought. He'd probably heard her name about a hundred times in the last twenty-four hours. "My family's like royalty, you know; we basically run the entire town."

The corners of his mouth twitched. *"Really?* I had no idea I was face to face with a real-life Princess."

"Well, now you know."

Gavin followed her eyes as they shifted to Prater, approaching them with a baffled look on his face. "Sorry to break this up, but June wants us home."

"Aww... Jim! Gav and I were just getting to know each other." She hiccupped again and waggled her finger. *Holy shit, was she's gonna hate herself in the morning.* An image of her curled up in front of the toilet, moaning her regret, flashed in his mind. "But we do not cross June Prater if we know what's good for us."

Prater's eyes moved down to Hayley's hand, which now rested on Gavin's thigh. Bushy grey eyebrows bounced to his hairline. "Ummm... *okay...* thirty minutes?"

Gavin looked at Prater with eyes that screamed *HELP*, but wasn't he the one who had just stopped her from walking away? He felt disoriented and in way over his head. "Yeah, it's getting late..."

"We'll take it!" Hayley exclaimed.

The old foreman looked back and forth between them with eyes as big as saucers before a tickled smile formed on his lips. "Alright then, I'll... leave you to it." He made his way back to the table.

"It's crowded in here." Hayley stood, gripping Gavin's shoulders to steady herself. His hands instinctively went to her hips.

"Get a room!" some asshole yelled from across the bar. An enthusiastic "Woo-hoo!" cried out from Hayley's drunken squad.

"Wanna get some air?"

Hell no, was his thought as he nodded his head yes.

When they left the warm confines of the bar and stepped into the chilly night air, she pulled on the sleeves of Gavin's jacket and slid it off of him. "You don't mind, do you cutie pie?" She swung it animatedly around her shoulders and laughed, like it was the funniest thing in the history of the world.

"Maybe I should drive you home..."

Grabbing a hold of Gavin's hand, she pulled him into the narrow alleyway between the bar and her father's hardware store. She pushed him up against the brick wall, her hands pressed to his chest as she stared up at him with heavy lidded eyes. "Who are you?" she whispered. Gavin stayed quiet, because fuck if he knew the answer to that loaded question.

She grabbed a fistful of his shirt. "Why were you such a prick to me?"

"Wasn't my intention."

"What was your 'tention?"

To make my daughter love me again, he answered himself honestly.

Her eyes struggled to stay open. "That's the saddest thing I've ever heard."

Did I just say that out loud, he thought in horror. *Thank God she won't remember this conversation.*

She stood on her tiptoes and pressed her mouth to his ear. "Your daughter's a super-duper special girl, so I'll forgive you on one condition."

The combination of her perfume and his cologne was a magical pheromone inducing concoction. "Depends on your condition." His voice was low, his breathing labored. His cock strained against the fabric of his jeans. *Pull it together, Gavin,* he chastised himself.

"Take me out on a date?"

A date? He turned the word over in his mind for half a second before concluding that his answer would be a resounding *hell no.*

"Take me to the harvest fistful. Maybe we can go out before then, give you couple chances to 'splay your honesty?"

She slid her palms up and over his shoulders, looping her arms around his neck. Gavin kept his firmly at his sides. His heart thrummed in his chest. Her eyes rolled closed, and she swayed sideways.

"You okay?" His hands moved to her hips, and a contented sigh escaped her lips. The sexually frustrated side of him was flipping tables in his mind, admonishing him for not taking her up against the brick wall right then and there.

"What are you thinking about, mystery man?"

He squeezed his eyes closed and heaved a frustrated sigh. "I'm thinking it's time to go home."

"Noooooooo," she pouted.

A smile took over his face. Even though this wasn't real and the evening had been torturous in its own right, he hadn't had this much fun in years. "Yes."

She reached between them and slid her hand over his cock. "I don't think you really want to," she whispered against his lips. His head fell back against the brick wall. He hissed through his teeth and tried to focus on every repellent thing he could think of: Prater naked, maggots, black licorice, spider eggs, rotten milk, vomit...

And then, she threw up on him.

SIX

Hayley

The crisp air smelled of the changing season, and the trees had begun dressing themselves for the occasion, their leaves turning vibrant hues, falling to the ground like oversized confetti. Being back in her hometown just in time for the start of the season had been cathartic for Hayley. Today, however, she felt as if she'd been hit over the head with a sledgehammer. Sunglasses covered her puffy, bloodshot eyes. She pulled the collar of her sheepskin coat up around her face and snuggled into a chair outside the local coffee house, Perks. It was cute and quaint, the way she preferred cafes. Chain stores weren't allowed inside city limits, and it was refreshing not to see a Starbucks on every corner, like in NYC.

Hayley couldn't stomach the idea of her usual pumpkin spice latte and had ordered a mug of turmeric cinnamon tea with honey, instead. She took a sip, appreciating the warm spiced liquid as it slid down her parched throat.

Smartly dressed in a designer hoodie and well-fitted jeans, his hair slicked back like a 1950's bad boy, her childhood friend Hunter Lynn sat across from her with a sympathetic gaze. After high school, Hunter had left for Emory, earning a degree in English Lit. He had initially set his sights on becoming an editor, but after a year working for a publishing group in Atlanta, he'd realized his passion was in writing and was currently

71

working on his first novel. He twirled a pen around with his long fingers. "I'm sorry, Hales. I could have come to your house for coffee; you didn't need to venture out when you feel like shit on a stick."

Hayley waved him off. "It's fine, I needed some fresh air. Ugh, I think I puked up a lung this morning, and you guys are barely hung over. You are wretched friends for letting me do this to myself."

"Blame your sisters!" Kinsley exclaimed, looking super cute in her oversized, off-the-shoulder, ribbed sweater paired with leggings. She was far too chipper for Hayley's liking. "They were ordering you doubles behind your back. When I finally caught wind of it, you were already long gone."

"Those bitches are dead," Hayley groused, tucking the errant strands of hair that had escaped her messy bun behind her ears.

"I needed a little break from your crazy and left to talk up the cute new bartender." She waggled her eyebrows. "Jake is Stan's nephew, visiting from Salt Lake City. He's helping out at the bar through the holidays. We have a date next Friday night," she squealed.

"Poor James." Hayley stuck out her bottom lip. "Oh, and thanks for rubbing in your good fortune in the midst of my pain," she chided. "I am declaring now that I will never drink hard liquor again. I haven't had that much to drink since college. I'm a lightweight now." She took another sip of tea, and a wave of nausea rippled through her. Blowing out a controlled breath, she pinched the bridge of her nose. "I didn't flash my boobs or start a bar fight, did I?"

"Bar fight?" Kinsley said. "Hunter, I'm gonna need you to paint me a picture of young Hayley."

Hunter set down his cappuccino and chuckled. "She was too young for bar fights, but Hales and her sisters were trouble with a capital T. Ain't no party like a Jackson party, and last night you were the star of the show, my friend."

"You were a member of our girl squad and every bit as bad as we were, Hunt."

"You hear that, Kinsley? Never was a man more politely friend zoned than by being called one of the girls."

"Oh! I kind of thought you were…"

"Gay? No. I was an exceptionally unfortunate nerd who had been mercilessly picked on since kindergarten. Hayley and I were lab partners in the seventh grade. When she befriended me, I officially became a platonic member of an all-girl crew, led by a member of Timber Creek royalty." He gestured to Hayley. "Which was basically like putting a dog in a meat locker and commanding it not to partake."

Kinsley busted out laughing. Hayley attempted to roll her aching eyes and propped her Ugg's clad feet on the empty chair next to her, snuggling deeper into her coat. "You never complained. And you did get to take me to prom after Declan… Anyway, I'll always love you for that, Hunter. Thank you."

Kinsley gasped. "Does he know the Declan story? Hunter, you have to tell me the Declan story."

"Pfft, are you kidding me? No one knows that story. And you're welcome, Hales. Even though I tried to kiss you that night and you rejected me, then come back to town single and looking like a fashion model temptress, it's more than fine. I am content with becoming a famous author and traveling the world." He stroked his chin as if in deep thought. "I'm thinking I'll land in either Paris or Tokyo."

"Hunter, noooo, you can't leave. You are so close to becoming my BFF." Kinsley scooted her chair closer to him and looped her arm through his.

"You two deserve each other," Hayley grumbled.

"Alright, enough about me." Hunter leaned back in his chair and stretched out his long legs, crossing them at the ankles. "Let's talk more about your adventurous evening."

Hayley held up a hand. "Wait a second, wait a second... back up. What did you mean earlier when you said I was the *star of the show*?"

Hunter looked at Kinsley. "You wanna do the honors?"

"You mean it's time! I can tell her now?" Kinsley bounced in her chair.

"What in God's name are you two talking about?"

Hunter cringed while looking in Hayley's direction.

A wide grin spread across Kinsley's face. "Oh, let's just say you had yourself some major fun with a certain mysterious gentleman."

Hayley sat up in her chair and set her mug on the table. "Please, tell me it wasn't Declan."

"Hell no. You told Declan off, and it was fucking brilliant. Seriously, you would have been so proud of yourself. And Gavin? Holy shit does that guy hate Declan. I laughed my ass off witnessing their alpha male exchange. I was waiting for them to whip out their dicks and compare sizes. You really don't remember any of it?"

Hayley frowned. "Who's Gavin?"

"Oh, this is so much fun." Kinsley clapped her hands together gleefully, eliciting a glare from Hayley.

"Thank you for finding so much joy in my suffering."

Kinsley placed her hand on Hayley's. "I'm so happy that you're finally interested in someone, but I must say I'm a little shocked you'd choose the prickly, aloof asshole. Although, he did turn out to be hot as sin."

Hayley lifted her sunglasses and pegged her eyes on Kinsley. "Who *the hell* are you talking about?"

"The homeless looking dress guy. He's an odd duck, wouldn't even tell me his name. The only reason why I know it is because you said it about a thousand times when we were driving home. And when I helped you from the bathroom to your bed. I don't know what happened between you guys in that alley, but you were quite proud of yourself. Said Gavin was hung like a mule."

Gavin. Declan had told her his name when she'd inquired about him after the store incident. Panic rose inside of her.

"Alley? What alley?"

"And you kept calling him an outsider. It was comical."

"Slow down! Ouch." She held her pounding head with both hands. "I'm not following you. You are all over the place with this bullshit story."

Kinsley scrolled through her phone before handing it off to Hayley. "It's not bullshit. I'm telling you, there was a spark there that went beyond alcohol consumption."

Hayley's jaw dropped. The back of Gavin's head was facing the camera but there she was, over his shoulder, smiling at him like a drunken idiot. Next was a picture of his profile. It was a little fuzzy, but she could see what Kinsley was talking about. This guy was definitely good-looking behind all that scruff. She placed the phone on the table and slid it back to her friend.

"That is an I've-got-a-crush face if I've ever seen one," Kinsley sing-songed.

Hayley buried her face into her hands. "This cannot be happening."

"I may not have grown up with you or seen drunk off her ass Hayley Jackson in action before, but I'm telling you there was something there. You did not want to leave his side."

"Kinsley, this means nothing. Hunter, stop writing this down!"

"What? This is great book material." He finger-framed Hayley's face. "The princess falls for the made over vagabond."

"If you ply a human with enough alcohol, their baser instincts always take over. Doesn't mean I'm in love with the asshole."

"Damn, I wish your sisters hadn't commandeered so much of my time," Hunter replied. "I feel like I missed so much."

A whisper of a memory came back to Hayley. "Holy shit," she breathed. "I think I may have asked him out."

"Oh, I know you did," Kinsley said. "You kept saying it over and over again. I asked Gavin to take me to the festival, I asked Gavin to take me to the festival. But you called it a fistful."

Hunter's face was turning red from holding in his laughter.

"And may I remind you this is the same guy you yelled at twenty-four hours prior?" Kinsley couldn't suppress her smile.

"You think this is funny?" Hayley scowled at her. "You're the worst, you know that? I think this town has had a bad influence on you."

"Hales, this is a good thing! You know how badly I want to see you get back on the dating horse again. And if you happen to mount a stallion or two before finding the right one, no harm, no foul."

"Ew. Kinsley, you're talking about my *sister*." Hunter air quoted his emphasis on sister.

Hayley's cheeks burned. "There will be no mounting of stallions." She set her forehead down on the metal table with a clang. "Dammit. Now I have to find this guy and attempt to explain myself," she mumbled despondently.

"I wholeheartedly agree. Oh, and while you're there, you should also apologize for puking on him."

Hayley's head shot up. "Please tell me you're joking." She grabbed a fistful of Kinsley's sleeve. "I didn't really do that, did I?"

Kinsley sucked in air through her teeth. "Afraid so, sweetie. In the alleyway next to the bar."

The door to the coffee shop opened, and a man stepped out, interrupting Hayley's private mental horror show. He was well-groomed and well-tailored, his round belly buttoned up inside of a grey wool pea coat.

Don't look hungover in front of the Pastor, Hayley, for the love of God! She planted on a sunny smile. "Good morning, Pastor Bradley."

"Hayley! I was just on my way to your shop. I see you're keeping Saturday hours."

Always appreciative of a well-timed snarky comment, Kinsley giggled.

Hayley gave her a disapproving look from behind her sunglasses before turning her attention back to the Pastor. "I'm afraid we're closed on Sunday's, but we can certainly make an exception for you. Are you looking for anything in particular? Something for your wife?"

"I actually wanted to speak with you about the fall festival. It's two weeks away, and we need to fill the last of the vendor spots. Your daddy's been kind enough to help out, but I was hoping maybe y'all would consider signing up as well?"

Kinsley spoke up before Hayley could formulate a reply. "Hayley has a date, but I would be proud to represent Country Chic." Hayley kicked Kinsley's leg under the table.

"Congratulations, Hayley, who's the lucky guy?"

"She has a date with Gavin. From the Miller Farm, I think it's called?" Hayley kicked her again. "Ouch!"

"Gavin Taylor? Really? That's interesting..." He sipped on his to-go cup of coffee, looking genuinely pleased.

"Pastor, I can assure you, I do not have a date with that man." Hayley ran her finger around the rim of her mug. "But, out of curiosity... what do you know about him?"

He gave a short laugh. "Very little, I'm afraid. I know he likes baseball. I assume he likes horses and steering cattle, since he works on a ranch. He has a daughter." Bradley hesitated before continuing. "He seems to be a man in need of some... healing."

"Healing?" Hayley's curiosity piqued. "How so? Sorry, I know I'm being nosy."

"Well... I can't speak to what I don't know, but, in my experience, people who don't like to share things about themselves have been through a lot of pain, and if that pain is brought to the surface, they can't deal with it. I've only had one conversation with Gavin, and I could see that kind of pain in his eyes. But there was also a tiny spark of life in them, buried beneath miles of trauma, I'm sure."

Kinsley rested her chin in her palm. "Wow. That's deep."

Hunter scribbled away on his notepad.

"I've probably said too much. I'm no mind reader, so take what I say with a grain of salt. But if you do date the man, tread lightly. I'd better be on my way. I'm actually headed over to the farm right now to see if Prater and his boys would like to join us at the festival. Maybe provide horse rides for the kids. Chances are slim, but you never know unless you ask."

After the preacher said his goodbyes, a dispirited Hayley was more than ready to go home and crawl back into bed. They hugged Hunter goodbye and made plans to meet him for dinner one night that week. Kinsley was uncharacteristically quiet as they made the short drive home.

"Why did you leave me alone with him, knowing I was plastered?"

"I'm sorry, okay?" She signaled and turned down their street. "You were having such a good time. I tried to pull you away from him when you started to get touchy feely, but you weren't having it."

"And then you just sat back and watched me make an idiot of myself with the town drunk?"

"He wasn't drunk last night, and I was keeping an eye on you."

"By letting him take me into an alley to do God knows what?"

"I had to pee! When I came out, you guys were gone. I went looking for you."

"What did he say when you found us?"

"Well, he was covered in your vomit and I was dragging you into a cab, so we didn't have a chance to discuss the ins and outs of what happened. But I can tell you what I witnessed in the bar, and that was drunk Hayley having herself a good time with a brooding, yet seemingly harmless and exceptionally good-looking man. I'm telling you it was like night and day; the guy who walked into our store looking like a nomad and the clean-cut hottie from last night. That picture I showed you does not do him justice."

Hayley kept her eyes straight ahead, working her jaw.

"He tried to play it cool, but there was something about the way he looked at you. I was curious to see how it would all play out."

Arms crossed in front of her, Hayley glared at Kinsley as they pulled into their garage.

Kinsley put the car in park and threw up her hands. "Holy shit, you're overreacting! It's no big deal. Just go to the ranch and talk to him."

"Oh, like it's that easy." Hayley flung off her seat belt. "God, I seriously *puked* on him?"

"Afraid so." When I accused him of luring you into a dark alleyway, he assured me that he was the victim."

"Oh. My. *God.*"

"I say you go to the ranch and apologize for puking on him, yelling at him, and fondling him–although I'm sure he didn't mind that part. Then you can ask him out for real."

"I am not asking him out! Oh, and like he'd really go out with me after I made such a fool of myself." But Kinsley was right, she did owe him a major apology. She had an epiphany. "I'm going to make Madison a dress."

"Oh, you mean your new lover boy's daughter?"

"Shut up! I'm serious. Let's see if we can get hers and maybe even a few more designs over to Johnathan by Tuesday. I already have her measurements, and she can model the dress at our booth."

"You're thinking about pre-orders for an actual line?" Kinsley pulled her cell out of her purse and started typing out notes.

"Yes. The girl will be over the moon happy, and it will be my way of apologizing to this Gavin guy while, at the same time, potentially creating another clothing line. If we can get enough pre-orders that will help with the financial side of things."

"Damn, you must feel guilty as hell."

The Pastor's words played back through Hayley's mind. "In my defense, he was an asshole to me, and I was plied with alcohol against my will at the bar, but yes. I do."

SEVEN

Gavin

Gavin's thoughts lingered on the events of the night before as he absent-mindedly polished the same spot on his boot repeatedly. He couldn't stop thinking about his crazy encounter with Hayley Jackson. It had felt good to smile and laugh again, but their exchange also left him feeling unsettled. He didn't want to be attracted to her. Something told him she was dangerous. The kind of powerhouse woman you couldn't ignore or dismiss just because she didn't align with your closed off, brooding, pity-party-of-one lifestyle.

It had thrown him when she called him out on his lie about working for Prater, and then again when she asked him who he was, moments before the puking incident. She had no doubt heard rumors about him around town and, even in her drunken state, was trying to connect the pieces—fit his square-peg mysteriousness into a round hole. The night they met, he had on nice clothing and flaunted his money like a prima donna douchebag, while, at the same time, he was half drunk, out of line, and looking like he belonged in a soup kitchen. Last night, he was clean cut, quiet, and mostly sober, so he could understand her confusion. As for her behavior at the bar, something told him it wasn't a common occurrence. No mystery to be solved there, just a simple case of overindulging in revelry with friends. Round peg, round hole.

He rubbed his boot harder with the cloth. The sound of an ATV in the distance broke him from his thoughts. A minute later, Prater pulled up in front of the porch steps and killed the engine.

"You trying to rub a hole in that boot?"

"Your friend ruined my brand-new boots. Don't even know why I'm bothering, these things are trashed." Gavin couldn't help but smile, remembering the smitten look on Hayley's face right before she emptied her stomach on him. Although her attraction toward him was most likely alcohol induced, it was still flattering. It had been many years since a woman looked at him like that, and he had to admit it felt really damn good. "She's... something else."

Prater pulled off his wide brimmed hat, a stern expression fixed on his wizened face. "She had herself a bad night, but she's a good girl. Even when she was raising hell as a teen, I knew she was something special. I wouldn't want to see her hurt, you hear me, son?"

"I was a perfect gentleman, Jim. I hope you know me well enough to know that I'd never take advantage of a drunk woman." He tossed his boots aside and pushed himself up to stand.

Prater chuckled. "Boy, I've never seen you so much as glance at a woman in the five years I've known you."

Gavin wasn't about to tell him that his balls were so blue he had to rub one out in his truck last night while covered in Hayley's vomit. For the first time in seven years, it wasn't Carly he'd thought about, but a woman with lead lined, honey-colored eyes and plump lips, her ample breasts pressed against him as she cradled his cock in her palm. He'd broken down afterward. Went home and popped some sleeping pills to stop himself from getting drunk.

"So, you didn't ask her out?" Prater asked, shooing away a horsefly.

Gavin screwed up his face. "Of course not. I'm not interested in dating, and even if I had, she wouldn't have remembered it."

"Ah," Prater said sagely. "Good. Wasn't the time." He gave Gavin a sly smile. "Doesn't mean it won't ever be, though."

Gavin squinted his eyes and scratched the back of his neck. "I'm confused. Did you not just warn me against hurting her?"

Prater lit a cigarette and took a long pull. "Son, you can be dimmer than a faulty light bulb. Asking a woman out and not hurting her can be achieved, you know. This is not a pat your head and rub your stomach type scenario. I'm just asking that you go about it the right way, when you're both sober."

Before Gavin had a chance to formulate a rebuttal, the front door swung open. "Holy shit. Where's your beard?"

"Madison, language!" He couldn't stand it when she cussed, knowing she'd heard every curse word under the sun come out of his mouth. It was just one more thing to add to the already mile long list of things he had to feel guilty about. He took in her appearance, surprised to see she was wearing overalls and a long-sleeved flannel shirt, and nodded to the baseball cap clutched in her hand.

"What's that?"

She shrugged a shoulder and slid the cap onto her head. "Dunno, found it in my closet."

Emblazoned on the hat were the letters S and D. He blinked, wondering if he was seeing it correctly or if he'd lost his mind all together. His muscles tightened, heart rate skyrocketing from the shock of adrenaline that nearly knocked him off balance. "Madison Ann Taylor, where *the hell* did you get that hat?"

Madison curled her lip at him. "I just told you, I found it in my closet. It was in a box of old clothes. God, what's your problem?" That look of disgust was in her eyes again. The one she reserved just for him.

Prater's eyes ping ponged worriedly between the two of them.

Gavin hadn't told her he'd played professional ball, because he didn't want anyone to know. That part of his life had been punctuated with a hell of a lot of hurt, pain, and humiliation that he didn't want unearthed. And kids talk.

Gavin's cell phone buzzed, and he dug it out of his pocket. Looking down at the screen, he cursed under his breath. Denise Lawson. Carly's mom, Madison's grandmother, and a major thorn in his side. After silencing his phone, he shoved it back into the front pocket of his jeans and fixed his attention on his daughter. Her tiny head swam in her mother's baseball cap. His mind was playing tug of war with either ripping it off her head and running away or bawling like a fucking baby and spilling everything right then and there. Instead, he stayed stock still, his eyes fixed on the brown and gold cap. A tangible reminder of his heartbreak.

"*God*, here. Take the stupid hat if you're so obsessed with it." Madison threw the hat at Gavin and it bounced off his stomach, landing in front of him on the cedar planked porch. "Not gonna lie, dad, you get weirder and weirder every day." She turned to Prater. "Papa Jim, I was thinking of riding Pegasus down to the old fishing shed by the creek; I left my book there. But maybe first I can help you with the cows?"

Clearly ready for the awkward exchange to be over, Prater nodded. "I'd love the company."

He put on his hat and scooted back on the seat, patting the empty spot in front of him.

"Wanna drive?" Without a second thought, she jumped on the ATV and turned the key. The engine roared to life, and Jim's hands went behind him to grip the seat. Madison squealed as they lurched forward and picked up speed.

When they were out of sight, Gavin pried open a loose floorboard on the porch and pulled out Prater's secret stash of Tennessee whiskey. Jim would kick his ass if he caught Gavin drinking his most coveted libation, but he needed a swig of something before he had to hear the wretched woman's grating voice. He pulled his phone from his pocket and sat down on a porch step, heaving a deep sigh.

After the accident, Denise's true colors showed themselves like never before. She had never liked him, so he wasn't surprised when she'd blamed him for Carly's death, instead of the driver who had plowed into them, dying on impact. But he'd been shocked by how far she was willing to go to destroy a man who had already lost nearly everything. The father of her only granddaughter, to boot. Denise's dream had been for Carly to marry her social and economic equal, live in a mansion, and raise boarding school brats. She hated that Carly would travel with Maddie to games, thought Maddie's life should be more consistent and stable. Denise had gone ballistic when he moved her across the country to live on a ranch. The first year she had been relentless in her attempts to reach him, and he was equally as persistent in ignoring her. When she showed up at the ranch four years ago, demanding to see Maddie, Gavin had threatened to sue her for trespassing, and she finally backed off. Why she'd think for a second that he'd let her spend any amount of time with Madison after what she'd done was beyond him.

He pushed the speaker button and pressed play on her voicemail.

"Gavin, this is Denise Lawson. It's been far too long since we've spoken, and I'm hoping we can set our differences aside for the sake of my granddaughter. Jack and I would love for Madison to visit us this Christmas. I'm not trying to make things difficult; we just want to see her. Please, call me back."

"Not a chance in hell, Denise," he said to his phone before taking a long pull from the whiskey bottle. "Now you're ready to be cordial and set aside our differences?" Denise used the word *visit*, but Gavin knew that if he gave her an inch, she would do her best to take Madison away from him. He and Madison's nearly nonexistent father-daughter relationship wouldn't stand a chance against Denise's brainwashing.

Carly had loved her parents in her own way, but he knew she wouldn't want them raising Madison. She had always thought they were too controlling. Too structured and rigid. Sure, he'd been far from perfect, but he was ready and willing to work on himself… soon.

Gavin stood and rested a hip against the porch railing, once again pondering just how badly he'd messed up with his daughter.

Admittedly, he had lied to Madison. More than once. He never told her about his baseball career, although that wasn't so much a lie as it was an omission of truth. And now, as a reminder of that huge omission, she'd found Carly's hat. He had no idea how it had ended up in her room.

For the past two Christmases, Maddie had asked Gavin for a smartphone, and he had told her she was too young. While he believed that to be true, Gavin's resistance primarily stemmed from a fear of what she would find. The internet was a powerful thing, and Madison was a smart and curious girl.

The lie had happened two years ago. In a fit of drunken idiocy, he'd told Madison that all of her grandparents had died. Even though he was drunk, he remembered how much it had caught him off guard when she inquired about them. He'd meant it as a twisted joke at the time, but perpetuating the lie was easier than attempting to explain things to Madison. He knew what he'd done was wrong, no matter how pissed off he was at them, it was a shitty thing to do. Now that his mind was clearer, he felt the weight of his lies and omissions heavy on his shoulders.

He looked down at the bottle in his hand. "Enough," he mumbled, setting it back in its not-so-secret hiding place. Although it was an unnerving feeling, unraveling the chrysalis of protection he'd built around himself, he needed a clear head. Especially if Denise was up to her old tricks again.

A white pick-up truck made its way up the long gravel driveway. When he saw that it was Pastor Bradley, he groaned, wishing he'd tended to the cows instead of daydreaming about a woman he would never have and pushing his daughter further away. He liked the Pastor, and he could tell he was a good man, just a little too nosy for Gavin's liking.

"Gavin!" Bradley shouted as he closed the truck door, dressed in his Sunday best. "I was hoping to see you at church today."

"I slept in." *Also, never going to happen,* Gavin thought, walking down the porch steps to shake Bradley's hand.

"I heard about all the excitement last night. Seems the entire town is even more curious about you now, which is saying a heck of a lot."

Gavin cast his eyes down, kicking at the gravel driveway with the steel toe of his work boot. He thought it best to play dumb. "Nothing happened." He wondered then what the penalty was for lying to a Pastor. *Oh well,* he thought. *I'm most likely going to hell anyway.*

The Pastor chuckled. "All I can say is that the men in town are jealous that Hayley Jackson has shown an interest in you, and the women are all talking about that face of yours. I must say, you clean up quite nice."

Gavin hung his thumbs from the front pockets of his jeans, squinting against the late afternoon sun. "Aw shucks, Pastor Bradley, did you come all this way to flirt with me? Or are you here to butt into my personal life like the rest of this town's nosy busy bodies?"

Bradley's perpetual smile faltered. "Gavin, opening yourself up to others can be a powerful thing. Takes you down avenues of healing and hope. I think, in this world, we could all use a little bit of both. Now, I know the people of this town can be a bit opinionated and overzealous at times, but if you give them a chance, you'll see they are only human and have struggles of their own." The Pastor's expression softened. "I came to see if y'all would be interested in helping us out with the festival. I'm thinking maybe horse rides would go over really well with the kids, bring them some extra cheer. I don't know if you knew this, but times have been tough for a few of our families. I'm hoping to raise enough money to help them out some this Christmas."

Gavin hadn't known that. He'd been too busy being the town Grinch to notice or care. Shrugging, he feigned disinterest. "I'm sure we can work that out, but Jim's the man in charge, so you'll have to take it up with him.

He and Madison are in the stable." He gestured to the horse barn. "You might catch him before he heads out to herd cattle."

"Sounds good. I'll swing back by the house to say goodbye before I leave."

Gavin pursed his lips and gave the man a two-finger salute. "Pastor Bradley, I admire your persistence."

When Bradley walked away, Gavin pulled out his phone to text Prater.

Let's gift Pastor Brad $3,000 for the Christmas toy drive. Take it out of my savings. Oh, and let him know we'll be at the festival.

He took the porch steps two at a time with a self-satisfied skip in his step. The sound of gravel crunching under tires stopped him from reaching the door. "Son of a bitch, what now," he mumbled, turning around to see a black Ford Explorer pulling up in front of his house.

A familiar Hispanic gentleman exited the driver's side with outspread arms. "Pendejo, why the hell have you been ignoring my text messages and calls?" Gavin blinked. *Xavier Hernandez.* He'd received several texts and phone calls from his old friend last week, telling him he needed to speak with him and that it was urgent. True to form, Gavin had ignored them.

His adrenaline kicked into high gear, eyes shifting to the stables. "You need to go."

"Seriously, man?" Xavier replied with a wounded look in his eyes as he walked toward the house. "That's all I get after five years?"

"Come with me." Gavin hurried down the porch steps and motioned for Xavier to follow him to the pole barn. Fumbling with the keys, he unlocked the padlock and slid open the door, ushering his friend inside.

"It's nice to see you too, asshat." When the lights flickered on, Xavier's dark, widely set eyes looked around the space, disbelieving. "You mother fucker," he breathed. "I knew it. I had a dream you were throwing."

"Xavier, only a small handful of people around here know I played ball, and I'd really like to keep it that way. And you know why, so don't give me

87

shit about it. A nosy man who happens to be a huge fan of yours is on my property right now, and I don't want him in my business."

Xavier furrowed his brow. "Are you running from the law or something, man?"

"No, of course not."

"Then why the secrecy? You have to let that shit go; everyone knows you didn't do what she accused you of."

Gavin sat down on the weight bench and scrubbed his hands over his face. "You don't know the people of this town." His eyes rolled up to meet Xavier's. He felt a twinge of sadness, because the man's expression was unreadable, and he used to know what his friend was thinking just by looking at him. "Why are you here?"

"Look, I'll cut to the chase," Xavier said. "I've got a two-year deal coaching St. Louis. Our hitting is decent, but we are desperately in need of arms. Come in, throw a few sessions, and let's see what you've got." Gavin had to fight not to smile at the way Xavier still talked so animatedly with his hands. "Even if you're half of what you were, that's still a hell of a lot better than the jokers I'm working with now."

"I'm not interested," Gavin replied firmly, hoping he wouldn't push.

Xavier motioned to the pitching cage. "Then what's this all about?"

Gavin's eyes followed his gaze to the cage. "Just my way of burning off steam."

"If you don't want to pitch, then be a coach. I need someone I can trust. Your baseball IQ was off the charts, and you had a natural feel for game management. I can have Mack come out and write a contract right now."

"Just like that?" Gavin quirked a brow. "It's been seven fucking years, man."

Xavier smiled widely. The skin around his eyes crinkled pronouncedly at the corners, the result of both age and too much time in the sun. "Yes. Just like that."

Gavin grunted, unconvinced. "Like I already said, the answer is no." He stood up and extended his arm to Xavier. "It was really good to see you, man. I wish you nothing but the best, I mean that. But now is not a good time."

"You in here, Gavin?" The preacher peeked inside the barn. "Oh, hello. I'm sorry to interrupt you gentle… Wait, is that a pitching cage?"

"Jesus Christ, Bradley, why can't you let a man have his privacy!" Gavin bellowed. Remembering who he was addressing, he immediately backpedaled. "I'm sorry, Pastor, I didn't mean to yell. But this area is off limits."

Pastor Bradley pointed a finger at Xavier. "Have we met?"

Gavin gave Xavier the side eye. A nonverbal equivalent of *you better not say a damn word.* "No, sir."

"Well, as I live and breathe… You're Xavier Hernandez, aren't you?" Excitement built in his voice. "Bless my stars, Xavier Hernandez in Timber Creek? Gavin, you know this man and never said anything? Mr. Hernandez, I am a huge fan."

Always gracious toward his fans, Xavier thanked him.

"Wait!" Pastor Bradley took a long look at Gavin's face and then around the barn. "A pitching cage, a former catcher for the Padres, and Gavin Taylor. Holy Jehoshaphat jumping frogs in a shark tank, you're the young pitcher that got San Diego into the playoffs! You were in an accident, weren't you? Stopped playing shortly after? Are you thinking about making a comeback?"

"I'm working on it," Xavier said.

"No!" Gavin countered. "Pastor, I'm counting on your discreetness here. Please be sensitive to the fact that I lost my wife, Madison's mother, in the accident and that I was injured. Don't tell anyone who I am or what you saw here today. I'm not going to play again, and I want to be left alone. That's one of the reasons why I moved here."

"I'm so sorry, Gavin," Bradley replied genuinely with sympathetic eyes, resting his hand on Gavin's shoulder.

"Pastor," Xavier spoke up, "would you by chance like to see a pro pitcher and Hall-of-Fame catcher in action?"

"Not today, Xavier," Gavin groused, pegging him with another warning stare.

"Does it hurt to throw?"

"No, Xavier. It doesn't hurt when I throw."

His friend untucked his dress shirt and removed his tie. "Well, if you're not hurting, play catch with me."

"I'm not in the mood."

Xavier grabbed a glove and a couple of balls and entered the cage, taking his position behind home plate. "Humor me. Throw a few pitches, and I'll leave you alone. And don't tell me it's been a while either. Looks like you're in decent shape; I think your pretty boy ass is being dramatic."

The two men looked at him expectantly. Gavin rolled his eyes and sighed, reluctantly conceding. He grabbed his glove and took the baseball from Xavier. The Pastor leaned against the fence; a boyish grin stretched across his chubby face.

Xavier called ten pitches of various types and locations. Gavin threw better than he had in a long time. Pitching across from his old friend brought out a fire in him that had been long extinguished. That extra something that took his pitching from therapeutic to legitimately powerful. But none of it mattered, because one thing still rang true in his mind. He didn't want to play professionally.

When their session was over, Bradley whistled and clapped his hands. "That was magic."

Xavier tossed the glove onto a nearby table and picked up his tie. "Man, I know you've been through so much, and I can't pretend to know what it's been like, because I haven't walked in your shoes. But I feel like I can be blunt with you, because you've always been like a younger brother to me. There's nothing wrong with your arm, my friend. Your problem stems from self-pity and stubbornness. That's what's holding you back, Gav. You need to make peace with yourself. Until then, you'll never be what you were."

"How many times do I have to say it, man," Gavin fumed. "I don't want to go back." He turned to Bradley. "Pastor, I'm going to ask you not to break my trust. Tell no one about this. Please."

"Gavin, I give you my solemn promise," Bradley replied. "Just let me say that I believe what I've witnessed here today is a gift from God above, and it'd be a crying shame to see you squander it away."

EIGHT

Hayley

"Stop being such a chicken shit, Hayley Jackson." More than a week had passed since the bar debacle, and Hayley still hadn't worked up enough courage to face the illusive Gavin Taylor. She was unaccustomed to being in such a vulnerable position, lacking the reassurance that all was forgiven and forgotten, even though he was a stranger to her, and it shouldn't matter. Yet her thoughts had wandered to him often over the past week, wondering what he must think of her or if he even thought of her at all. Given the fact that she had vomited on him, both literally and figuratively, she imagined she'd crossed his mind a time or two. Every time she thought about what a fool she'd made of herself, she wanted to hide her typically confident and self-assured head in the sand.

The festival was only a week away, and beyond locating Gavin to apologize for making an ass of herself, she needed to speak with him about his daughter. It had been a slower week at the boutique, which had freed up time for Hayley to design a dress for Madison and send it off to her production manager, Jonathan. Since Jonathan was a rock star, it had been delivered to the boutique yesterday.

So, now she stood in front of what would always be known to her as the old Miller Farm to inquire about Gavin, marveling at how well the Prater's had done for themselves in the time she'd been gone. She inhaled a lung full of air, attempting to calm the hummingbird fluttering around in her chest, as she smoothed down her hair and made her way up the pumpkin lined porch steps. The front door opened before she had a chance to knock, revealing June Prater.

"June, hello!" Hayley was reminded then just how much she'd genuinely missed this woman's sweet face and effervescent friendliness.

"Hayley Jackson, what a wonderful surprise! Come in, come in!"

Madison appeared in the entryway, dressed in tie dyed leggings and a teal sweater, her long hair brushed smooth over her shoulder, breathtaking eyes as wide as saucers. "Hayley!" She threw her arms around Hayley's middle and squeezed tight.

Hayley giggled. "Just the young lady I wanted to see!"

"I made a pot of my homemade hot chocolate; would you like some?" June offered.

"You have to try some, it's soooo good," Madison said, pulling Hayley by the arm toward the kitchen. "She uses three kinds of chocolate."

"That actually sounds amazing, thank you."

"I've also got a pie in the oven," June said. "Should be ready soon."

Madison licked her lips and rubbed her hands together. "It's praline pumpkin crumble, my favorite."

"It smells phenomenal in here," Hayley replied, following June and Madison into the cottage style kitchen.

Madison scraped back a kitchen chair. "Sit here, next to me, Hayley."

"So, to what do we owe the pleasure of your company?" June asked from the stove as she stirred the pot of hot chocolate. A rush of warmth came over Hayley as she wondered if June had heard about her behavior at the bar. Gossip spread like wildfire in their town. "I've been meaning to stop by the boutique and pay you a visit, but between the pie shop, experimenting with festival recipes, and caring for this cutie pie, my schedule's been hectic."

Hayley remembered Declan saying that the Prater's basically raised Madison. Not that she trusted that asshole as far as she could throw him, but she looked around the space and saw the built-in cubbies in the corner of the dining area filled with children's books and art supplies, the refrigerator covered in whimsical artwork, and several pairs of Madison's shoes next to the back door. All signs pointed to this being Madison's home. She wondered if Gavin lived there as well.

"Well," Hayley began, turning to Madison. "I need to get your dad's permission first, but I've got some really exciting news. I designed a dress for you, and it came in yesterday! I thought you could model it for our booth at the Harvest Festival."

"Really?" Madison replied on a breath.

"Really! And that's not all. I'd love it if you'd help me create some designs for a junior's line. We want to make you our official Brand Ambassador. What do you think?"

Madison squealed with joy, clapping her small hands in quick succession. "Yes, yes, yes! Did you hear that, Nana June?"

Hayley noticed that June was quiet and looked slightly uneasy, giving them a smile that didn't quite reach her eyes.

"May I see the dress?" Madison asked.

"You're in luck, I just so happen to have it in my Jeep! I'll be right back."

A minute later, Hayley presented a bright pink box to an extremely excited Madison, who lifted the lid and gasped. The asymmetrical mesh dress was elegant, yet fun, with a ruched one-shoulder top and high-low puffy skirt. A large mesh bow was highlighted at the shoulder. It was covered in autumn-colored butterflies, representing both Madison's personality and the beauty of the season.

June inhaled a sharp breath. "It's gorgeous!"

"Hayley, it's the most beautiful dress ever!" Madison exclaimed, holding it up. "Thank you, thank you, thank you!"

"I'm thinking black tights, arm length fingerless gloves, and some brand new shiny black combat boots. The bow is removable, so maybe even a cardigan for later in the evening, when it gets chilly," Hayley suggested.

"That sounds A-mazing!"

"Well, what are you waiting for?" June said. "Try it on!"

Madison ran down the hall to her bedroom. She reemerged two minutes later, twirling around the kitchen, looking like a whimsical dream.

"I love it so much!" Madison's eyes welled up with happy tears, and Hayley felt a surge of pride.

"There *is* one downside to wearing this dress," Hayley warned her in jest. "You'll have to beat the boys off with a stick at the festival."

Madison stopped twirling and twisted up her face in disgust. "Ugh, Matthew Davis has a huge crush on me. He's one of the only kids at school I can tolerate, but he started acting all googly eyed and weird. I forced it out of him and then punched him in the arm."

Hayley and June laughed in unison. *God, I love this kid,* Hayley thought affectionately.

"You look absolutely fabulous, Mads." June plucked a tissue from a box on the counter and dabbed under her eyes. It warmed Hayley's heart to see the deep affection they had for one another.

Madison's mouth turned down. "What do you think dad will say?" she asked June.

"Is your dad here now?" Hayley inquired, keeping her tone casual, while her heart rate accelerated.

"No," June replied. "He's out with the boys, herding cattle."

"Wanna see my horse?" Madison asked Hayley.

"Sure! But you better change out of that dress first."

"I never want to take this dress off, but you're probably right."

It was a gorgeous yet windy day. A playful kind of wind, such as one drawn in swirls across the page of a children's book, ruffled Hayley's hair. Madison chattered nonstop as they strolled through a large section of grass to the stable. The property was beautiful, rolling hills surrounded by autumn-kissed trees in the distance.

"So, tell me a little bit about your dad."

Madison eyed Hayley with open curiosity. "Why, you interested?"

"Ummm... no." Hayley felt her face flush. "Remember, I told you I need his permission or you can't work for me? I just want to know what I'm in for." She nudged Madison with her elbow and smiled.

"My dad is a prickly dude. He's been better lately, hasn't been drinking as much and doesn't look like he has a forest animal growing on his face anymore. But good luck having any kind of a real conversation with him. If you ever do have the hots for him, don't expect too much. The only things I've ever seen him show any interest in are whiskey, the ranch, and lecturing me."

Hayley's denim jacket suddenly felt like an oven. "Sweetie, I can assure you that I'm not interested in dating your father; I don't even know him. I simply need his permission and signature on some paperwork before we can make your title official."

"Okay, okay, just trying to give you a heads up."

When they reached the stables, Madison made a beeline for a beautiful white mare with a grey mane.

"This is my horse, Pegasus," she beamed proudly.

"Oh, Madison, she's gorgeous," Hayley said, patting the horse's side. "I really miss riding. When I was your age, I would ride for miles and miles when I needed to get away and think. They are so therapeutic." She stepped back from the horse and leaned back against the stall wall, running her fingers down a long piece of hay. "So... does your dad always work on Sundays? I was really hoping to speak with him today so we can get the ball rolling before the festival."

Madison shrugged, brushing Pegasus's mane in long strokes. "I dunno. He kinda comes and goes. I really hope he's not in one of his ultra-grouchy moods today. If he says no, I'm disowning him."

"Wow, that's a big statement."

The intense look that Hayley had seen on the girl's face when they first met was back. "He's not really much of a dad, anyway."

Hayley grew quiet, unsure of how to respond to Madison's bleak observation of her father. A melancholy silence settled over them.

Madison set down Pegasus's sparkly pink brush and turned to Hayley. "Why don't you take Pegasus out for a ride? I think my dad's watering the cattle; just follow the creek and you'll come across him eventually. Miguel and Alejandro should be with him. They are *really* loud, so you'll know when you're getting close."

Hayley's first thought was to decline the offer, but then she thought about what a beautiful day it was, and she really did miss riding. She kept meaning to go by her parent's stables to take one of her dad's stallions out for a trail ride but hadn't found the time. And, although she wasn't looking forward to it, she really needed to talk to Gavin.

"I just might take you up on that."

Riding Pegasus felt natural to Hayley. As easy as breathing. Well trained, the snow-white horse amicably galloped along the trail leading to the wooded area that ran alongside Timber Creek. Once they reached the riverbank, the mare was on autopilot.

The foliage had reached its glorious peak and would soon succumb to pre-winter winds. Autumn in New York had been beautiful in its own right, with its lush, vibrant trees in central park, which signaled the start of holiday magic in the Big Apple. But it was soothing for her, being away from the hustle bustle of the City with its multitude of claustrophobic skyscrapers, as she flew through untouched, bucolic nature, filling her lungs with pollution free air.

A flood of memories came rushing back to Hayley as she rode on. Visions of family picnics along the banks where she and her sisters would explore the creek every Sunday after church, and kayaking and canoeing when the creek swelled and the water was at its deepest played through her mind. She had missed it so much, being on the back of a horse with the wind whipping through her hair. A steady rhythmic gallop reverberated through her, an electric feeling that enlivened every cell of her body.

The unmistakable pungent scent of cow stung her nostrils. Her dad had been a cowpuncher at one point, and the smell of cow patties was something she did not miss.

Up ahead, she spotted three men on horseback and urged Pegasus to slow to a trot. Cows moseyed along the edge of the creek, stopping to drink its fresh offerings. Perched tall in a saddle was a man Hayley assumed to be Gavin. The two men he was with were demonstrating some impressive lassoing skills. Madison was right, they were *loud*.

She stopped Pegasus far enough back from the men that she wouldn't be seen. It was Gavin's turn with the lasso. His accuracy and speed getting it around the neck of his intended target was impressive and earned a round of applause from his boisterous friends. He was riding to retrieve the rope from around the cow's neck with a self-satisfied grin on his face when a sharp crack akin to gunfire slapped the air. Hayley nearly jumped out of her skin. Pegasus reared back slightly and whinnied. Gavin's friends drove the cattle from the creek with whips. Hayley gasped when the cow Gavin had lassoed jerked away from him, pulling him off his horse and into the water.

The cattle moved quickly up the bank, stepping in time with the crack of the whips.

"Sorry, boss!" one of the men yelled, continuing up the bank. The amused looks on their faces told Hayley they had done it on purpose. "It's Sunday, man. We promised Maricela and Bianca we'd only work a half day. If it's okay with you, that is."

After pulling himself up to stand in the knee-high water, Gavin flipped them the bird. "One of these days I'm gonna fire you dickheads, for real."

He sloshed his way up the bank and pulled off his shirt, squeezing out the excess water. Hayley nudged Pegasus forward as the other men steered the cattle away from the creek, bantering animatedly in Spanish.

"Holy six-pack, look at those abs," Hayley muttered. She felt her skin flush, the cold gust of wind that blew over her was no match for the warmth of desire.

He stopped mid-wring and looked up; his eyes locked on her. A look of confusion, then realization, then surprise morphed on his face as he made his way toward her on foot. Kinsley was right, Hayley thought, those pictures did not do him justice. His tanned skin was smooth, muscles defined but not bulky. He was classically handsome, in a manly boy-next-door kind of way. She recognized his deep brown eyes as he approached her, so different from Madison's. A hazy memory flitted across her mind, her hands pressed to his chest as she looked into those very same eyes. Such a surreal thing, she mused, having touched a stranger intimately yet having no recollection of it.

"May I ask why you're riding my daughter's horse?" Gavin asked, rubbing Pegasus's muzzle. His drenched shirt was slung over a broad shoulder. She noticed his eyes were framed in dark circles, like he hadn't slept in a couple of days.

"Madison let me borrow her." She hated how small she sounded in comparison with his gruff, deeply timbered voice.

Twin lines formed between his brows, and he drew his head back. "So, you came to my house to visit my daughter and borrow her horse?"

So he does live at the ranch...

"I actually came to find you." *Stop looking at his abs, Hayley,* she admonished herself.

"Well, I hope you brought cash. You own me a hundred and fifty bucks."

Hayley's eyes darted up to his face. "What are you talking about?"

The corners of his mouth twitched. "You threw up on my shoes."

She covered her heated face with her hands. "I'm so sorry." *Kill. Me. Now.*

"I suppose you're forgiven, Pukey."

Hayley dropped her hands to her sides. "I'm fairly certain I deserved that."

Gavin shrugged, running a hand down Pegasus's coarse mane. His playful smirk turned slightly somber. "You were drunk. We've all been there."

Her unbound hair whipped behind her on a breeze.

Gavin shivered, and his naked skin broke out in goosebumps.

"You must be freezing."

"I am." He slid into his wet, long-sleeved plaid shirt and snapped it closed, much to Hayley's displeasure. "No thanks to those assholes." He held a hand up to her.

"Walk with me to get my jacket?"

She accepted his hand as she dismounted the mare. Although his skin was calloused and cold, a thrill shot through her at the tactile connection. Gavin grabbed ahold of Pegasus's reins and tugged, urging her to follow behind them.

Hayley fell into step next to him as they walked along the edge of the bank to his horse. "Just so you know, I'm not normally like that," she said after a few minutes of awkward silence. "Apparently one of my sisters thought it'd be funny to order me doubles."

Gavin laughed softly through his nose. "Well, what are you normally like?"

Her arm brushed against his as she moved to dodge a tree branch. "Sorry."

"No problem. Well?"

"Umm... The opposite of who I was that night."

"You were... entertaining. And *loud*."

She pressed her hand to her forehead. "Oh, God. Please don't give me details. Kinsley already told me the gist of it, and that was enough to make me want to channel an ostrich."

His handsome face twisted in confusion. "An ostrich?"

"You know how they bury their heads in the sand?"

He chuckled. "Oh, yeah. Got it."

She touched his arm, but only for a second. A tiny offering, adding sincerity to her words. "Look, can I just say I'm deeply sorry and I'd love it if we could put all of this behind us and start over?"

Gavin pursed his lips and kicked a rock into the creek. "Hmmm... not sure I'm gonna let you off the hook that easily. You were quite rude to me."

She looked over at him, incredulous. "Ha! Talk about rude! You were awful to me that night at the boutique."

Gavin nodded. "I was."

"You're... different now."

"It's amazing what a razor and a pair of scissors can do."

"While this is a much better look for you, that's not what I'm not talking about."

"I'd had one too many that day. Like I said, we've all been there."

Hayley's eyes moved back and forth between Gavin and the path in front of them. He was quiet for a beat, looking down at his wet work boots. "You mentioned that a lot. How different I looked. His eyes flicked over to her and then back down at his feet. "You seemed to um... really appreciate it."

Hayley sighed despairingly. "That's it. I'm never drinking again."

Gavin belted out a laugh, so loud and unexpected it made her jump, yet also helped her feel at ease. He had a great laugh.

When they reached his horse, he pulled a tactical jacket out of a pack strapped to the saddle.

Hayley ran her hand down his horse's muzzle. "Your stallion is gorgeous."

"Thank you," he replied, shrugging into his jacket.

He pointed to a large, flat rock sticking out over the edge of the creek. "Sit with me?"

Hayley nodded, following close behind him. She felt so unlike herself, as if she were under some sort of spell. This man was basically a stranger, and yet she'd probably rob a bank with him right now if he asked her to.

Gavin sat down about a foot away from her in a ray of afternoon sunshine that filtered through the trees. Speckled shadows danced across his face as the leaves rustled in the breeze. She could feel the pensiveness and tension radiating off him and wanted so badly to hear him laugh again. He pulled up his legs and rested his forearms on his knees. "You also called me a liar." He was full on frowning now, his voice lower.

Hayley scrunched her face. "Why would I do that?" She thought back to the wad of cash in his wallet, his expensive clothing, and the way those two men spoke to him. There was no way he was just a ranch hand. Not that it mattered. But he was a like a thousand-piece puzzle with no picture to refer to, and she wanted to connect the pieces.

Gavin was quiet.

"Well, are you?"

"No."

"Do your employees always tease you so mercilessly?"

"My employees?" He toyed with the zipper of his jacket; his eyes fixed on it.

"Those men referred to you as their boss. I thought Prater was in charge."

Gavin's expression hardened. "Miguel and Alejandro are vaqueros. They've spent the last five years teaching me how to be a decent cowboy. They are also asshole pranksters." She noticed that he evaded the question. He seemed about as forthcoming as a shady politician.

"So… you live on the farm with June and Jim Prater?"

He paused for a long moment before answering her cut and dry question. "Not exactly. June helps out a lot… with Maddie."

"She's an amazing woman," Hayley said.

"She is."

"She and Madison seem really close."

He nodded, stony-faced. "They are."

"Madison mentioned that her mom passed away?" She cringed, immediately wishing she could take the words back.

His eyes flew over to her, but he looked more surprised than upset. "She did?"

Gavin's cell phone vibrated from his jacket pocket. He pulled it out and glanced at it before sliding it back into his pocket, clearly unhappy with whatever he saw.

"I'm sorry, I shouldn't have said that. I know it's none of my business."

"You're right, it's not," he snapped, clenching his jaw, and scratching the back of his neck.

Wow… She'd obviously pushed him too far. It was definitely time for her to go. But even with his sour mood, the spell cast upon her stayed firmly intact, and she wasn't ready for her time with him to end.

A thick, uncomfortable silence settled over them.

"Well, I guess I should be getting back. I'll drop Pegasus off and get out of your hair…"

Gavin raked his fingers through his hair and sighed. "I'm sorry. My wife… my late wife, Carly. She died when Madison was four. Car accident."

Hayley noticed the hard bob of his adam's apple when he swallowed. She felt so awful for bringing up such a painful subject. One that was decidedly none of her business.

She turned to face him, sitting cross legged on the rock, and rested a hand on his leg. "I'm so sorry. She must have been an amazing woman, if Madison is any indication."

"She was." He looked down at her hand, and she pulled it away, folding her hands into her lap.

Clouds rolled in underneath brilliant blue sky, the atmosphere changing its countenance on a whim. Hayley wrapped her arms around her body and shivered.

"Damn, it's getting really cold," she said.

Slipping out of his jacket, he slung it over her shoulders and tucked her into it. He kept his hands there, gripping its zippered edges while his gaze roamed over her features.

Her heart beat in time with the rise and fall of her chest, quickening as her breathing thinned out, as if the oxygen had been sucked out of the air between them. She licked her parched lips, and his eyes flicked down to her mouth. "I'm so incredibly sorry," Hayley said. "For what happened at the bar, I mean."

"It's okay, seriously. No harm done. Well, except to my shoes." A grin took over his face, flashing her a perfect set of white teeth, and her stomach did a slow flip.

His back-and-forth moods, snappy and brooding to smiling and charmingly funny, had her perplexed. He was both darkness and light in varying measures, and she'd never met anyone like him before.

"I'll totally pay for them."

She bit her bottom lip. His eyes landed on her mouth again and flared. "Nah, don't worry about it," he murmured. "I'm just giving you a hard time." Pastor Bradley had said he saw pain in Gavin's eyes, but what Hayley saw now was nothing but pure, unadulterated lust. She felt it, too. Never had she felt such toe-curling attraction toward a man.

"You can kiss me, if you want," she heard someone say. Someone who sounded just like her.

His eyes widened, and he shook his head no. The response was too fast, like a reflex rather than an outright dismissal. Still, it was enough to make her stomach sink and her face heat with embarrassment. She was about to pull away, but then he reached out and fingered a tendril of her windblown hair. The gentle look in his eyes felt like a caress on her skin. The moment hung suspended.

"You're so beautiful," he whispered, watching his thumb as it grazed across her lips. A pained expression crossed his face before he cupped her cheek and leaned in to capture her mouth. His jacket slipped from her shoulders. She leaned forward and wrapped her hands around his biceps, moaning as he slid his tongue inside her mouth. A sound reverberated through him, a strange combination of pleasure and grief that almost made her pull away. But then he tangled his fingers and thumbs through her hair, tilting his head to gain better access to her mouth, and devoured her like he'd been starving for years and she was a gourmet meal. One hand cradled the back of her head while the other slipped inside her denim jacket and under her blouse. His hand splayed across her back, kneading her skin. Liquid warmth pooled low in her abdomen; her entire body was a heartbeat slamming against her skin as he continued his exploration of her mouth. "Hayley," he panted, "I need you closer." She climbed onto his lap to straddle him and nearly came undone when he slid his hands under her t-shirt and cupped her breasts over her bra, sliding his thumbs across the hard peaks. Gavin's hands glided down her skin to her denim covered hips. He grabbed her ass and pulled her forward until she felt him rock hard against her center.

"Gavin," she breathed, her eyes rolling back into her head while he brushed her hair aside and kissed the base of her throat. "You feel so fucking good. I want you inside of me."

He pulled away from her abruptly, like a bucket of ice water poured over a blazing campfire or a broken spell. His eyes squeezed shut. They were both panting, like they couldn't breathe fast or deeply enough.

"We should go. It's starting to rain."

She slid off his lap, her body aching and deflated, her ego bruised.

He dropped his chin to his chest and sighed. "I'm so sorry, Hayley."

"No, I'm sorry," she replied, willing away tears of shame and embarrassment. "I let myself get carried away. Please know... I'm not usually like this."

"I just... I can't... go there, right now."

"I understand." She stood up, unstable and throbbing between her legs. "Let's go back to the house, looks like it's about to pour."

"You go on ahead of me. I'm gonna need a minute."

She hauled herself up and walked to Pegasus, admonishing herself for going there with a man who clearly had issues. But kissing Gavin was the best thing she'd felt in a long time, maybe ever. Her swollen lips already missed the feel of his, so pillowy and warm, and her sex deprived body felt the absence of his hands – rough, calloused, and capable.

They arrived back at the house just before the steady drizzle turned into legitimate rainfall. Saying nothing, they averted their eyes from each other as they put Pegasus and Zeus back into their respective stalls.

When Hayley followed Gavin into the house through the back door to collect her purse, they were greeted by a small crowd congregated at the kitchen table with slices of pie in front of them. The group appeared surprised to see them. The men, whom she thought to be Gavin's ranch hands, were there, along with two kind-looking women she assumed were their wives. "Hey, amigo! Did you have a nice swim?" one of the men said with a teasing smirk.

"Oh, yay, everyone's here," Gavin mumbled sarcastically. Hayley saw the way he eyed Prater, who was giving him a knowing smirk.

"Hayley, this is a mighty pleasant surprise," Prater said, walking around the table to hug her.

Madison strutted into the kitchen wearing her new dress, as if the kitchen floor were a catwalk.

"What do you think, Dad? Hayley made it for me! She wants me to be a Brand Ambassador and model it at the festival!"

Everyone seated at the table ooohhhed and aaahhhed.

The word *Shit* blinked in neon across Hayley's mind, as she realized she hadn't spoken with Gavin about Madison's dress or her representing the new line.

"Pie, dear?" June asked her. Hayley heard the hint of worry in the woman's voice, which made her feel even more nervous.

"No... thank you, June."

She chanced a look at Gavin who looked like he was seeing red. She remembered Madison's warning: *My dad is a prickly sort of dude.* "Please, explain to me what the hell a Brand Ambassador is," he bellowed.

Hayley's heart pumped harder in her chest. "Ummm... Madison inspired us to build out a junior's line. We would like her to be the face of that campaign on social media and model some of the pieces for our website. With your permission, that is. It's a great opportunity, but nothing's set in stone. I was going to ask you..."

"My daughter is not going to be your Brand Ambassador."

"Dad!"

"You stay out of this," he barked at Madison.

"Son, maybe you shouldn't do this here," Jim intervened.

"Fine. Hayley, let's take this outside." Gavin marched to the back door and pushed it open, waiting for her to join him.

"Hayley, it's best to let him cool down," Prater said quietly. The others looked on with eyes as big as saucers. She felt her face heat and her eyes burn as she followed Gavin outside, closing the door behind her. They stood underneath the awning as rain fell around them, so hard that the sound blurred into one long, whirling noise.

"What do you think you're doing?" he groused. It was hard to believe that this side of an hour ago she'd wanted to have sex with this hostile man more than she wanted to breathe.

"I'm doing something nice for your daughter." Hayley felt the sudden urge to defend herself, and Madison, for that matter.

"I offered you hundreds of dollars to make her a dress, and you told me you didn't have the time. Then you did it behind my back, taking all the credit?"

"That wasn't my intention, okay? I'm sorry..."

"I'll pay you for the dress and she can wear it to the festival, but this Brand Ambassador social media thing? Not happening."

"But, Gavin, she wants this so badly."

He squeezed his fists at his sides. "I am her dad, and the answer is no."

Hayley's blood boiled. "For starters, you don't get to be a prick to me. I did nothing wrong, and I was planning on asking your permission before moving forward. Secondly, you are being an unreasonable asshole about this." She stabbed a finger in the direction of the door. "You have a daughter in there who needs more than a dictator for a father. Take an interest in what she wants. Let Madison be Madison."

Gavin curled his hair into his fists, holding his breath like a toddler having a temper tantrum. "I was trying to, and you stole it from me!"

Hayley paused then, her demeanor softening. She hadn't looked at it that way, and he was right. "I'm sorry... I didn't realize." She reached out her hand to touch his arm, but he took a step back from her.

"Let me be perfectly clear, Hayley. You are not her mother. You are nothing but a nosy stranger who thinks she knows what's best for my daughter. I know what's best for her."

Gavin's words cut deep, and she had to fight back tears as she attempted to regain her composure. "I hope every time she looks at that dress, she thinks about how amazing I am and what a jerk you are." She pushed past him to the door.

"Hayley, wait." She looked down at his hand wrapped around her wrist. It felt oddly familiar.

"Fuck you, Gavin." She ripped her arm away and flung open the back door, ignoring the multiple sets of eyes staring at her as she collected her purse from the coat tree in the entryway. Madison was nowhere to be found.

"Hayley!" Gavin pushed through the back door and darted past the stunned-into-silence onlookers to the entryway.

She held a hand up in front of her to stop him from coming any closer. "Never step foot in my store or come anywhere near me again."

NINE

Gavin

Gavin's eyelids slowly opened, and he winced against the blinding glare of a streetlamp. He had a vague recollection of driving to the dive bar far outside the city limits. The seedy structure in front of him was dark, his truck the only vehicle left in the parking lot. He reached for his phone to check the time before remembering what he'd done to it.

It was a frigid night. Although he was bundled up, that didn't stop the cold from seeping into his bones. Unable to stop thinking about how it had felt to be intimate with such an extraordinary woman after so many years of abstaining and how quickly he'd fucked it all up, he'd fallen back into his mind-numbing ways and passed out cold in his truck. He wasn't good for anyone, especially not the likes of Hayley Jackson. He had lost all sense of human decency, had forgotten what it was like to interact with people on a healthy level, and he had proven to himself that he was too far gone to change his ways.

He turned the key in the ignition, his truck roaring to life, and cranked up the heat, closing his heavy eyes.

What felt like a minute later he heard voices, followed by a cold rush of air. Was he being robbed? He was too tired to care, but when he felt a hand on his shoulder, instinctively he swung and kicked in that direction.

"Woah! Gavin! It's okay, buddy. I'm not going to hurt you."

The blurred image of the Pastor came into his line of vision. "Oh, hey there, Pastor. What are you doing here?" Gavin muttered. "I'm sleeping. You'll need to come back in the morning."

He had a vague notion that his truck was moving. An unsettled feeling grew inside of him as queasiness took over, but then everything went dark again. When the movement stopped, he opened his eyes just long enough to realize he was home.

He was weightless for a moment and then felt gravel beneath him.

"Where's your wallet?"

Gavin registered the gruff voice as Prater's and shrugged his shoulders. "Dunno, why the fuck do you care?"

"You kept mumbling that you needed more to drink but lost your wallet."

He'd crammed a fifty in his pocket before he left the house, just enough to get him good and plastered on cheap, dive-bar whiskey. Apparently his barely conscious brain had wanted more on the drive home and remembered that his wallet was still missing.

"Dammit, Gavin, where's your phone?"

"I chucked it. Bitch keeps calling me."

"Son, you better not talk about Hayley Jackson that way..." Prater warned.

Gavin snorted. "Not her. She doesn't want to talk to a loser like me."

Miguel pulled Gavin's listless arms over his shoulders piggyback style and dragged him up the porch steps on his back. "This pendejo weighs a ton."

June opened the screen door and followed Miguel, Prater, and Pastor Bradley down the hallway to Gavin's room. His eyes rolled open.

"Why the hell are all of you here? Jesus, I have to take a piss," Gavin grumbled.

"Shhhh! You want Madison to see you like this?" June chastised him.

Gavin stumbled to his bathroom and slammed the door shut, relieving himself before he even had his pants down. He fell and landed face first on the cold tile floor, just coherent enough to hear the conversation happening right outside the bathroom door.

"Thanks for coming, Pastor, Miguel," Prater said solemnly. "We've got it from here."

"Of course," replied Bradley. "He'll be in my prayers; call me if you need me."

"Later, boss," Miguel said.

"I'm done with him, June. I can't keep playing nursemaid to a drunk."

Gavin blinked open his eyes, processing Prater's words.

"Jim, he's hurting."

"No one knows that better than me. But dammit, how do you fix a man who doesn't want to be fixed? Always taking one step forward and falling five steps backwards. And his backwards gets worse every time."

"Think about Madison."

"I love that girl as if she were my own granddaughter, but Gavin should be raising her, not us. If he can't step up and be that man, he'll need to find someone else who'll take her."

"Shhh, Jim you don't mean that! You're angry."

"Damn right, I'm angry. We should be enjoying our golden years, not raising a child all over again and caring for a drunk. I hear Stan is looking to sell the bar. Working with Declan would be a less dramatic investment than this. Stop your crying, now. We'll talk more about this later."

Gavin instantly sobered. A searing fear gripped his soul. He couldn't fathom being abandoned again. Not only had Carly left him, but his mom had left when he was a young child, and his dad had been too concerned with rising within the ranks of his military career to be a decent father. He knew he'd pushed his own luck with Jim and June over the years, but abandoning Madison? The fact that Jim would say such a thing, knowing how much he cared for her, spoke volumes to Gavin. Meant the man was officially at his wits end.

Gripping the porcelain bowl, he pulled himself up and emptied the contents of his stomach. He curled himself around the toilet and wept. The bathroom door creaked open and closed, and he felt a cold rag pressed against his neck. June knelt beside him and laid a gentle hand on his shoulder.

"Please don't leave us, June." A sob tore from his chest.

"Breathe, Gavin," she said, her voice soothing like a mother's should be. "Like I said before, I'm not going anywhere."

"I can't do this anymore," he cried, his body shaking uncontrollably. "He should have taken me, not Carly."

June rubbed her hand down his arm. "Gavin, what happened was an accident that occurred because of someone else's stupidity. Free will caused it, not God. There is no rhyme or reason behind it. We must learn to move on and make the best of the life we have left. Madison needs you," June said tenderly.

He shook his head. "I'm a failure, I'm no father. Madison deserves better, she deserves her mom. You and Jim deserve better. I didn't even know about Daniel. You had a son…"

"Shhh," she said, patting his arm. Don't think about that now."

"It should have been me, June." Exhausted, he closed his eyes. He felt his head lift and then sink into a soft pillow. A heavy blanket was laid over him, warming his shivering body. He let sleep pull him under, instantaneous and profound, unable to fight with himself anymore.

Gavin was conditioned to the aftermath of binge drinking. What hurt the most and weighed heavily on his shoulders when he woke up at noon the next day was the shame and embarrassment, knowing he had once again hurt and frustrated those closest to him. Gavin remembered every harsh word Prater had said. Determined to make amends, to start anew, he peeled off his vomit and urine-stained clothing and stepped into the shower.

When he joined June in the kitchen a half hour later, the aromatic smell of pumpkin turned his stomach. *Ugh.* He'd be glad when she moved on to baking apple pies again, those were his favorite. There were at least a dozen of his now least favorite pies scattered on the table.

"Gavin, you scared me!" June pressed a hand to her chest, catching her breath.

"Sorry about that."

She examined him from head to toe and beamed. "Someone looks like they're feeling better." He noticed her eyes were puffy and red rimmed. That alone hurt his heart enough to make him want to change his ways, once and for all.

"About last night..." he began.

She put a hand up to stop him. "Let's not rehash all of that right now. Today is a new day. An exciting day, at that!"

"Gavin pulled a glass down from the cabinet and filled it with water from the sink. "Why is that?"

She looked at him like he had two heads. "It's day one of the festival, silly!"

Shit, he thought as he popped an aspirin into his mouth and drained the glass of water. "Day one?"

"Yes, tomorrow is the carnival!"

"Thrilling," Gavin mumbled, pouring himself a cup of coffee. "Is Jim around?"

She gave him a tight smile. "He and the boys left hours ago to set up the booth. The pie contest isn't until later this afternoon, so I stayed behind to finish up baking."

He thought about Hayley and the awful things he'd said to her. And then Jim and how overburdened he'd sounded. "I think maybe I should sit this one out."

"I don't think so, young man." She placed a hand on his arm. "Part of letting go of the past and forgiving yourself is putting yourself out there, even when it feels uncomfortable. Facing things. Also, this is your ranch, even if no one knows it. You should want to represent it proudly."

Gavin sighed. "June…"

"I don't want to hear excuses. I need your support, and the boys need you." She pegged him with stern eyes. "And you need to fix what happened between you and Hayley Jackson."

"I need to fix a lot of things."

She looked at him thoughtfully. "Yes, I suppose you do. All the more reason to go and be a part of things." She pulled a tissue from her pocket and dabbed under her eyes. "Alright, now that that's settled…" Gavin suppressed a groan when she set a piece of pie on the counter next to him. *I never want to see another damn pumpkin pie again for as long as I live*, he thought, scratching the back of his head.

"I'm thinking of submitting this one, but I need your opinion one last time. Eat up, then help me load all of these pies into the truck. You're gonna drive Maddie and me to the festival."

Gavin looked at the table, confused. "Why so many?"

"Samples for my booth, of course."

His daughter appeared in the kitchen, expressionless. Her hair was pulled back into a ponytail, and she was wearing her work overalls.

"Why are you wearing *that*?" Gavin asked.

She put her hands on her hips and glared at him. "What, now you have a problem with overalls too? I might as well help Papa Jim with the horses. Nothing else for me to do at the festival."

He studied her for a moment. The look on her face and the pain in her eyes made his heart ache. He knew it was time to offer her that olive branch.

"Madison, Miss Hayley made you a dress and meant for you to wear it. I want you to put it on and work at her booth today."

She eyed him warily.

"Well, what are you waiting for?"

"You're serious?"

"As a heart attack."

Maddie ran to Gavin and flung her arms around his middle before racing to change. He stood, shell shocked, while June stood in front of him with a knowing smile.

"See what a little bit of give can do?"

His heart swelled. It was amazing how much lighter that one little act of kindness made him feel. It was a highly addictive feeling, far better than whiskey. "You were right. Thanks for your support, June."

She nodded to the pie. "Now it's your turn to support me."

Turning his attention back to the pie, he took a hesitant bite. "Yeah, that one's great." At that point they were all starting to taste the same to him.

She put her hands on her hips, mouth agape. "Gavin Taylor, that is store-bought pie. I have fed you countless pieces for the last month, and you can't tell the difference between my home-cooked pie and a pie out of a tin? The texture and flavor is one hundred percent different."

He dropped his fork on the plate with a clang. "Then why the hell did you feed it to me?"

"I'm hoping you'll be chosen as a judge. I was testing you!"

"Nana June, can you braid my hair?"

Gavin breathed a quiet sigh of relief, grateful for Maddie's interruption.

"I'll braid her hair; you load up the pies and think of a way to right your wrongs, and grow a decent set of taste buds," she said with a wink that made him chuckle.

After loading up the pies, he came back inside to find June in the entryway, helping Maddie with her gloves. His daughter looked much older than her eleven years. Images of her future flashed before his eyes – prom, her wedding. There were so many important milestones ahead that he would need to show up for.

He opened the car door for Madison. His eyes lingered on his daughter as she slid into the back seat.

"What?" she asked, clearly perplexed by his change in demeanor.

"You look so much like your mom." He knelt next to her and took her tiny hand in his. "And she was the prettiest girl in high school."

A genuine smile crossed Madison's lips. She hadn't smiled at him like that in ages, and it warmed him from the inside out.

"Really?"

"Yup. I want to tell you all about her, Madison... I will, soon. I promise. And I hope I didn't mess things up between you and Hayley... I know how much she means to you."

"Nah. She still loves me, even though you were a major dum-dum."

Gavin cringed. "So... she talked to you about me?"

Madison shrugged a bow-clad shoulder. "Grownups don't give me details, but she said enough to let me know she's not happy with you. Maybe if you're not a grump she'll change her mind and want to hang out with you some today?"

"I seriously doubt it, but thanks for the pep-talk, Mads."

"Anytime, dad."

The Harvest Festival was in full swing. Once Gavin dropped June's pies off at her booth, he shouldered his way through the sea of jovial

117

strangers to find his own. It didn't take him long, as his was the only one with a corral and two horses. He apologized to a seemingly surprised Jim for being late, and his foreman shook Gavin's outstretched hand without meeting his eyes. He knew it wasn't going to be easy getting back into Prater's good graces, and that he was going to have to prove himself. Make some real changes.

Gavin took in the long line of children, bouncing on their toes with excitement as they waited for their turn to ride. He chuckled when he saw that Pegasus was dressed up like a unicorn, knowing it was more than likely his daughter's idea, and a smart one at that. People of all ages gathered around the corral, oohing and aahhing as Miguel and Alejandro demonstrated their impressive lasso skills. They even had their two older boys, Jorge and Mateo, who were eight and nine, respectively, helping.

But Gavin noticed that not everyone was impressed by the show. Declan and his band of assholes sat off to the side, pointing and laughing. Determined not to cause trouble, Gavin clenched his jaw and averted his eyes from them. *They aren't worth it,* he thought, crossing his arms in front of him and leaning a casual hip against the booth. He allowed his eyes to roam the festival in search of a certain honey-eyed woman.

His heart rate kicked up notch when he spotted Hayley at her booth. Women scoured the racks of clothing lined up under a sheet of canvas and paraded in and out of a makeshift dressing room. Hayley's face lit up with excitement when she saw Madison running toward her in the dress. Gavin smiled at the two of them together, seeing how much she seemed to genuinely care for his daughter. She had been in their lives for such a short amount of time and yet had already made such a big impact on Maddie. He had a lot to learn from Hayley Jackson, and he realized then, with alarming clarity, that he wanted to get to know her better. A *lot* better. Once the crowd thinned, Gavin decided it was time to start groveling.

Hayley did a double take when he approached her booth, her wide smile morphing into a frown. He swore to himself then and there that he would never be responsible for putting that look on her face again. Not if he could help it, anyway. She grabbed his elbow and led him behind the dressing room.

"I'm not about to make a scene in front of everyone," she spat out, "but I thought we made our positions clear?"

Gavin slid his hands into his pockets and smiled. It was a reflex, like a flower unfurling to the sun. His smile only widened when he saw how furious she was trying to be, yet he could tell she was affected by his proximity. Her breathing had changed, and her cheeks were flushed pink. She seemed to be at war with herself, her demeanor fluctuating between pissed off and turned on.

He gave a small shrug. "My position has changed."

"Well, mine hasn't."

She crossed her arms in front of herself. Even from a foot away, he could smell her intoxicating scent. He wanted to pull her to him and nuzzle his face into the hollow of her neck for a more concentrated hit.

"You're an asshole, and I should have never allowed myself to think otherwise." When she started to walk away, he grabbed her arm gently to stop her.

"Hayley," he said calmly. "Just hear me out. Please."

She pursed her lips. "Fine. You have one minute."

"What I said was wrong and ungrateful. I really do appreciate what you've done for Madison." He sighed and ran a hand through his hair. "I have issues. Things I haven't dealt with. I get confused, and I lash out. I feel inadequate, and I lash out." He pointed a finger at his chest. "But those are *my* problems. You did nothing wrong." As he reached for her hand he breathed an internal sigh of relief when she didn't pull away. "I'm so sorry I hurt you."

Hayley's expression softened, and he watched the tension leave her body. "Thank you for letting Madison wear the dress and work the booth."

A thickness formed in his throat. "I'm ashamed to say it was the first good decision I've made in many years concerning my daughter. But I'm determined to be better."

"I don't imagine it's easy being a single dad to a smart as a whip, sassy girl like Madison. I'm sure you have your own ideas about what kind of person you want her to be, and that they don't always line up with hers." She squeezed his hand. I'm sorry, too. "I shouldn't have butted in."

"To be honest, I've been too busy telling her what I don't want her to be instead of listening to her. That's not parenting. I've done a shit job with her."

She nodded over to a happy looking Maddie, proudly showing off her dress to the townspeople. "Well, this is a wonderful first step."

He let go of her hand and tipped up her chin with his finger. "I really like what I know about you so far, Hayley Jackson, and I'd like to get to know you better. Please believe me when I say that I *thoroughly* enjoyed kissing you."

The pink flush of her cheeks grew more pronounced. He wondered if she was a natural blusher or if he brought it out in her. That was just one of the many things he was looking forward to finding out. "I wasn't sure... I thought I'd done something wrong."

He drew his brows together. "Ummm... no. Quite the opposite. I just... I haven't kissed anyone since Carly, and I got overwhelmed."

Hayley's jaw dropped. "Wait a second. Are you telling me I'm the first woman you've kissed in *seven years?*"

He nodded slowly, reaching up to brush the pad of his thumb over her bottom lip. "And I would love the chance to redeem myself. Try it again sometime?" Tears pooled in her eyes, and he immediately wanted to back pedal for whatever it was he'd said wrong. It had been a long time since he'd had to read a woman's emotions.

He wrapped both hands around her arms, examining her. "What's wrong?"

"Hales, I need you out here! What the hell are you…" Kinsley stopped short when she saw Gavin. She took one look at Hayley's face and ran to her side. "What did you do to her?" she asked him accusingly, wrapping a protective arm around her friend.

Hayley sniffed and swiped under her eyes with the tips of her fingers. "He didn't do anything." Kinsley eyed Gavin skeptically, while the reassuring smile on Hayley's face put him at ease.

"I have to go," she said. "We'll talk later, after the pie contest?"

Gavin returned her smile and nodded. "Looking forward to it."

Pastor Bradley's megaphone-amplified voice hushed the crowd. Gavin walked to get a better vantage point of the small stage positioned at the heart of the festivities. He couldn't help but notice the looks he was getting, specifically from women. As a ballplayer, women had flocked to him after every game, begging him for autographs in the most… interesting places. Needless to say, Carly had hated it. But that had been so long ago, he'd forgotten what it was like. The very same people who had spent the last five years eyeing him with fear and disgust now had admiration in their eyes. And Gavin was truly shocked to discover that he liked how it felt. Sure, he still wasn't happy with the way they had treated him, but he realized that was mostly his fault. He may as well have been wearing a sign around his neck for the past five years that said *stay the fuck away from me*. Looking around at the swarm of people, he attempted to see them through a new lens. As actual human beings and not just thorns in his side. The words of the Pastor came back to him, *everyone has their own struggles*. He thought of June and Jim. Life had dealt them a similar hand, yet they hadn't chosen to forfeit their lives because of it. It gave him pause then, made him wonder what struggles the people of Timber Creek had gone through and were going through now.

Pastor Bradley was playing up his role, animatedly cracking jokes. *He really is a good man*, Gavin thought. And yet another person he owed an apology to. The Pastor acknowledged and thanked the town patrons who had helped make the festival possible and the vendors who had donated so generously. Gavin's heart swelled with pride.

When Bradley announced the start of the pie contest next, the crowd cheered. He called up the pre-selected judges: the mayor, the sheriff, an older woman Gavin didn't recognize, and Hayley Jackson. She looked amazing in her skinny jeans and fitted crimson sweater. His mind flashed to his hands and mouth on her, something he hoped to repeat as soon as possible.

The judges sat at a long, white table lined with pies. Hayley was adorably contrite as Pastor Bradley hailed her as Timber Creek's hometown golden girl. He made a joke about Hayley being the one to blame for the increase in traffic, but that it was well worth it, considering her store was starting to bring in more revenue for the town. Declan and his friends were just to the right of the stage, gesturing and making remarks to one another. He glared at them with clenched fists, knowing their banter was most likely directed at Hayley and sexual in nature.

"Per tradition, I will select a fifth judge from the crowd." A huge smile stretched across his face. "Gavin Taylor from the Miller Farm! Please come on up and take a seat next to Hayley Jackson."

A murmur ran through the crowd, and Gavin felt the weight of a thousand sets of eyes on him. If he could have shrunk down to the size of a mouse, he would have. Sensing his nervousness, June appeared by his side and gently nudged him forward. The crowd parted like Moses and the Red Sea as he made his way to the stage on shaky legs. He climbed the stairs and sat down in a white plastic chair next to Hayley.

Anxiety gripped his chest as he looked out at the crowd of stunned faces. June was bouncing on her toes with nervousness.

Hayley leaned into him. "You're looking a little green over there, Gav. Everything okay?" The scent of warm vanilla briefly dissipated his anxiety, bringing up thoughts of their kiss instead. "You can thank me for this," she said with a wink, clearly letting him know that she had arranged for him to be a judge.

The woman was not to be messed with.

"Mayor Davis, Tommy Jones, Holly Hammond, Hayley Jackson, and Gavin Taylor, I hope you brought your sweet tooths!" the Pastor exclaimed. "The rules are simple. The judges will taste each of the numbered pies and submit the pie they like best."

The judges dug into the slices of pie in front of them. Two stood out to Gavin, as they both tasted familiar.

"What do you think?" Hayley asked him.

He swallowed and wiped his mouth with a napkin. "I think it's between numbers two and three."

"I personally like number three," the mayor interjected with a wink. He reached around Hayley to shake Gavin's hand. "I'm Mayor Thaddeus Davis, remember me in the next election."

Hayley rolled her eyes when the mayor looked away and leaned into Gavin. "I always thought my daddy should have been mayor. And two is definitely better," she whispered in his ear.

While he agreed with her, he was confused. He knew he had tasted both pies before.

The mayor and the unfamiliar woman were hard pressed to support number three, whereas Hayley and the sheriff were adamant about number two. Gavin took a bigger bite of each, hoping for a revelation. He chewed thoughtfully, allowing the flavors to linger on his taste buds.

Pastor Bradley picked up the megaphone and told the judges it was time to reveal their picks. Gavin was officially in panic mode.

"Mr. Taylor! All of the votes are in except for yours, and it appears to be a tie! The winner of the pie contest is in your hands." Gavin was sweating in places he never knew existed. Disappointing June was not an option. His eyes darted back and forth between the two pieces. "Number...two?" he squeaked out.

"June Prater is the winner!" shouted The Pastor.

Gavin exhaled with relief and wiped his brow with the back of his sleeve. Hayley squealed and wrapped her arms around his neck. Cheers erupted from the crowd, most noticeably from Prater, Madison, Miguel, and Alejandro.

They surrounded June and exchanged hugs and kisses while Ann Davis stood close by, casting them dirty looks.

"Of course he'd side with Hayley Jackson. He's smitten with her and had no business being a judge."

Ann Davis was really starting to grate on Gavin's nerves.

June ran up to him with open arms and enveloped him in a warm hug. "Thank you! I knew you wouldn't let me down!"

"Yeah right, you were sweating just as much as I was," he said, pulling her in tighter. "Congratulations, June; you deserved the win."

Gavin watched Declan and his friends gather around Ann Davis, consoling her as she continued to gripe about how she deserved the win.

"I knew I had tried both pies," Gavin said to June, loud enough to ensure that Ann and the boys would hear him. "But how would I have tasted similar pies from one baker, when only one entry was allowed per person?"

Ann turned to them and glared at June. "She must've stolen my recipe." Knowing Gavin had figured it out, she was clearly trying to gain the upper hand.

"The other pie had a consistency that I've had before," Gavin said. "But this is a pie baking competition. You're supposed to bake them from scratch, Miss Davis. I've tasted dozens of June's pies, enough to know that yours wasn't from scratch, was it? It was store bought."

A crowd had gathered, watching their heated interaction in stunned silence. Little did Gavin know, no one had ever challenged Miss Ann. Her cheeks reddened. "Well, I never." She walked off in a huff while Declan and his crew took a step closer to Gavin.

"You talkin' shit about my boy Beau's grandma?" Declan hitched a thumb at the stocky one of the four-man douche crew.

Determined to keep his cool, Gavin held his hands up in front of him. "Don't want to make an issue out of it, I'm just saying what I tasted."

Beau approached Gavin and pulled a wallet out of his coat pocket. "I found something that belongs to you. Probably dropped it while you were drunk." He slid it back in his jacket pocket and crooked his finger, gesturing Gavin forward. "Come and get it."

"I'm not going to fight you, man."

Hayley walked over to stand in between them, facing the boys. "Leave him alone, assholes."

"You need your uptight girlfriend to fight your battles for you?" Declan heckled. "Move out of the way, Jackson. This guy has had it coming for a long time."

"Hayley, this is my fight," Gavin murmured into Hayley's ear.

"Why don't you tell your girlfriend here how you lost your wallet?" Declan said with a smirk.

If Declan's goal were to humiliate or provoke Gavin, he had a long way to go. Seeing that Madison was within earshot, there was no way he was going to bite. "It must have fallen out of my pocket."

Beau tossed the wallet a few feet away from Gavin and scoffed. "Yeah, because you were drunk. Don't you recognize this asshole?" he yelled to the crowd of people who had gathered around. "This is the town lush. A drunk who cleans up nice."

A chubby boy, no more than Madison's age, sidled up to Beau's side. "That's Madison's dad."

Beau curled his lip. "That weird girl who's always snitching on you? No wonder she's such a loser. Runs in the family."

Austin smirked up at his dad. "Yeah, Madison's a real loser."

"Shut your fat mouth, Austin!" Madison screamed. Sensing she was about to charge, Gavin wrapped his arm around her waist.

125

"You shut up, bitch," the boy retorted.

Gavin's blood boiled. Messing with him was one thing, but there was no way in hell he was gonna let this snot-nosed bully speak to his daughter that way. He stabbed an angry finger in his direction. "Apologize to her. *Now.*"

Beau lifted his chin and puffed out his chest. "Don't tell my son what to do. How about your drunk ass and your brat daughter take a long ride out of town and never come back."

Madison struggled to pull away from Gavin. "Hayley, please take Maddie to June," he said firmly, letting go of his daughter to approach Beau. Hayley did as she was told and stood off to the side with Maddie and June, her expression a mix of anger and worry.

Beau sneered, planting his legs wide and cracking his knuckles as Gavin stepped closer to the four men. Declan moved to stand in between Gavin and Beau and rolled up his sleeves. "Sorry, Beau. This asshole is mine."

Gavin swerved so that Declan's first punch missed him by a mile. Then he swung back, slamming a right hook onto Declan's jaw, knocking him backwards on his ass. Beau grabbed Gavin by the arms from behind. A left hook from Declan caught his face. It stung, but Gavin's adrenaline surged. A well-placed kick brought the man to his knees.

Miguel flew into the fray and slammed into Beau, knocking him off balance before turning to land a punch on the jaw of another one of Declan's friends. Alejandro joined in, swinging at all four of them.

Gavin continued throwing punches, some effective, some not. Prater tried separating the men, but when he was accidentally hit, he lost his temper and started throwing punches too.

Gavin sent a hard right against Declan's temple, landing him in a pile of mud. The Sheriff and his Deputies began pulling the men off each other. Gavin and Declan, who were still tangled up, were told that if another punch was thrown, they would be spending the night in jail.

The men were bloody, bruised, and covered in mud. Madison marched over to Austin and held out her hand. At some point the boy had snatched Gavin's wallet. He crossed his arms in front of him, daring Madison to do something about it. Madison reared back and punched Austin in the nose. He screamed, dropping the wallet to cover his bleeding nose with his hands. "I think she broke my nose!" he sobbed, running to his dad's side. Madison picked up the wallet and walked it over to her dad.

"Thanks, Mads. That was a really good punch." He looked down at her admiringly, and she smiled up at him, lifting her shoulders. "I have good genes."

Gavin gave a black-eyed Prater a pat on the back. "Thanks for having my back, man."

"We're family," Prater said gruffly, with a twinkle in his eyes. "And although families go through trying times, we will always have each other's backs."

"They had it coming," Miguel added, shaking out his hand.

"That Austin kid is such an asshole," Madison said.

Gavin chuckled, letting her foul language go this time.

He found Hayley with her arm wrapped around a frazzled looking June, who had just spotted Jim and was running over to check on him. When Hayley saw Gavin walking toward her, she rested her hands on her hips and bit down on her smile.

"Go out with me?" he asked as he closed the gap between them. "After all, isn't it tradition that the man who wins the fight, wins the girl as well?" He brushed her hair behind her ear and smiled.

"That is a ridiculous and archaic tradition, Gavin Taylor." She reached up to wipe a smudge of mud off his cheek. "But yes, I'll go out with you."

TEN

Hayley

Running a hand down her freshly flat ironed hair, Hayley scrutinized her reflection in the full-length mirror. "Be honest. How do I look?"

Kinsley stretched out on Hayley's queen-size sleigh bed and took a bite from the apple in her hand. "I'd definitely do you," she said around the mouthful.

Hayley chewed on her bottom lip and knit her brow.

"Stop worrying! You look smoking hot, as always."

"Do you think this is a good idea?" Hayley asked, turning to face her friend. "There's still time for you to talk me out of it. I can totally fake a stomach flu."

Kinsley burst out laughing.

"What?"

"Awww, your relationship already has a theme! Vomit!"

Rolling her eyes, Hayley slid into her olive-green cargo jacket. "Ha, ha."

"In all seriousness though, Hales." Kinsley pulled herself up to sit cross legged on the bed. "While I'm not thrilled with the way he treated you, I know you enough to know that you wouldn't be going out with him if he hadn't redeemed himself on some level."

Deciding then and there to shove her negative thoughts and flight instincts aside, Hayley nodded in agreement. "You're right. The man's got a lot of unresolved issues, but he's been through hell. It can't have been easy for him to put himself out there with me. He's allowing himself to feel vulnerable, and that's not a small thing." She selected a small boho bag from a hook behind the door and slung it across her body. "A lot of guys try to come off a certain way to hide their douche-like tendencies. I think Gavin's a good guy who's trying to come off like an asshole and push people away to protect his fragile heart."

"Look at you, poetic Doctor Hayley. I say you tuck him in nice and cozy tonight." She pointed a finger at Hayley and winked. "That's the prescription."

Hayley dropped her head back and groaned. "I'm trying to have a serious conversation with you. I swear to God, you have a one-track mind."

"You're right, I'm sorry." She tossed the apple core into the trashcan next to Hayley's dresser. "I totally get what you're saying. It was super sweet the way he stood up for Madison at the festival."

"It was, wasn't it? Their relationship is definitely strained, but I can tell he really loves her."

Kinsley dragged a fluffy throw pillow onto her lap. "And I know how much you enjoyed watching him fight Declan. That alone should earn him some lovin'."

"While I hate that he got hurt in the process, yes. I thoroughly enjoyed watching him pummel the douche nozzle." Hayley sat down on the edge of the bed and zipped up her boots. "So, what are your plans for the evening?"

"Sexy times with Jake," Kinsley replied, playing with the tasseled trim of the pillow.

"Why am I not surprised? How's that going?"

Kinsley twisted up her mouth and tilted her head from side to side. "Eh. He'll do, for now. Anyway, have no fear. I'll be at Jake's place, so you and your broody lover boy can have the house to yourselves."

"You really think I'm going to sleep with him on our first date? Do you not know me at all?"

She didn't tell Kinsley that if Gavin hadn't put a stop to it, she would have most definitely had sex with him on that rock.

"Well… considering you already let him feel you up and stick his tongue down your throat, something you haven't let anyone do in over a year, I figured sex was the next logical step."

"Even if I wanted to, I know he's not ready."

"Pfft. He's a guy, of course he's ready."

"Okay…" Hayley bent her knee and scooted further up on the bed to face Kinsley. "If I tell you this, you have to promise not to bring it up. In front of Gavin, I mean. I know how you get."

Always up for a juicy piece of gossip, Kinsley sat up a little straighter and widened her emerald eyes. "What is it?"

"Well… Let's just say I'm the first person he's had intimate contact with since his wife died. *Seven* years ago."

Kinsley's jaw dropped. "You're shitting me."

"I shit you not."

"I don't understand how that's possible," Kinsley shook her head, slow and disbelieving.

"He *really* loved his wife."

"And, after all of these years, he chose you!"

Hayley stood up and walked to her dresser in search of her favorite earrings. "I have to admit, it's flattering."

"For the love of God, put the poor guy out of his misery, Hales."

The doorbell rang. They simultaneously gasped, looked at each other, and squealed like seventh graders.

Kinsley darted up from the bed. "I'll get it!"

"You better be good!" Hayley yelled after her.

Drawing in a calming breath, Hayley shook out her hands and willed her heart to stop racing. She checked her appearance in the mirror one last time then clicked off her bedroom light.

Gavin stood in the entryway with Kinsley, holding a bouquet of flowers and looking slightly like a deer in headlights. He also looked sexy as hell in his black collared shirt tucked into dark washed jeans, charcoal suede jacket, and boots. The bruises on his face mixed with his day-old stubble and combed back hair gave him a bad boy vibe.

"Look how sweet you are, bringing our girl flowers!"

Gavin handed Hayley the bouquet. The sweet gesture made her feel warm and tingly inside. She couldn't remember the last time she'd received flowers from a man. "Thank you so much, Gavin, they're beautiful."

"I wasn't sure what your favorites were. Hope they're okay." He wrung his hands and rocked back on his heels. Oddly, his nervousness made Hayley feel more relaxed, like they were in it together.

"They're perfect," she replied, sniffing the plush, pink roses.

Kinsley took the bouquet from Hayley and ushered them out the door. "I'll put these in water, you guys go! Be safe! Don't do anything I wouldn't do. On second thought, do what I would do, but don't get caught!"

"Your home is beautiful," Gavin commented as they made their way down the front walkway to his truck.

"Thanks. We love it."

Gavin opened the door for Hayley, and she climbed inside.

"I'm sorry about Kinz," she said, after Gavin slid into the driver's seat, filling the cab with his warm and spicy scent. "She can be a little overenthusiastic at times. But bless her heart, she means well."

"I can never tell if that phrase is meant to be sincere or passive aggressive," Gavin mused, turning the ignition over. The V8 engine roared to life.

Hayley giggled, securing her seatbelt with a click. "When it comes to my best friend, it's a little of both, for sure." Her phone dinged from inside her purse. "Shoot. I'm so sorry. I know this is incredibly rude, but I need to check my Instagram account really quick. It's a work thing."

Gavin grunted. "Social media. Definitely not my thing."

"Bless your heart. Why does that not surprise me?" She gave him a teasing grin before pulling her phone out of her purse and scrolling through the *Country Chic* account. Her smile grew wide when she saw the progress her team had made on the page revamp they'd discussed during their Zoom meeting last week.

"So, what do you have, like a million followers?"

"Close to two hundred thousand."

Gavin's jaw dropped. "Seriously?"

"Social media is a must in my line of work." Her thoughts moved to Madison and the new line. Unsure if it was the right time to bring it up, a jolt of nerves shot through her. She looked up from her phone and over at him. "Speaking of work, would you mind if Madison sat down with me next week to help with designs for the new line? No pressure at all. We're moving forward no matter what, but if you'd rather her not be a part of it, I totally understand."

He turned up the heat and adjusted the vents. "That'd be fine," he said congenially.

"Really?" She was pleased and surprised by his laid-back attitude, the antithesis of his initial reaction.

"I overreacted before. If she still wants to do it, it's fine by me."

Hayley did an internal jig and gave him a big smile. "Thank you, Gavin." She tucked her phone back into her purse, ready to not think about work for once and focus on her date. She turned her body toward him. "So, Mr. Taylor. Where are you taking me?"

He put the truck in reverse and backed out of her driveway. "I thought we'd head over to the carnival. I haven't done the first date thing in a really long time, so I hope that's okay."

"That sounds wonderful! I was actually hoping you'd want to go, I loved it as a kid."

She watched his shoulders relax as he turned down a brightly lit and festively decorated Main Street. "Great."

"As long as you're not planning on taking part in another fist fight," she reproached him mockingly. "I'm pretty tough, so I could definitely help out, but I'm not really dressed for it."

Gavin cringed. "No fights tonight, I swear. I don't really feel like spending the night in jail." His expression hardened. "I'd do it all over again, though. Declan had it coming." He looked over at her and then back to the road. "Speaking of Declan, I noticed he's not exactly your favorite person either."

Hayley frowned. "Declan Reynolds is nothing but a two-bit snake."

"Preaching to the choir."

"Let's not talk about that prick."

"Gladly."

He kept his focus on the road, drumming his thumbs against the steering wheel. She took a moment to examine his profile, the gentle curve of his nose, long thick lashes any woman would die for, the freckle near his ear that she suddenly had the urge to kiss, and the stubble on his cheek she wanted to scrape her nails over. She hoped he'd lower his guard enough for her to find out if what they had was more than just superficial attraction.

His eyes flicked over to her and a slow grin took over his face. "What are you thinking about over there?"

Busted. "Nothing."

"You look amazing tonight, by the way. I mean, you always look amazing…"

Warmth spread through her at his words. "Gavin Taylor, I do believe there's a soft heart buried underneath that hard exterior." Her cheeks burned with embarrassment, realizing how that must've sounded. Gavin was blushing as well, his smile wide and knowing.

They pulled into the open field that served as the town's fairground. The small-scale carnival was bustling with people. Memories came flooding back to Hayley as they walked through the entrance and she took in the nostalgic scene before her. She had created so many memories on this quarter mile of patchy grass turf: causing mischief with Hunter and her sisters, her first kiss with a boy named Jimmy Jones (whom she cried over after he moved away a week later), and how she'd won the first prize ribbon in the livestock competition three years in a row. She had been thrilled when her dad let her keep Lily the pig instead of sending her off to the slaughterhouse when she retired.

Her life had evolved profoundly over the years, it almost felt to her as if those memories happened to someone else.

"Aunt Hayley!" Her nephews Kyle, Andrew, and Phillip waved from the vintage carousel, perched on wooden horses, holding sugar spun clouds of pink and baby blue. Two of her sisters, Amy and Candace, who rode along with them, did a double take when they saw that she was with Gavin.

Ibrahim, the kind and lively man who ran the general store, stopped to say a hearty hello as they passed by. "I still can't believe it's really you, Mr. Taylor. It's good to see you looking so well." Hayley thought it was sweet how genuinely pleased the man appeared to be. Gavin cleared his throat, visibly uncomfortable. "I appreciate that, Ibrahim."

Soon they spotted Madison and June walking toward them.

"Dad! Hayley!" Madison flung her arms around Hayley who glanced nervously at Gavin, afraid he might be hurt by his daughter's affection toward her. She was relieved to see that he was smiling.

"Are you two having a good time?" June asked with a wink. Hayley wanted to laugh when Gavin gave her a look that said, *don't start.*

"We just got here," replied Hayley, running her hand down Maddie's mermaid waved hair.

"Come now, Madison, let's leave these two alone to explore. We'll get some cotton candy."

"And a candy apple?"

"You can pick *one.*" She took Maddie's hand and waved goodbye. "Have fun, you two!"

"Can we stop over here for just a second?" Hayley pointed to a booth surrounded by a large crowd of people. "Every year my dad heads up a charity game called Knock 'Em. I'd love for you to meet him… unless that would be too weird for you."

"No. That'd be fine." He cleared his throat and swiped a nervous hand through his hair.

"Don't worry, my dad's harmless. I got really lucky. A lot of small-town southern dads are outrageously overprotective, controlling pieces of work. He's totally cool, I promise."

"Daddy!" she called out as they approached him.

Shea Jackson's face lit up. "Ah, there's my princess!"

His strong arms enveloped her, and she breathed in his familiar scent of cedar and mint. Although he would never admit to it, Hayley knew she was his favorite daughter.

Stepping back from Hayley, he looked Gavin up and down with kind eyes and the hybrid *it's genuinely nice to meet you, but I've got a gun and know how to use it* smile he had given to all of her boyfriend's growing up.

"Where's mama?"

"She was feeling run down. Nothing major, just a little head cold. Who do we have here?"

Hayley ushered Gavin forward. "Daddy, this is Gavin Taylor."

"Don't think I've seen you around before," he said, extending his hand for Gavin to shake. "Are you new to Timber Creek?"

Gavin looked about as comfortable as a kid in the principal's office. "In a way, yes."

Hayley smiled at his answer.

"This is a cryptic one you've got here, Hales."

Tell me about it, she thought, smiling up at Gavin.

Her dad hitched a thumb over his shoulder. "Well, I gotta get the game started. It was nice to meet you, Gavin."

"You as well, sir."

"See you later, daddy!"

Shea Jackson stepped behind the booth. "Step right up, folks, this is for a great cause. If someone can knock down all six sets of stacked jugs, I will donate one thousand dollars to the local charity of their choice."

The crowd cheered.

"You guys gonna give it a go? Like Mr. Jackson said, it's for a great cause."

"Pastor Bradley, hello!" Hayley greeted the kind, yet slightly eccentric man.

Gavin gave him a tight smile and a nod. "Pastor."

"How's it going?" Hayley asked him. "Have you collected enough donations for the families in need program?"

The Pastor beamed. "Yes! We were fortunate to receive a large sum of money from an angel donor."

"That's wonderful!"

"We're putting the other donations into our Meals-on-Wheels program, which should be up and running soon. He patted Gavin on the shoulder. "That extra thousand dollars would go a long way. I'd love to see Gavin here give it a go."

Hayley caught the hostile look Gavin gave Pastor Bradley, and her eyes moved back and forth between them curiously.

"I don't think so," Gavin replied in a clipped tone. "It's not really my thing."

Hayley looped her arm through his. "Oh, come on. I'm no good at this game either, but I'll do it if you will. And it really is for a great cause. We should show our support."

Pastor Bradley looked at him with pleading eyes.

Gavin gave a long sigh. "Yeah, fine. Okay."

Hayley tugged him by his hand to the back of the line. When it was his turn, Shea lined up six balls in front of him. Gavin locked his focus onto the bottles and threw the balls in rapid succession, knocking down all eighteen jugs within seconds. He hit them so hard most of them flew out of the booth.

The crowd gasped and applauded.

Pastor Bradley whistled his approval.

Hayley's mouth hung open. "Holy shit! Sorry, Pastor…" She turned to Gavin. "Ummm… you're really good."

"He is, isn't he?" said Bradley.

Ignoring their praise, Gavin directed his attention to Hayley. "Where to next?"

Shea Jackson walked up to them and patted Gavin on the back. "Son, that was amazing. What local charity would you like to support?"

"Pastor Bradley here said the Meals-on-Wheels program could benefit from it," Gavin replied.

The Pastor looked at him with a proud gleam in his eyes. "That would be amazing, Mr. Taylor, thank you."

Gavin turned back to Hayley who remained standing stock still, stunned into silence by what she'd just witnessed. "Hayley?"

"Yeah, sorry. Ummm… Oh! Let's go on the Ferris Wheel!"

Gavin groaned. "I should probably tell you that I'm not great with heights."

"Come on, you big baby," she said, pulling him by his arm.

"Not sure you're gonna enjoy seeing me break out in a cold sweat," he said. They walked toward the Ferris Wheel with its teetering white carriages and spools lit up with hundreds of flashing neon bulbs.

"Don't worry, I'll distract you," she said with a wink. The thought of being with Gavin alone on a Ferris Wheel gave her all the feels.

When it was their turn in line they slid into an empty carriage. They started moving right away, and Gavin curled his fingers around the bar. Hayley giggled at the terrified look on his face and settled back into the red padding of the seat.

"I appreciate you braving your fears for me," she said, leaning forward to rest her hand on his knee as they climbed higher.

"I'm sorry, I know I'm acting like a huge pussy. It was awful when I had to fly a lot. I sedated myself every..." His voice trailed off, and he stared straight ahead as if in a trance. Hayley's heart rate sped up, wondering what was going on with him, sensing it had nothing to do with the Ferris Wheel.

"You doing okay over there?"

Shadows danced over Gavin's taut features as they slowly moved higher. "Yeah, sorry."

Hayley took her hand off his knee and tilted her head. "So, you used to fly a lot? What was your profession?"

He dropped his chin to his chest. She put her hand on his back. "Gavin, if we're gonna do whatever this is, we need to open up to each other."

"You're right," he said, swallowing hard.

"Look," she began, rubbing her hand down his back, "I don't want to pressure you, because I know you've been through a lot. Thank you for telling me about Carly. For trusting me with that when we've only really just met. But I like you, Gavin... probably more than I should." He looked over at her and she smiled, letting him know she was teasing.

"I haven't been through the level of pain that you have, but I've been hurt before. My ex lied to me. All the time. That's why honesty is so important to me. I say all of this to say that I'm putting myself out there as well, and I know how scary it is. But I'm willing to set aside my fears and get to know you. To find out what you're thinking about when you make this face for instance." She slid a finger down the crease between his brows and smiled. "Pastor Bradley sure seems to like you. He didn't grow up here, so I don't really know him, but he seems like a good guy."

"He is."

"I sensed some pretty one-sided hostile vibes back there. What was that all about?"

He remained quiet, picking at the cartilage on his left thumb. She tried not to take offense, knowing that he and his mood swings were a package deal.

"What were you like as a kid?" Hayley asked, sensing a subject change was in order. "You must have been into sports, based on what I witnessed earlier. Did you play baseball in high school? Or college? I enjoy baseball. The camaraderie, the hot dogs." She giggled. "My friends and I would go to Yankee Stadium from time to time to watch the games."

Gavin's posture stiffened. She braced herself, gluing her eyes on his lock-jawed profile. He looked over at her, opening his mouth to speak and then closing it again. A breeze caught the cart and it rocked. He white knuckled the bar. "I…played ball in high school," he finally said. "Carly got pregnant our senior year, and we got married right after we graduated."

Hayley nodded. "You look young, so I figured you guys were teenagers when you had her. That would make you, what, 29?"

"Yeah. How old are you?"

"I'm 25," Hayley replied. "Go on. I'm sensing there's more to this story."

He let out a controlled breath. "After high school I was on travel teams and played some in Latin America. It was tough with a baby, but we made it work. I was eventually picked up by the Padres and rose steadily through the organization. Suddenly, I had it all. Dream career, a beautiful wife and daughter. I thought my life was set."

Hayley's mouth dropped open. "You seriously played for the *Padres?* Gavin that's huge!"

"The next part you know." The depth of sadness that radiated from his eyes was almost too much, but she didn't let her eyes break away from his. She took it all in, allowing herself to imagine what this man had gone through, but unable to fully understand, having not been through it herself. Her heart cracked for him, nonetheless. His watery eyes shimmered pink in the fluorescent lights of the Ferris Wheel, his beautiful face bruised, his heart not yet stitched up with time.

She pulled his hand into her lap and clasped it between her own. "I'm here, if you want to talk about it."

He nodded, looking away from her and inhaling a shaky breath as he swiped at his eyes with the back of his free hand. Wetting his lips, he stared out into the night, his body limp, no longer afraid of the distance between their cart and the ground when measured against the pain of his loss. "I had just pitched the most important game of my career. We were on our way home and another car collided with us. We rolled. I watched her die."

His expression hardened. "And before you ask if I had been drinking, I hadn't. The guy who hit us, however, was three times over the legal limit."

"Oh no… I wasn't going to…"

He dropped his chin and arched a brow. "Hayley, come on. I know you've heard rumors about Gavin the town drunk." He took a deep breath. "Full disclosure? What they say about me is true. I didn't drink at all back then, not even on special occasions. The drinking came later, after I spent months in rehab trying to claw my way back to some semblance of my former life." He lifted a shoulder. "But it was all for naught."

"What brought you to Timber Creek?"

"Carly had money…a lot of it. Because of that, she drew up a will the second she became of age, leaving all her money to me. That mixed with the money I made playing pro ball for a season, I was more than set financially. After she died, I set up a trust fund for Maddie and bought the ranch. It had been Carly's dream. And I wanted to…escape. From baseball and the pressure to perform. The media. My horrible excuse for human being in-laws. But all I succeeded in doing was creating a deeper level of despair by finding the bottom of bottle after bottle."

"Gavin… I'm so sorry."

"No one's fault but mine. I gave up, and part of giving up means hiding away. I turned myself into a pathetic cliché. Let my appearance go and became a sorry excuse for a human. Pushed my daughter away."

She put a hand on his arm. "Hey, raising a daughter isn't an easy thing for any parent to navigate; don't be so hard on yourself. My dad did it times four, and I know it wasn't easy for him. We were pretty wild, a lot wilder than Madison. She's doing okay."

"Don't you see, Hayley? Your dad and I are night and day, because he actually tried. I haven't tried with Maddie in a long time." Hayley brushed a lock of hair from his forehead and cupped his cheek. Closing his eyes, he leaned into her touch. "I know I have it in me to be better." He opened his eyes and looked into hers as he continued. "I used to love people, fed off of their enthusiasm and praise. I thrived off of pitching a game in front of fifty thousand people." Hayley reveled in his openness, the warmth of his voice. The way his eyes lit up as he spoke about the sport he had obviously loved very much. But then his face fell, and his eyes grew dark.

"After the accident, I had microphones and cameras shoved into my face for months, people asking how I was coping and what it was like to watch my wife die. My in-laws and the media... their insensitivity astounded me. They picked at my wounds and watched them bleed. It got to the point where I couldn't differentiate between my mental state and Carly's non-existence. I was a dead man walking. I lost my faith in humanity, didn't have the proper support system because I pushed everyone away. It was a very lonely place. I don't want to think about where Madison and I would be without the Prater's."

"Do you ever think about the possibility of playing professionally again?"

"No."

"Does Maddie know?"

He looked at Hayley intently. "No. I'm going to tell her, though; I've kept too much from her, and it's time, but part of me is afraid that, if I tell her, it will leak. Very few people around here know about my past, and I'd really prefer to keep it that way."

"But why hide it? What you achieved at such a young age is massive. You should be proud."

"I know it sounds like I'm being dramatic, but I really want to leave that part of my life behind me. I won't get into it right now, because it's a lot, but things happened. Also, and I don't mean to sound boastful or conceited, but I was a pretty big deal. The next up-and-comer. I'm not interested in ESPN knocking on my door asking for an interview."

"You really think they would, after all these years?"

Gavin shrugged. "Maybe not. But I don't care to find out."

"People do love a good human-interest story."

His laugh was self-deprecating. "Nothing interesting about me now."

She looped her arm through his and snuggled in, tipping her head up to look at him. "I beg to differ. I wouldn't be here with you if I didn't find you interesting."

"You don't know me," he murmured, looking into her eyes.

"Everyone deals with grief differently."

His hand slipped into her hair, and he stroked his thumb along her jaw. "Thank you, Hayley."

When they got off the Ferris Wheel and began walking around the carnival, Gavin took her hand and entwined their fingers tightly, so that their palms were pressed together. A warm glow spread through her.

"I love your hands."

"Really? They're like sandpaper."

"I like the feel of them. Means you're a hard worker. Capable." She blushed, hearing how seductively she'd said the word.

His mouth turned up at the corners. "Or I'm a man who doesn't moisturize properly."

"Well, which is it?"

"A little of both, for sure." His smile was sweet. His face lit up in the red glow of the flying rocket ride.

They earned curious looks from the townspeople. Every head turned as they passed. There were a mixture of shocked expressions and knowing smiles. Hayley noticed quite a few women ogling Gavin, which left her feeling giddy, proud, and slightly territorial.

She found him to be quite funny, which surprised her. It was like he was unknowingly showing her glimpses of what he was like before his life was turned upside down in the most tragic of ways.

After a full five minutes of her begging, he reluctantly agreed to give the mechanical bull a go. Much to his chagrin, he only lasted about ten seconds. Hayley stifled a laugh when he approached her, looking red faced and dizzy.

"What a racket."

She wrapped her arm around his middle, and he slung an arm over her shoulders for balance. "Awe, did that bruise your masculine pride?"

"That and my ass."

"At least this time it didn't involve water." Hayley looked up at him and belly laughed, earning her a sheepish yet brilliant smile. She thought he was breathtaking when he fully let his guard down.

A band started to play in the distance and Hayley gasped. "Let's dance!"

"Ummm… no."

"Why not?"

"Because, I can't dance."

She stuck out her bottom lip and tugged on his hand again, but this time his feet may as well have been stuck in concrete. "Please? I've managed to coerce you into everything else, so you may as well give in."

He shook his head slowly and tsked. "Your powers of persuasion are weakening, Miss Jackson. It's gonna take a *lot* more than that to get me on a dancefloor."

She stood up on her tippy toes and placed an opened-mouthed kiss on the freckle next to his ear. "Pretty please," she whispered in his ear. Someone whistled in the distance.

He rested his forehead on hers, the rise and fall of his chest quickening. "I take that back."

She stepped back from him, clapped her hands, and squealed. "So, you will?"

"You're evil, you know that?"

She laughed and pulled him toward the makeshift dance floor, smiling to herself when he adjusted himself as they walked.

He wasn't lying, the man had two left feet. But, bless his heart, he tried, and his arms felt so good around her.

After the carnival died down, they drove back to her house. She couldn't remember a time when she'd had more fun with a guy, and she wasn't ready to say goodbye. Despite his initial reluctance to open up, she felt so comfortable with him. That rare occurrence when you've only known someone for a short amount of time but it felt like you've known them forever. It had taken Hayley a full month before she'd slept with Derrick. With him it was a slow burn that, over time, became a flame and eventually led to the kind of epic sadness and disappointment one felt when they were cast aside and cheated on. What little bit of sentiment she had left toward that shit bag of a man diminished to nothing as she walked hand in hand with Gavin up her porch stairs. She wanted to ask him inside but wasn't sure if he was ready to take that step.

In the golden glow of the porch light, his long lashes fanned shadows across the tops of his cheeks. He towered over her, head tilted, dark eyes holding her gaze. Her stomach fluttered with excitement and nerves while her heart galloped wildly in her chest.

"I had a wonderful time."

"So did I," he replied, his voice barely above a whisper.

He reached out and touched her face, trailing his fingertips down her cheek. Hayley's eyes fluttered closed, and her lips parted as a wave of pleasure coursed through her in anticipation of his mouth on hers. She reveled in the warmth of his body as he closed the gap between them, the gentle press of his lips on the corner of her mouth, the pressure of his hand resting on her hip, the other cradling the back of her neck. He brushed his mouth over hers, catching her bottom lip between his teeth. Hayley's breath quickened as a magical, dizzying euphoria swirled around her. She grasped a fistful of his shirt, tilted her head, and opened her mouth to invite him in.

A warm ache settled between her thighs as he savored her, drawing up her desire with each sweep of his tongue. His hands slid down her back and over her ass. He grasped her thighs and lifted her as if she were weightless. She wrapped her legs around his waist and squealed when, in one fluid motion, he swung around and thrust her against the front door. His grip tightened, roughly urging her on as he continued exploring her mouth. The feel of him against her as his hips started to move made her mindless with lust. She couldn't remember anything ever feeling so good, and he wasn't even inside of her yet.

Her hands reached down to fumble with the button of his jeans. "Gavin," she gasped. "I want you."

"Stop." He squeezed his eyes closed and dropped his forehead to the door. Their breathing fell together in an uneven, choppy rhythm. She started to pull away from him, her heart sinking to her feet.

He gripped her hips tighter. "Is Kinsley home?"

A relieved smile stretched across her face. She shook her head.

"Inside. *Now.*"

"You're so damn bossy." She nipped at his bottom lip. He growled before releasing her so that she could unlock the door.

Once inside, she ripped off her jacket and he backed her up against the door, pressing his palms next to her head on either side, caging her in. "Say it again," he whispered against her mouth.

"Say what again?" she asked, breathless.

"Tell me that you want me."

"I want you, Gavin. You know I do."

He nestled his face into the hollow of her neck. "You smell so fucking good." Dropping to his knees in front of her, his work roughened hands slid up her skin, lifting her shirt to expose her stomach. He kissed a trail from her navel all the way up to the center of her breasts and back down again. Meanwhile, his fingers worked to unbutton her jeans and pull down the zipper painstakingly slowly. "Holy shit. You have a tattoo. That's so damn sexy." He brushed his thumb over the butterfly tattoo she'd gotten after high school graduation. She wove her fingers through his hair and moaned as he placed open-mouthed kisses along the satin lining of her underwear. Tugging her jeans, he pulled them down just enough to push her panties aside and slip two long fingers inside of her. She threw her head back, slamming it against the door. "Gavin," she panted. "That feels so good." He picked up the pace, thrusting his fingers in and out while circling the pad of his thumb over her clit until an orgasm ripped through her. She wanted to fall into a puddle on the floor, but instead, she pulled him up to stand and unbuttoned his jeans. Her thumbs slipped into the waistband of his black boxer briefs and she pushed them, along with his pants, down. When his erection sprang free, she drew in a sharp breath and wrapped her hand around the base.

He hissed through clenched teeth. "Hayley. I'm going to cum right now if you do that, and I *need* to be inside of you. Please, tell me you have condoms."

"No. But I'm on the pill and I haven't had sex in over a year." She smiled wryly. "I'm fairly certain you're clean. I trust you."

That was all he needed to hear.

She peeled off her jeans and he lifted her again, propping her up against the door as he positioned the tip of his erection at her opening. "Fuck," he moaned, sliding inside of her an inch at a time until he filled her completely, gripping her thighs and pumping into her harder, faster. Bright points of light burst behind her eyelids with each upward thrust.

"Hayley, I'm so sorry. I promise I'll make it up to you."

They came violently and in unison. His head buried into her neck, her teeth biting down on his shoulder.

"Oh my God."

"I know," she panted, kissing up his shoulder to the base of his throat.

He moved his head back to look at her, his dark eyes predatory, still wanting.

"Where's your bedroom?"

ELEVEN

Gavin

Two weeks later, Gavin woke, once again, inside a cocoon of blankets, Hayley's body wrapped around him. An hour later, as he stepped inside the ranch house, his mind was distracted by visions of her lush mouth, soft curves, and the way it felt to be inside of her. He'd forgotten what it was like to give himself up to someone so completely. Once he'd had a taste of Hayley Jackson, he was greedy for it, like someone who'd been wandering through the desert seeking an oasis. The stress and anxiety he typically dealt with on a daily basis had been quieted as of late. Instead of getting drunk off whiskey, he'd been lust drunk for the past two weeks. But it wasn't just the sex. Gavin really enjoyed spending time with Hayley, in general. He was surprised by how much he'd allowed himself to feel for her in such a short amount of time. Any decent therapist would tell him to take time to work on himself before diving into a relationship, but being with her felt right, and he thought that maybe she could help him on his journey to becoming a better man. She was already so good with Madison and could teach him a thing or two about being more patient, attentive, and caring toward his daughter.

He was in the kitchen, making himself a cup of coffee, so lost in thought he didn't notice Miguel leaning a casual hip against the counter, watching him.

"Shit!" Gavin yelled, nearly dropping his full mug of coffee. Fucking hell, Miguel, you scared the life out of me."

"Sorry, boss. I ran out of coffee and wanted one of your snooty K-cups." Miguel held up his steaming mug of coffee. "Where's June?"

"Not sure... haven't seen her yet this morning," Gavin hedged, not wanting to admit he'd just gotten home.

Miguel shook his head. "Man, I'm so glad we're past the pumpkin season. Way too much of a good thing, ay yi yi. June with all the pies."

"Past it?" Gavin chuckled and bent down to wipe up the coffee that had splattered on the floor. "Halloween and Thanksgiving are around the corner. I have the feeling there will be many more to come."

"No." Miguel waggled an emphatic finger. "There will be much flan and sopapillas. If I have one more bite of a pumpkin, I will quit and return to Mexico."

"Oh, so that's how I get rid of you! I'm glad you told me. I'll make sure to pick up some pumpkin coffee pods next time I'm out to make your departure more imminent." Gavin snickered at his friend's chagrined expression. Apparently, he could dish it, but he couldn't take it.

Miguel eyed him warily. "I'm not so sure I like this new and improved Gavin."

Gavin walked to the fridge and pulled out a carton of creamer. He held it up and nodded to Miguel. "Si, gracias."

"Totally messing with you, man. I'm right there with you on the pumpkin. Tell Maricela to bring on the flan, I welcome it."

The two men sat on the porch together, enjoying the rare moment of quiet. They watched the sun bloom on the horizon, but it would soon be hidden by cloud cover. After several mild days, the news anchors predicted cold rain and windy conditions for their region, starting that afternoon. The temperature was steadily dropping. Gavin nestled deeper into his coat and sipped his coffee. The puff of steam curling up from the mug warmed his face. He breathed it in, basking in the rich aroma of the comforting brew.

"You seem at peace, boss. I take it your date was bien?"

Gavin couldn't help but smile. He hadn't been this happy in seven years, and Hayley was the reason. "Muy bien."

Miguel's grin was wide and genuine. He raised his mug to Gavin. "I'm happy for you, man."

Gavin crossed an ankle over his knee and leaned back in the rocking chair, rubbing his thumb and index finger over his lips to contain his cheesy smile. "Thanks, man. I really like her. She's headstrong and independent but also honest and genuine. What you see is what you get, you know?"

Miguel nodded. "I do know. Maricela is the most genuine person I know. It's one of the things I love most about her. It sounds like you found something special, too." He dropped his whiskered chin and arched a brow. "Don't mess it up by being yourself."

Gavin shook his head and grinned. "Thanks for the vote of confidence, Miguel."

They sipped their coffee in contented silence until Prater tromped up the porch steps. He took a seat in the empty rocking chair next to Miguel with an early morning sigh and lit a cigarette. "Morning, boys."

"Morning, Jim," Gavin replied, powering up his phone. He'd shut it off last night when Denise Lawson had called him for the third time that day. "Shit," he muttered when he saw that there were two more missed calls and voicemails from Denise and three texts from Xavier. Determined to stay in his happy Hayley bubble, he slid his phone back into his coat pocket.

"How's it going with Miss Jackson?" Prater inquired in the same gruff manner he'd been addressing Gavin with for the last two weeks. Gavin knew Jim was happy for him, but he got the feeling he was also waiting for him to fuck it all up. "You've been seeing a lot of her."

"Just fine, Jim, thanks for asking," Gavin replied nonchalantly before tipping back the last of his coffee. There was no way he was going to delve into his sex life, which was most definitely none of their business. Not that he thought Prater would be interested in that aspect of their relationship. Miguel, on the other hand? He'd be all ears.

"Don't worry, boss," Miguel said. "I already gave him some sound advice."

"Damn, it's getting cold," Gavin said, deciding it was time to veer off the topic of his love life. *Love.* Is that what he was feeling? He zipped up his coat as far as it would go and took in the ominous clouds that were building on the horizon. His warm breath turned to plumes of white steam as he spoke. "We're gonna get a lot of rain and high winds in the next day or so, which means flooding." Gavin raised his empty mug to the men. "To fun times ahead."

"Speaking of a fun time, I have some good news," Prater spoke up. "Lucy has booked several families for riding lessons, and June is making plans for a summer camp." Prater held up his hand preemptively, expecting Gavin to protest. "Now, before you start your whining, hear me out. This is a smart idea, Gavin. Would bring in a windfall of money. We could offer a variety of outdoor activities, such as camping, archery, and horseback riding. Maybe even a gun safety course. People would come from all around."

Gavin scraped a hand through his hair and sighed. "Well, it's certainly ambitious." He leaned forward and rested his forearms on his thighs, tapping his thumbs together. "But necessary, I suppose."

Prater arched a bushy brow. "And as your foreman, I know best."

"Yes, Jim. You know best," Gavin said, an eye roll implied in his tone, an amiable smile on his lips.

Gavin could tell that Prater was taken aback by his response. He leaned back in the rocking chair and stretched out his legs, crossing his ankles. The look on his face was one of both surprise and relief. "Well, alrighty then. We actually had someone sign up for this morning. Our first paying customer."

Miguel was quick to reply. "I vote Alejandro takes them on account of him not waking to join us. He and Bianca had their 10th anniversary yesterday, so he was muy busy last night." Miguel waggled his eyebrows. "If you know what I mean."

Ignoring the innuendo, Prater snubbed out his cigarette on an ashtray sitting on the table next to him. "Nah, I reckon Gavin should take this one."

When Gavin objected, the foreman threatened a day of working on the cold range, so he begrudgingly relented. He pulled his vibrating phone from his pocket as he made his way to the stable.

Denise Lawson again. He took a deep breath and steeled himself, knowing it was time to rip off the bandage.

"Yeah?" His greeting was clipped.

"Gavin?"

"Yep."

There was radio silence on the other end of the line.

"Hello?"

"Um… yes. Sorry, I'm just surprised you picked up. I know things have been strained between us in the past, but I'm hoping for Madison's sake you'll allow us to see her. She needs to know her grandparents, and I want to resolve this without unnecessary drama."

The mechanical tone of her voice worked its way under his skin. It sounded to him as if she were reading from a script. "If memory serves, you were the one who started the shit storm of unnecessary drama, Denise."

Ignoring his barb, she continued. "We are planning to travel to Catalina Island over Christmas and thought it would be a great opportunity for her to spend some time with us."

"Denise, I've spent the last five years trying to forget the fact that you exist. I don't know what makes you think I would let Madison see you at all, let alone *vacation* with you." He kept his voice calm and even. He'd missed the feeling of being in control of his emotions, more contained.

Alcohol had made him clouded and angry, unable to properly articulate his feelings.

"Gavin, I'm her grandmother," she replied sternly. "And I've had zero contact with her for half of her life."

"Can you blame me, after the bullshit you tried to pull? Tell me, why should I trust you?"

"I had just lost my daughter, and you took my granddaughter a thousand miles away. What did you expect me to do?"

"Well, I lost *everything*. My wife. My career. My health. And you tried to take my *daughter* away from me. The one thing I had left." He unlocked the stable door and walked in. "You made your choices, and those shitty choices have led you down this path, not anything I've done. For as long as I have a say, you're not going to have contact with her."

"You started drinking. I was worried for her and only trying to do what I thought was best for her quality of life."

"I did what I knew Carly wanted for our daughter by honoring her wishes. I know it was hard for you to believe that Carly wanted to have a life with the likes of me, but she did. We built a life and started a family that you had nothing to do with. You couldn't accept her choices because you're just about the most selfish person I have ever known. Nothing I did was ever good enough for you. I wasn't always perfect, but I was nothing but loyal and loving to Carly, and you did whatever you could to try and tempt her away from me. You, Denise, are a monster."

Gavin felt a hundred pounds lighter. It was liberating for him to finally let it all out.

Silence hung over the line. "I don't know what to say."

He rummaged around for Zeus's saddle and blanket. "You're a smart woman, you'll figure it out. Leave us the hell alone, Denise." He hung up on her and shoved the phone into his back pocket. In an effort to calm down, he took a few deep, steadying breaths.

Once he found the saddles, he climbed up to the loft and tossed some feed down for the horses. Gavin still wasn't thrilled with the idea of dealing with the general public, but he promised Jim he'd try. He was just finishing up pushing hay when he heard a familiar voice say his name. Stepping down the ladder, he caught a glimpse of his student.

"Hayley?" He hopped off the last rung of the ladder and drank in the sight of his lover in faded jeans, riding boots and a worn, brown leather jacket. Her long hair was windswept around her shoulders, cheeks pink from the cold, and a mischievous smile danced on her plump lips.

"Aren't I a lucky girl," she said as she sauntered toward him, eyes twinkling with naughtiness. "When I booked this lesson with Prater last week, I was hoping you'd be my instructor." She stopped just short of reaching him and tilted her head. "Are you mad?"

Gripping her open jacket with both hands, he tugged her closer. "Why would I be mad?" he asked, smiling like a fool, examining her bright eyes.

She shrugged. "I know you must have been a little apprehensive when you heard you were giving a lesson. I told Prater to make damn sure it was you."

Gavin brushed the tips of his fingers down her cheek, and a small sigh escaped her lips. When he bent his head to kiss her, she scraped his bottom lip with her teeth. "Mmmm… you are a very naughty girl." He tipped up her chin with a thumb and index finger, his gaze flitting between her eyes and mouth. She didn't have makeup on today. He could see the tiny mole underneath her right eye and the faint scar on her chin that she must've gotten during her legendary Timber Creek tomboy days. He loved seeing her like this, natural and raw, comfortable in her own skin. She was always beautiful, but he thought she was prettiest just like this. "How is it that I left you three hours ago and I already missed you?"

"I missed you, too. And I had such a great time last night," Hayley said, glancing up at him from beneath her lashes.

He arched a brow. "Just great?"

Her smile was shy as she bit down on her bottom lip. *She knows exactly what she's doing*, he thought, feeling himself grow hard. He slipped his hands under her jacket, linking them together behind her back. "Amazing, spectacular, titillating, passionate, sensual, toe curling, orgasmic, deliciously naughty… I could keep the adjectives rolling, but I think you get the point."

He leaned down to kiss her again, and she opened her mouth to him, sweeping her tongue against his. Pushing her hair aside, Gavin trailed his lips down her neck to the base of her throat. The now familiar scent of her skin was a luxury and the feel of her wrapped in his arms a comfort. It had only been two weeks and yet, somehow, she already felt like home.

"Rain's coming soon," Gavin said. "We should probably get a quick ride in before the storm comes. I know for damn sure you don't need lessons, but you did pay…"

"We can postpone." She ran a long, pink fingernail down his jawline. "Find something else to do?"

He traced her lips with his finger. "There are worse things than being caught in the rain with Hayley Jackson. Plus, I kinda feel like taking a ride." His mouth went to her ear and she shivered. "I'm starting to feel like you only want me for my body."

She laughed softly. "You're on to me."

They put on warmer coats and outfitted Zeus and Pegasus. Together they led the horses out of the stable and were about to mount them when Hayley pointed at the pole barn. "What's in there?"

Gavin stared at the barn for a long moment before looking back at her. "A shrine to my past."

Hayley raised her eyebrows. "A shrine to Gavin Taylor's past, huh? I'm definitely intrigued."

He looked at the barn again, conflicted. She must have sensed his hesitation because she walked up to him and placed her hand on his back.

"Hey, it's okay. You don't have to show me."

He turned to her, his mind at war between wanting to fully open up to her and wanting to curl back up into his shell, like a snail sensing danger. But, in that moment, as he looked into her eyes, so soft and caring, he wanted her to see all of him. He'd already told her everything. What was inside that barn was merely a tangible representation of a past she already knew about. "No… I want to."

They led Zeus and Pegasus to the old barn. After turning on the light and ushering Hayley inside, he slid the door closed behind them. "So, this is where I work out and throw. It helps to clear my mind."

Hayley's gaze roamed the space as she walked further into the barn. "Gavin, this is *amazing.*" She went to the cage, curling her fingers around the chain link. "You come here every day?"

He nodded. "Most days."

She turned to him and smiled. "This is so incredibly cool. Thank you for showing me."

As she continued her perusal of the barn, her eyes landed on Carly's photos, which lay scattered across the weight bench. He intended to pick out a few to frame for Maddie and start initiating conversations with her about her mom and his baseball career. But, because both he and Madison had been spending so much time with Hayley as of late, Maddie helping with the clothing line and Gavin helping with some of Hayley's…other needs, he hadn't found the time. He would though, he told himself. Very soon.

Opening himself up to both the Praters and Hayley made him realize just how ridiculous and wrong it was to not be vulnerable with his daughter, the one who needed to hear it the most. It was time to put some trust in his daughter and earn hers in return. He had fostered a closed off environment, one where she no longer felt safe to ask him questions about her own mother. Gavin thought back on seeing Maddie wrapped in the blanket Carly had made and wearing the baseball cap she had found. He wondered if she knew they were connected to her mom in some way and had been drawn to them because of it.

Hayley picked up one of the photos of him and Carly. "Gavin, she was gorgeous. You two made a beautiful couple. Madison has her eyes."

Walking to stand beside her, he looked down at the photo. "This was the last picture taken of us together. God, my life was such a whirlwind back then. I didn't have time to really stop and appreciate everything I had." He looked at Hayley standing next to him, realizing just how important she had become. She lit him up inside, and, for the first time since that awful night, he could see a beacon of light in the darkness, illuminating a path. And she was walking right beside him, holding his hand. Turning to her, he cupped her cheek in his palm. "I still miss her. Every day. But I want to appreciate every moment I have now. With you."

Hayley set the photo down on the bench and wrapped her arms around his waist. "What do you say we make our own memory?" She pulled her phone out of her coat pocket and put it in selfie position with the batting cage behind them.

When he gave her a wary look, she set down the phone and put her hand on his arm. "This is just for us, Gavin, I promise. I'm not going to post it on social media, if that's what you're worried about. I respect your privacy."

Gavin relented, all feelings of trepidation swept away by the sincerity in her voice, eyes, and the sweet smile on her lips. He trusted her. They leaned against the pitching cage and snuggled together. She pressed her lips to his cheek and snapped the photo.

"It's perfect," she said, looking down at the photo.

"It is," he agreed, looking over at Carly's photo on the weight bench.

She rested her hand on his arm. "Hey, are you okay?"

He took a cleansing breath. "Yes. I think she'd be happy for me. You're good for me... and for Maddie."

Tears pooled in Hayley's eyes, but none escaped. "You are so surprisingly sweet, you know that? Thank you for this. For trusting me."

After turning the lights off and locking the up barn, the couple mounted their horses. They moseyed along in contented silence, glancing over at each other and smiling every now and again. She had a way of disarming him. The more time he spent with her, the more the wall he'd built around his heart crumbled.

"I spoke with Maddie's grandma today." The wall of protection he'd built around his heart concerning Denise, however, was one he didn't think would ever fall.

"Did you?" She looked surprised. "Look at you making so much progress in all areas of your personal life."

"I finally told her off, and damn did it feel great."

"Oh really? I'm surprised I found you in such good spirits."

"I thought it went pretty well. I was able to get my gun off and didn't feel the need to punch a wall or drink a fifth of whiskey afterward. Believe me, that's progress."

Hayley giggled. "I suppose that's true. You're definitely on the right path."

"She's being so damn pushy. Wants to see Madison over the holidays."

"What are you going to do if she pushes for it?"

"Oh, that's easy. I'm gonna keep telling her no. Even better, I'll block her number."

As they rode on, they happened upon a dilapidated old shack close to the river, which looked like it was held together by spit and a few nails. Gavin explained to Hayley that he and Madison used to sit on the bank to fish and would hide out in that shack when it rained. Now Maddie used it as a quiet place to read. Maybe he'd renovate it, he thought, and start fishing with his daughter again.

"I used to love to fish," Hayley said. A vision of the three of them standing on the bank fishing together made him smile.

They rode along the riverbank, making easy small talk as they went. Hayley shared the ins and outs of how she'd become interested in fashion during high school.

Gavin grinned at her mention of high school. "I bet Hayley Jackson ruled the school."

"My junior and senior years were glory days, for sure. Amy and Candace had graduated at that point but didn't go to college, so they hung out with us a lot. But Lainey, who is a year younger than me, poor Hunter, me, and a couple other girls who moved away after graduation made quite the crew at Timber Creek High. It was a fun time, for sure... for the most part."

"So, what's the deal with you and Declan?" Gavin knew it was a touchy subject for her, but he was so morbidly curious, he couldn't help but ask. "I mean, obviously the guy is the worst. I take it he wasn't much better as a kid?"

Hayley looked down at her hands gripping Pegasus's reins and grew quiet. A shock of alpha male adrenaline coursed through him. By the look on her face, the douchebag had to have done something pretty damn shitty.

"*Oh,* I see how this is gonna be," he teased, at war with wanting to find out what happened and dropping the subject for fear of spoiling their lighthearted mood. His curiosity won out. "I tell you my life story, and you get to maneuver around the unfortunate parts of your past." He moved his hands up and down like weight on a balance scale. "That seems fair."

"It's stupid, really," she replied quietly.

"It involves Declan so... obviously. But whatever happened seems to have caused you a great deal of pain, so you shouldn't underplay it. You are a mature, composed, put together woman, but when Declan's around it's like you're unleashing years of pent-up rage. Whatever the asshole did must have hurt you in some profound way."

She sighed. "Fine, I'll tell you."

Gavin laughed. "Hayley, you don't have to tell me. I'm just learning that it's good to get things off your chest. Makes you feel a hell of a lot lighter."

"It all started the week before prom," she began. "Okay, so I guess I should start by saying that I had a huge crush on Declan. All through high school." She paused and looked at him, as if measuring his response. He shrugged. "I mean he's a dickwad, but he's not a bad looking guy. And it was a high school thing, I totally get it. Go on."

Hayley shook her head. "Never mind. This is *so* stupid. You've been through so much in your lifetime, and this is nothing compared to that."

"No... but it clearly affected you. Trauma is trauma, no matter the level. This isn't a competition, Hayley, so take me out of the equation. We're focusing on you now." He steered Zeus around a large tree stump. "The scale of other people's problems doesn't make your own easier to live with."

She gave him an appreciative smile. "Okay. Well, like I said, it was the week before prom and I didn't have a date. It's not that no one asked me, as you know I was pretty tomboyish my freshman and sophomore year, but by my junior year I had..." She paused, considering her words." Let's just say the boys were suddenly... very interested."

"Oh, I believe it," Gavin said with an impish grin. Her cheeks, already pink from the cold, turned rosy red. Making Hayley Jackson blush was quickly becoming his new favorite pastime.

"Anyway," she said on the tail end of a laugh. "So, yeah, I had gotten a lot of offers but was too busy pining away for that ass-hat to care. And then, one day, it happened. I was walking to my car after school and there he was, leaning against a classic red car and staring at me all Jake Ryan from Sixteen Candles style. Have you seen the movie?"

"Ah, yes, I know who Jake Ryan is. Carly was a big fan."

Hayley nodded. "Right, exactly. What woman isn't? So, anyway, he beckoned me over with his finger."

"Ooohhh, the sexy finger crook."

"Yes, that. So, I went over to him and he said, 'Hey, Jackson.' He used to call me Jackson."

"Yes, I knew that."

"You did?" Hayley scrunched up her face. "Huh. Okay. Then I walk up to him and he says, 'Hey, Jackson. Janie's being a bitch, so I dumped her. Go to the prom with me?'"

"Classy."

"Janie was his girlfriend at the time, but everyone knew they were like oil and water. Fought constantly. Plus, she was a year older than us, headed off to college, and way out of his league in terms of life potential."

"You were out of his league, too."

"Aww, you're so sweet. And you're right, I was. But focus."

Gavin gave her a two-finger salute. "Yes ma'am."

"So, needless to say, I was over the moon excited. I even made my own dress."

"Oh, like Molly Ringwald in Pretty in Pink!"

"First of all, you're adorable and I love that Carly indoctrinated you in all of the best eighties chick flicks, and second of all...yes. But there was a lot less pink. Hunter was my Duckie."

Gavin pulled his riding gloves out of his pocket and slipped them on. "So, if you had a Duckie that means the fucker must have ditched you?"

"Worse, actually. He asked if we could go out the night before prom. Of course, I said yes, so he came to pick me up in the red car, but he was acting super sketchy and anxious. Not in an *I'm nervous to go out on a date with you* kind of anxious, but an *I'm in a shit load off trouble with the law* kind of anxious."

"Was he?"

"Yup. Turns out he *borrowed* that red car and *forgot*," Hayley air quoted the words borrowed and forgot, "to give it back."

"Sounds about right. Then what happened?"

"The cops tailed him on his way to my house, so he took a backroad and ditched them."

"What a dip shit."

"It gets even worse."

"Suddenly, putting Declan in the hospital would be worth the jail time."

"He's definitely not worth it. Anyways, the cops pulled us over and Declan was sweating up a storm, begging me to take the blame because my dad basically owns half the town and could get me out of it."

"That selfish mother fucker. What did you do?"

"I took the blame."

"Seriously?"

"Yup. And before you go judging me… nah, go ahead and judge. I was an idiot. It was awful. The Sheriff questioned us in one of those little rooms with a spotlight shining down on the table."

"First of all, no judgment here. I'm just processing. Second of all," Gavin arched an eyebrow, "they have an interrogation room in Timber Creek?"

Hayley laughed. "I'm not really sure if that's the technical name for it, but it sure felt like it at the time. Then they called my dad and Stan, so I continued to lie off my ass saying that I was to blame. I did have a wild streak back then, but I had a bright future ahead of me. My dad knew I wouldn't have screwed that up, and that I wasn't a thief. So, he totally saw through me. He stared down a very frightened Declan the entire time."

Gavin shook his head. "The man's got a lot of restraint."

"My dad is protective in his own way, but fairly low key and pragmatic. I think he knew it would all resolve itself."

"What happened next?"

Hayley hesitated. "I'm gonna skip ahead now if that's okay, because I'd rather not say the next part."

"Oh, come on. You've come this far, may as well go all the way."

She cringed. "Such a coincidental choice of words," he heard her mumble. "Gavin, I'm afraid if I tell you, you'll murder him. I don't want to live with that kind of guilt, and I'd miss you way too much if you went to prison."

"Did he take your virginity then dump you?"

Hayley gasped "How did you guess?"

Gavin gave her an incredulous look. "It's a Declan story, so of course it was going to take that turn."

"So yeah, we had sex that night. Even after all that, I slept with him. That's how stupid and lovesick I was. The next day they found proof that Declan had stolen the car. He begged me to talk to my dad about getting him out of it, and when my dad refused, Declan dumped me and got back together with Janie."

Gavin's jaw ticked. Just thinking about the fact that that smug mother fucker was inside of Hayley, let alone the shitty position he put her in, made Gavin want to find him and kill him, but he tamped down his anger. "I'm still not surprised, but yeah, I'm really gonna have to make an effort to stay away from him, because I do want to murder him in a slow and violent fashion."

"As you know, news spreads faster than fire on gasoline in this town, so I made him promise not to tell anyone, or my dad would cut off his balls and feed them to his dog. And then Hunter took me to prom. So, now you know why I don't like to talk about it and why I didn't want to tell you about it. It's not that I don't trust you, it's just something I'm not proud of."

"Hey, I get it. If anyone knows what it's like to do something you're not proud of, it's me."

Raindrops began to fall. He lowered his voice and looked at her. "My house is empty right now. I can make you forget all about that asshole."

TWELVE

Hayley

Hayley lay languidly in bed under crisp sheets, her restless hands roaming over warm skin as she imagined it was Gavin who was touching her. Indulgent and intoxicating, his touch was like an expensive bottle of wine that you never wanted to find the bottom of. He made her feel lust filled and alive. With him, every sensation was heightened, and each point of pleasure a live wire. Sex with him the night before had been the best of Hayley's life. They'd slept together several times over the past two weeks, taking advantage of the stable when an empty house wasn't available, and each time had been unbelievable. But opening up to him about Declan yesterday had detonated what few inhibitions remained. She'd only left his bed a few hours ago and already wanted more. Biting her bottom lip, she opened her nightstand drawer and pulled out her favorite toy.

Kinsley and Hunter's hoots of laughter from the living room split through her desire. She sighed, put the toy back in the drawer, and pulled on a tank top and sleep shorts before reaching for her robe. The plush fabric against her sensitive, tingling skin felt decadent. After sliding her feet into fuzzy slippers and tightening the belt of her robe, she made her way into their open-concept living room.

"Hey there, you naughty girl," Kinsley said, perched on a bar stool at the kitchen island with her hands wrapped around an oversized mug of coffee. "I'm assuming your date went well, since you slinked in here all covert-op style before the sun came up."

Hayley bit down on her smile a second too late. "Aww! Look at that smile, Hunt. She's smitten! Considering I had to man the boutique alone yesterday so you could hang with your boyfriend, I think I'm owed some details."

Ignoring her overzealous friend, Hayley walked to the kitchen, pulled a mug from the cabinet, and poured herself a cup of coffee, adding a substantial amount of pumpkin spice creamer.

"You two have been humping around town for weeks now, and I've gotten nothing from you." Kinsley pouted her bottom lip. "What kind of best friend are you, Hales, keeping this kind of information to yourself. I've had to rely on Hunter's gossip."

Hunter looked at Hayley and patted the empty spot next to him on the sofa. She eyed him warily before plopping down next to him, tucking her legs underneath her.

"Honestly, I should start writing romance novels." Hunter smirked. "You and your boy toy provide all the juicy content I need."

Hayley felt her cheeks flush as she ran her palm up and down the soft fabric of her robe. "I have no idea what you're talking about," she stated firmly, feigning innocence as she blew into her mug of hot coffee.

"I'll ignore that bullshit and go heavy on the tea. Everyone knows things between you and Gavin have been hot and heavy. You've been seen sucking face and copping feels all around town."

Hayley rolled her eyes. "That's an extensive vocabulary you've got there, Hunt. I think Emory needs to give you a refund."

"Ha, ha," Hunter said, pinching Hayley on the wrist.

"Ouch!" she yelled, pinching him back, just as hard. "Stupid small towns," Hayley muttered, rubbing the sore spot on her wrist. "Why can't people just mind their own business? And you two are no better you... pot stirrers."

"So, yesterday, when you left me high and dry at work, did you actually ride the horse or just play mount the stallion again?" Kinsley asked.

Hunter stood up and walked to the fruit bowl on the counter. "You are legit out of control with these horse references, Kinz." He tossed an orange in the air and turned back to Hayley. "So, purely from a research perspective, what does he have that I didn't? And are there wedding bells in the future?" he asked with a teasing grin.

"Hunt, I can assure you there are no wedding bells in the future." An image flashed into her mind then, Maddie walking in front of her throwing flowers, Gavin standing at the end of the aisle looking impossibly handsome in a tux. She shook off the ridiculous thought. "We do have a connection, but right now we're just having fun." But not so deep down, she knew it was more than that.

"I think we need another night out to really delve into this. Maybe some wine with your sisters will make you talk," Kinsley said, reaching for her cell. "I'm gonna make this happen."

"Hell no, Kinsley." Hayley jumped up to snatch the phone, but her nimble friend was too quick. Thumbs flying, Kinsley began texting Hayley's sisters. "Hayley Jackson is finally dropping her guard down and letting someone in. Speaking of letting him in, how's the sex?"

"She only asks in the spirit of research," Hunter added from the kitchen, peeling his orange over the sink.

They were like thirsty little wolves, eager for Hayley to drop a tiny sordid morsel. Shaking her head, she walked back to her room. "I'm not telling you anything, and I'm not going out tonight."

"They're in!"

In the end, Kinsley had won, and much to Hayley's displeasure, they were back at The Republic, joined by her sisters Amy and Candace, with Hunter in tow. Her younger sister, Lainey, was at home with a sick baby.

Hayley wished to God that there was another bar close by and had even begged them to go to the seedy one outside of town. But they had refused, adding that they had no interest in contracting hepatitis. That meant she was once again subjected to Declan the douche and his band of misfits. But, because she had just opened up to Gavin about what Declan had done, she found that her anger had dissipated and morphed into something more positive. She was learning how to trust again. A smile stretched across her face at the thought of Gavin's sexy smile, his fingers entwined with hers, his strong arm wrapped around her, his breath tickling her neck and making her giggle.

"Earth to Hayley! Oh, yeah. You were right, Kinsley. She's got it *bad*," Hayley's oldest sister Amy teased.

Apparently, a girls night *was* much needed, because beyond Hayley's crew's morbid curiosity over her love life, her sister Candace, who went by Candy, seemed to be going through a hard time. She was quiet, which was very unlike her, and stared down at the table with a sullen expression. Candy was dressed to elicit attention, which was also unlike her. Her mini skirt and low-cut, skintight top didn't leave much to the imagination. Hayley noticed that she and her sisters were getting quite a few curious looks, but she thought it probably had less to do with Candy's outfit and more to do with the town's increasing fascination with her love life. Hunter had been right, it seemed that all of her business was now public domain. She couldn't care less who knew but worried more for Gavin, knowing what a private man he was.

Unsurprisingly, Declan approached their table. Hayley had insisted they get a table instead of sitting at the bar, where there was easier access to alcohol and Declan's attention. A pretty redhead named Talia, whom Hayley had gone to high school with but didn't know very well, was waitressing that night, but Declan had apparently left the bar to Jake and volunteered to take their table.

167

"Evening. What can get for you lovely ladies?" he asked with a sadistic smirk and a wink. "Can I start you off with some drinks?"

They took turns ordering drinks and food. Hayley grimaced when Candace ordered a round of tequila shots. It was going to be a long night.

"Men are such assholes," Candace proclaimed, once they had gotten their shots. She immediately downed one of them and, when Hayley pushed hers aside in favor of her glass of Merlot, Candy downed that one as well. "Except for you, of course, Hunter."

Hunter lifted his shot glass. "Men are indeed assholes, and I am happy to be a part of this fine girl squad."

"Woo!" Candace exclaimed, slamming her glass down on the table. "I'm suddenly feeling very brave." She stood up and wove her way through the crowd, stopping to openly flirt with Declan's friend Sam. Hayley felt a pang of worry for her.

"Her hatred of men lasted all of thirty seconds," Kinsley teased. She took a sip of her fruity drink of choice before turning to Amy. "Are you still with your man?"

"Yes. It's not perfect, but we're happy. We respect each other and allow each other our freedoms. He likes fishing for hours; I like online retail. It works out pretty well." She took a sip of her Shirley Temple. It was her turn to be DD. "Until we see each other's credit card statements, that is."

The group of ladies went on bantering, eager for details about Gavin. Amy wanted to know about his character, while Kinsley wanted to know if he had any friends. Hayley resisted the urge to tell her she should get back with James.

Hunter took it all in stride. While he did interject here and there, he mostly just sat and listened to the ladies talk and occasionally typed on his phone. He had decided to stay in Timber Creek to draft his novel, and Hayley was really starting to worry that it would be less fiction and more of a biography on her love life. She may have to steal his phone and delete a few things.

A local country band started to play, and Candy was back at the table, insisting Kinsley and her sisters join her for the two-step. It was law in any country bar that when a two-step song came on, every woman had to show off their drunken dance skills. Kinsley caught on fast, being well-versed in New York's club scene. When Hayley caught a glimpse of Candace pressing up against Sam, she knew something was up.

Beau Davis's wife Mallory made eye contact with Hayley and flashed her a smile that didn't quite reach her eyes. She was a bullish woman who looked more like Beau's sister than his spouse. "Let's head back to the table," Hayley said, ignoring Mallory.

When they sat back down, Hayley polished off her glass of Merlot. She was sticking to wine tonight, no shots for her, but she had just finished her second glass and was feeling a little floaty.

"Let's take a selfie!" Kinsley proclaimed tipsily. She picked up Hayley's phone. "Is your password still Chic? Awwwwweee! Look at this picture! Hales, you guys are so freaking cute! Hunter, look!"

"Is that a batting cage behind you?" Hunter asked, examining the photo. "Where the hell were you guys?"

"Okay guys, this is just between us." Warning bells went off in Hayley's head, urging her to keep her mouth closed, but the wine was making her loose lipped. She had debated using that picture as her wallpaper, but she was proud of her man.

"He played pro ball for the Padres, but he doesn't want anyone to know about it. His daughter doesn't even know, so you have to promise, promise, promise me you'll keep quiet."

Hunter's jaw dropped. "Seriously?"

"I bet he looked great in a uniform," Amy said, biting into a chicken wing.

"Kinsley, what are you doing?" Hayley asked, reaching for Kinsley's phone.

"Googling Gavin Taylor and Padres baseball. Holy shit!" she exclaimed, fingers scrolling, eyes widening.

"Can I get you ladies anything else to drink?" Hayley thought Declan was acting suspiciously sweet, especially for someone who'd just had his ass handed to him in a fist fight with her boyfriend two weeks ago.

"We'll have some fried Oreos," Amy responded.

Kinsley made a gagging noise. "Fried Oreos?"

"They are *so* good Kinsley. You'll love them," Amy said.

"If there's one thing the South can do right, it's fried Oreos," Beau's wife Mallory spoke over Kinsley's shoulder. She dragged a chair next to Hayley and sat down with an obviously fake smile planted on her masculine face. "I'm so sorry about what happened with your boyfriend at the fair. Beau can be such an ass at times, but I think they all learned their lesson. I know Austin learned his. Madison Taylor is not to be messed with."

"I appreciate you saying that, Mallory..." Hayley trusted this woman as far as she could throw her. "Let's just put all of that behind us and move forward."

"Sounds good to me," Mallory replied with a saccharine sweet smile before taking a swig from her beer bottle. "So! I heard something about a cute picture?"

Kinsley brought Hayley's phone to life. "Kinsley! Give me back my phone."

"Oh, I'm sorry. I don't mean to pry. I've just heard so much about you two. Mallory scrutinized the picture and handed the phone back to Hayley. "Y'all are adorable. Damn, he sure is a looker. Are y'all baseball fans?"

"Um, yeah. Something like that." Hayley slid her phone back into her purse, which was hooked on the back of her chair. "Watch my stuff will ya, Kinz? I'm gonna hit the ladies." Hayley rolled her eyes as Kinsley's attention was distracted by a decent looking, middle-aged guy in a cowboy hat who looked like he belonged in a Camel Cigarette ad.

"Shots at the bar ladies!" she heard Jake yell. "On the house! Amy, you too. One shot's not gonna hurt you!"

On her way to the bathroom, Hayley saw that her sister was doing shots with one of the local married men. Hayley marched over to them and grabbed Candy by the arm, pulling her into the empty restroom.

"Candy, what the hell is going on with you? Are you and Rhett having problems?"

"He's been cheating on me," she hiccupped, "so I'm gonna cheat right back."

"Are you serious? *Rhett?*"

Candy hiccupped again. "Yup. Been going on a while, apparently."

"How did we not know about this already?"

"I don't know; he's a cop. Probably pays people off. If I hadn't overheard him on the phone, I would never have found out."

Hayley rubbed her sister's arm. "Sweetie, I am so unbelievably sorry. But how will the way you're behaving tonight make things any better?"

Her sister remained quiet, playing with an unruly sequin on her mini skirt. Hayley could see the sadness and frustration in her hazel eyes. "You jumping from bed to bed isn't going to help matters. All that's going to do is cause more innocent people pain. Harry Belton? Really, Candy? His wife is Peggy, the sweet librarian? Not okay."

Candace sniffled. "I wasn't really gonna do anything with Harry. He was more for attention. I'm an aging, stay-at-home mom with three kids under ten whose husband is cheating on her." Ripping a paper towel from the dispenser, Candace dabbed the tears beneath her eyes. "I think I'm entitled to a little fun." She covered her face with her hands. "God, Hales. What the fuck am I gonna do? I don't have the money to fight him in court."

"Talk to Daddy, he'll help you. He's always been there for us."

"I don't have the heart to tell daddy, he really likes Rhett. He got ordained just to marry us, for Christ's sake."

Hayley pulled her sister in for a hug. "We have your back, Candy. You can lean on us, okay?"

"I hope this Gavin guy isn't a dirtbag," she mumbled into Hayley's hair.

"He's not."

"Well, you look really happy."

The two sisters walked out of the bathroom together, linked arm in arm. Declan walked past them and winked.

"Don't worry, Hales. I would *never* have sex with that dick bag."

Hayley belly laughed. "That's great to know, Candy."

When they got back to their table, Hayley was relieved to see that Mallory was gone.

Amy took in Candace's makeup-streaked face and Hayley's arm wrapped securely around her. "Okay, what the hell is going on with you."

Candy hiccupped, yet again. "I'll tell you on the ride home. Can you take me now?"

Amy looked at Hunter, knowing she was his ride as well. "Looks like I'm heading home, too. He lifted his glass to Hayley, proffering a toast. "Hales, you have a lot of phenomenal things going for you. As much as I jest, I'm sincerely happy for you."

They clinked glasses and Hayley's thoughts drifted back to Gavin. His eyes, his smile, his palms splayed over her skin, his naked body. And then, as if he morphed from her thoughts, the bar door opened and there he was, beckoning her with a sexy finger crook and a smile.

THIRTEEN

Gavin

The sky loomed grey over low hanging clouds. Prater had the men winterizing pipes and storing hay in the loft for winter, protecting them from moisture with tarps. Feeling the strain of a cold, industrious morning, the four friends walked inside the toasty-warm ranch house and sat around Gavin's kitchen table for a lunch of burritos and beer.

Taking a generous bite, Gavin savored the cooked-to-perfection carne asada and fresh avocado mixed with rice and beans. "Maybe we should open an authentic Mexican restaurant. I'd totally back your wives. We could call it Marianca's."

"Ha! Oh, believe me, we've tried," Alejandro replied. "They're actually thinking about going to school for their nursing degrees."

"Really? That's great! Good for them." Gavin leaned back in his chair with his arms crossed behind his head, full and content.

Miguel went to the sink and washed his plate, dried it, and put it away.

"Maricela's got you trained well, my friend," Gavin said.

"Expecting someone, boss?" Miguel asked, hitching a thumb to the living room window.

He whistled through his teeth. "Nice vehicle."

The beer bottle in Gavin's hand hovered, forgotten, near his lips. He shot Prater a look. They both stood up at the same time and went to the porch.

Xavier exited the SUV, joined by none other than Jamie Mack. "Of course he'd bring Mack into this. A closer for the closer," he muttered to Prater before striding down the porch steps.

Stretching his back, Jamie's wanderlust gaze took in the ranch. "This is a gorgeous homestead, Gavin. Very impressive." He stepped forward and extended his arm, smiling his million-dollar smile when Gavin accepted his handshake. "Good to see you again, man. It's been way too long."

"Good to see you, too, Jamie," Gavin said warily while shooting daggers at Xavier with his eyes. "Unless Xavier brought you here to bully me into signing a contract. If that's the case, you two can go right back where you came from."

Jamie smacked a hand on Gavin's back. "We aren't at the contract stage yet, but from what I hear, baseball is where you belong! I came all this way, the least you can do is throw one session for me." Gavin noticed the man's hair line had receded significantly over the last five years, otherwise; he hadn't changed a bit. Same expensive suit, spray tan, and relentless desire to get what he wanted.

"Absolutely!" Miguel exclaimed, taking the porch steps three at a time.

"We have never seen him do this," Alejandro added, fast on Miguel's heels.

Prater came to stand by Gavin, a silent wall of moral support.

Gavin rubbed his forehead and sighed. "Xavier, you do know that beating a dead horse is a pointless waste of everyone's time, right?" He turned to Jamie. "I'm sorry he dragged you all the way out here, Mack. It really is nice to see you, but we have to get on with our workday." He shook Jamie's hand again. "Whatever it is you thought you were going to accomplish today isn't going to happen."

"What if we promise not to pressure you," Xavier said, pulling in his chin and holding his hands up in front of him in an act of contrition. "Just throw for him, man. For old times' sake."

Gavin's annoyance grew as his eyes moved over the small circle of men, willing him to relent. He gave an exaggerated roll of his eyes. "If it means you assholes will leave me the hell alone, fine."

Everyone hooted and hollered, except for Prater who simply patted Gavin's shoulder with just a hint of smile, his atta-boy face. A simple, fatherly gesture that said more than words could.

When the men gathered in the pole barn, Gavin sat down and took off his boots, replacing them with his old cleats, which hung on the cage behind him. He unbuttoned his plaid work shirt, exposing his abs. Xavier and Jamie whistled their approval.

"Hot damn, someone's been staying in shape," Jamie said, clapping his hands together. "This is good, Gav. This is very, very good."

Ignoring him, Gavin slipped on a t-shirt and walked into the cage to stretch out, then he went through his cadence to ensure elasticity and looseness. Xavier picked up the catcher's mitt and joined him.

"Alright, fastballs only. If you feel up to it, you can mix in the sinker," Xavier said, kneeling into position.

Gavin nodded and took a cleansing breath, while everyone outside of the cage found themselves a place to sit. Slinging the ball forward, he blocked out the words of encouragement from his entourage. Once he received the signs from Xavier, he threw, again and again and again. Adrenaline surged through him, lunging him forward as he put his all into each throw with laser sharp focus. *Smack!* Nothing sounded sweeter than the ball hitting the inside of a catcher's glove. Xavier called for a fastball inside, but Gavin shook him off. He was thinking sinker. From outside of the cage, Jamie Mack stood up and linked his fingers through the chain link, assessing Gavin intently. Gavin's fingers once again turned the ball until he found the right grip. Winding up, he kept his eyes firmly on the glove. *Smack!* Confidence he hadn't felt in years rose like the sun breaking through a dark horizon.

"Well, fuck me," Jamie muttered after Gavin's final pitch. He looked at Xavier. "I thought you said his head wasn't in it." He whistled. "That was a thing of beauty."

Xavier approached Gavin and spoke into his ear. "You still drinking?"

"Not lately."

"Oof!" Xavier knocked the wind out of Gavin with his tight embrace. "Good for you, man. I can see the difference." He patted his back before pulling him back at arm's length. "You've got it. I'm telling you."

Miguel and Alejandro were at a loss for words for once, seemingly shocked by what they'd just witnessed.

Swaggering like he did when they first met a decade ago, Jamie Mack made his pitch. "Let's see you in action against some batters. Come to spring training and make the squad, you'll start out in Triple-A then be fast tracked back to the major leagues. Think about it. St. Louis is only four and a half hours away. You could go back and forth to the ranch, be here full time in the off season."

Gavin shook his head with a sardonic smile. "You guys are such fucking liars." He wiped his forehead with a towel and took a swig from the water bottle in his hand. "What happened to 'no pressure, we just want to watch you throw'?"

Jamie held his hands out to his sides, palms up. "Come on, Gav. You can't expect me to see something like that and not at least try. Think about it. Please."

"You really expect me to leave behind my ranch, my daughter and my..." he stopped himself from saying girlfriend. He was all in with Hayley, but they technically hadn't labeled themselves yet, and he didn't want to bring her into this, "to be on the road for months at a time?"

"I think Maddie would be proud and happy to see her daddy doing what he was always meant to do," Jamie said.

Gavin felt Prater's eyes on him as he kept his own to the ground. The man had a way of communicating with him without saying a word.

"Speaking of Madison, we'd love to see her," Xavier said.

"She'll be home from school any time now, which is why I'd like to conclude your impromptu visit now," Gavin said.

Xavier deadpanned. "Dude, you still haven't told Madison?"

"Don't start with me, Xavier," Gavin replied with a warning look.

"I'm sorry, man, I'm just having trouble understanding what the big deal is."

"It's my business. I don't need you to understand." But he knew Xavier was right. Even if he wasn't going to play again, it was time. Things had been better between the two of them since Hayley came into their lives. Tonight, after dinner, he was going to bring her here to the barn and tell her everything. Show her the pictures and share stories about her mother. His annoyance with Jamie and Xavier's visit lifted as he thought about how good it would feel to be transparent with Maddie. And how proud Hayley would be of him.

"Can we at least meet for dinner later? Catch up a little?"

Gavin's countenance softened as he put his flannel shirt back on and walked to the barn door. "I would really like to, but a nasty storm's moving in overnight. You guys may want to head out soon."

"I'm staying in Nashville this week with friends, Xavier and Ann as well, so it should be no problem to grab a bite to eat and head back before it gets bad," Jamie said, as the six men made their way outside.

Unable to think of a good reason why he couldn't accept the dinner invitation, besides wanting to spend time with Hayley, he conceded. He'd talk to Maddie after dinner and make it up to Hayley tomorrow. "I'll text you a little later to let you know when we're wrapping up here. What are you city boys gonna do in the meantime?" Gavin teased, as they made their way to the front of the house. Everyone stopped in their tracks when they saw the slew of vehicles that surrounded his house, including a NASHVILLE NEWS 7 van. Gavin blinked, eyes moving from the reporters headed their way to the men standing next to him.

"Did you guys do this?" Gavin's tone was sharp and accusing as he glared at both Jamie and Xavier. They shook their heads in unison, seemingly just as confused as he was.

The journalists and photographers flocked to them, peppering Gavin with questions. Panic tightened his chest as he pushed his way past them to his house.

"Are you thinking about a comeback?"

"Have you been grieving over the loss of your wife all this time?"

"Word has it you're dating business mogul and fashion designer Hayley Jackson? For how long and is it serious?"

Gavin made his way up the porch steps just as Maddie opened the front door. It looked as if she'd been crying. Her watery eyes widened as she processed the scene in front of her.

"Maddie, I need you to go back inside, okay? I just need a few minutes and then I'll explain everything."

He pulled the door closed and turned to face the media. His anxiety spiked. He wanted to run inside, but, instead, he stood frozen as they continued drilling him with questions; some about Maddie, whom they'd obviously just seen, and snapping photos.

Mercifully, Jamie stepped forward to deflect. "Look, I don't know what you think is happening here, but I can assure you all that the sole purpose of our visit was to simply catch up with our good friend Gavin Taylor. We have been reminiscing about the old days and taking a tour of his beautiful ranch. There is nothing to announce, and I'd ask you to respect his privacy. Thank you."

With that, Xavier opened the door and guided Gavin inside. Once the door was closed, he doubled over, performing breathing exercises he'd learned in therapy long ago, in an attempt to calm down.

"I don't know how they could have known we were here," Xavier said.

"I can tell you." Madison appeared in the kitchen. "I learned a lot about you in school today from that jerk Austin. He showed me Hayley's Instagram page and the tabloid photos. So, you were a famous baseball player, huh? I got asked so many questions and couldn't answer a single one of them because I don't know anything about my own dad." Madison's face crumpled, tears welling up in her eyes.

"Hayley's Instagram page?" Gavin's heart turned to lead and sank to his feet. It couldn't be true. She had promised him she wouldn't post that picture. He reached for his daughter, but she pulled away. "Madison, I was going to talk to you about all of this tonight, I swear."

"Yeah, right. Nice to know how important I am to you." Maddie ran to her bedroom, slamming the door behind her.

Gavin's phone vibrated ceaselessly in his back pocket.

"Look, I don't know what's going on, but I promise you, Xavier and I had nothing to do with it."

Making a beeline for the liquor cabinet, Gavin poured himself a generous amount of whiskey and sat down at the kitchen table. He shot back the drink and did a Google search of his name.

The first article to pop up read: *Gavin Taylor, former pitcher for the San Diego Padres, has been living a secluded life of mourning on a ranch in the small town of Timber Creek, TN. Seven years ago, his beloved wife, Carly Taylor, died, and his career derailed due to an accident involving a drunk driver. However, it seems he's found love again with New York-based fashion designer and hometown sweetheart, Hayley Jackson. A source close to the couple says the two have been inseparable since her return to her hometown from NYC two months ago.*

Gavin stopped reading when the front door opened and Jim, Miguel, and Alejandro walked inside. They had managed to wrangle the paparazzi back to their vehicles, fitting, considering they wrangled herds of cattle for a living.

"You boys care to explain yourselves?" Jim addressed Xavier and Jamie with stern eyes as he entered the kitchen.

Jamie spoke up first. "Sir, we were telling the honest to God truth when we said we had nothing to do with this."

"It was Hayley," Gavin said flatly.

"Son, there has to be an explanation," replied Prater. "I don't believe for one second that Hayley would do something like this."

"Seems pretty cut and dry to me, Jim. She posted it. It's her account."

"You could call her and ask for yourself," Miguel chimed in. "In my marriage I've learned never to assume. Communicate." Alejandro nodded in agreement.

The booze had already worked its way into Gavin's system, removing his filter. "You're right. I should call and ask why the actual fuck she would do this to me. Dammit, why does she feel the need to meddle in things she has no business getting involved in? I asked her not to share it, and she promised me she wouldn't! Now my privacy is out the window, and Madison is upset." He rested his elbows on the table with his face in his hands. "I let myself get too close…"

"Boys, I think it's probably time for you to go," Prater said to Jamie and Xavier.

They nodded in agreement. "I'll call you, Gavin," Jamie said. "And I'm sorry about all of this. Once again, we are just as confused as you are."

"We'll take care of the media if they come back, boss," Alejandro said, Miguel nodding in agreement.

Once the men left, Prater scraped back the chair next to Gavin and sat down. "It seems to me that you knew this day would come. You're gonna need to own up to it and be honest with Maddie. Regardless of if Hayley messed up or not, your priority needs to be that little girl that ain't so little anymore. Also, it's really not that big a deal. The paparazzi will die down. You made it clear enough you're not going back anyway, so I don't see these folks pestering you much from here on out."

Gavin worked his jaw. "It's the principal, Jim. She betrayed my trust." His phone buzzed next to him and Hayley's picture appeared on his screen. He turned it off and got up to pour another drink, cursing himself for putting his trust in a woman he hardly knew and not opening up to Maddie a long time ago. His nightmare had officially come full circle.

FOURTEEN

Hayley

"Okie dokie, doll. All the invoices are filled, payments remitted, and the numbers are looking fabulous." Kinsley walked out of the back room of the boutique with a skip in her step and a satisfied smile.

Hayley stood behind the counter checking her phone for the tenth time that hour. It was odd that Gavin hadn't texted her once that afternoon. Their sexy back-and-forth banter had been constant the past couple of weeks, so his silence was odd. She hated that feeling. That irrational tap, tap on the brain telling her that something was off. The paranoia of the scorned.

"Let's close up shop early. It's the perfect night to snuggle on the couch and watch movies. I would kill for an Irish coffee right now."

"What happened to Americanos only?" Hayley replied absentmindedly.

Kinsley slipped a black suede jacket off its hanger and tried it on. "Hunter made me a believer. And if it involves booze, I'm not partial. I need this jacket."

"A movie sounds good. Is it alright if I ask Gavin to join us?"

Kinsley had her bangs pinned back today. It was quite a shock for Hayley at first, as she didn't think she'd ever seen her best friend's forehead. She was growing it out as well, and it was already a smidge below her shoulders. She looked like a completely different person. *New town, new look,* she'd said that morning when Hayley stared at her for a full minute with her jaw on the floor.

"Sure, but that means I'm gonna need someone to get snuggly with too." Kinsley hung up the jacket and walked to stand in front of the counter. I was thinking instead of Jake, maybe Hunter would like to come over?"

"Sounds good to me. Although we'll have to take control of the remote before he does, or else we'll be subjected to hours of silent films while he fills in the commentary." Hayley gasped, slow to process what Kinsley had insinuated. "Wait. Are you telling me you're *interested* in Hunt?"

"Maybe…" Kinsley averted her eyes from Hayley's and began folding a pile of already folded t-shirts.

"Kinsley, *no.*"

She dropped the t-shirt she was folding, and her upper body deflated. "We're two consenting adults, so what's the big deal?" she said, followed by a sharp intake of air. Her eyebrows shot up to her new hairline. "It'll be our first Timber Creek double date!" She bounced on the toes of her Ugg's and clapped her hands.

"Absolutely not. Literally every fiber of my being is rejecting this, Kinz. He's a good friend of mine, and I don't want to jeopardize that. Things could get really complicated and awkward really fast." She picked up her phone to send Gavin a text about coming over to her place later.

"God, you are such a major buzzkill sometimes, you know that?"

They planted on smiles as they greeted a customer asking about puffy winter coats, which they didn't carry, followed by two adorable college gals who had driven in from Nashville looking for party dresses. An hour later the store was empty again, and Hayley still hadn't heard from Gavin.

"Let's get out of here," Kinsley said, shutting down the register. Now I'm thinking multiple bottles of rosé, a binge-worthy show, and some strong arms wrapped around me."

"Not Hunter's!"

"Fine, *God*. I'll ask Jake," Kinsley said petulantly. "What's with the far-off look of concern? You're being so dramatic about this."

"No, it's not that," Hayley said, clicking off the twinkle lights. She looked pointedly at Kinsley. "Although I'm *vehemently* against anything romantic happening between you and Hunt." The comment elicited an eye roll from Kinsley. "It's just kind of odd that Gavin hasn't texted me today."

Plopping down on the stool behind the counter, Kinsley rested an elbow on the glass top, chin in hand. "Maybe he's busier than usual. Weather is predicted to be pretty bad tonight, so I'm sure he's doing whatever those ranch guys do to get ready for a big storm."

Hayley relaxed, knowing Kinsley was probably right. But five minutes later her impatience got the best of her, and she decided to call Gavin. It rang once then went to voicemail. "I think he just kicked me to voicemail. Either that or his phone is off, but I doubt that's the case."

"Stop worrying! Damn, he's got you whipped," Kinsley said, walking to the back room.

When Hayley's phone dinged a second later she smiled like a schoolgirl in love when she saw that it was from Gavin. But her bright smile quickly faded as she read his text.

I thought I could trust you. How could you do this to me? We're done.

Hayley froze in place while her heart rate skyrocketed. "He's breaking up with me?"

"What?" Kinsley yelled from the back room.

Thumbs flying, Hayley texted him back with unsteady hands.

What are you talking about? Is this a joke?

She waited for what felt like an eternity for his response.

I asked you not to post that picture. And that caption? You outed me. Media got a hold of it and they came to the ranch. Now my face is everywhere. My phone's blowing up, Madison knows everything. It's a shitshow.

"Everything okay out there?" Kinsley said.

Gavin, I swear to God I didn't post that picture. I would never do that to you.

Hayley held her breath while she waited for his response.

I don't believe you.

Hot tears pricked her eyes. Gavin's name appeared on the screen. "Gavin?"

"No, he's gone to the barn."

"Madison?"

"Why didn't you tell me first?" Hayley's anxiety grew when she heard the hurt in Madison's voice.

"Tell you what?" Hayley could tell she was crying. "Maddie, please talk to me."

"The picture of you and my dad on your Instagram account. A bunch of people came here to interview him and take pictures. My dad was a famous baseball player, and I didn't even know. You've been in our lives for like five seconds and he told you everything. My dad hates me, and I hate you!"

"No. Madison listen to me, please. It's not like that. We all just need to take a breath and talk about this."

"I have to go."

When the line went dead, Hayley shook like a tree, tears slipping down her cheeks. She fumbled with her phone, dropping it twice before finally managing to pull up her personal Instagram account. Sure enough, there was the selfie, posted to her account nineteen hours ago with the caption: *Me and my sweet ex-Padres ballplayer, the one and only Gavin Taylor, living the dream in Timber Creek, TN.* She hadn't seen the notifications because Gavin had teased her the other day about how much she was on her phone and bet she couldn't stay off social media for 48 hours. If she won, he said he'd go to Sunday dinner at her house. So she wouldn't be tempted, she'd moved the social media app icons to a different place on her screen. She didn't have near as many followers on her personal account, but it was public and had been shared. A lot. There were already thousands of likes and comments. When she saw the unusual number of twitter notifications, she knew it had been posted there as well. Hayley covered her mouth and inhaled a sharp breath. *How?*

Kinsley emerged from the back room with a WTF is going on expression on her face. "Was that Madison? Hayley, what's wrong?"

"There's no way I posted this." Hayley paced the storeroom floor. "I wasn't drunk, and I barely touched my phone."

"Posted what?" Kinsley asked, walking to stand next to Hayley.

"Someone posted the selfie of Gavin and me to my Instagram and Twitter accounts, making it look like I outed him as a former player. He didn't want anyone to know, he hadn't even told Madison yet, and now he's pissed as hell at me because he thinks I did it. Maddie's mad at me too."

Going back over her time at the bar, Hayley could only piece together one logical explanation. She turned to Kinsley and narrowed her eyes. "Did *you* do this?"

Hurt crossed over Kinsley's delicate features. "You think *I* did this?" she squeaked out, incredulous.

Hayley scraped her fingers through her hair. "No! Yes! I don't know. You had my phone; you know my password. Are you jealous of Gavin and me?"

"Hales, I'm gonna forgive you for this because I know you're really upset, but please know that I would never do that to you. You are my closest friend. I'm not jealous of you, I'm happy for you."

Hayley sighed and pressed a hand to her forehead. "I'm sorry. I know you wouldn't do that." She put both hands on Kinsley's shoulders and looked at her intently. "But I need you to think hard. At any point during my time away from the table did you leave my phone at the table and walk away?"

The look on her friend's face confirmed her fears. "Jake was offering free shots at the bar. I only talked to him for a minute, and your phone was on the table when I got back. Hunter and Amy were there at the bar too."

"But I remember putting my phone in my purse." *Declan.* Jake provided the distraction and Declan fucked with her phone. "It had to have been Declan. That's the only other explanation."

"But he doesn't know your password, how could he have gotten into your phone so fast?"

"I don't know, but I'm sure as hell about to find out." Hayley stormed out of the store and made her way across the street to The Republic. There was only one customer sitting at the end of the bar, looking like he'd seen better days. Declan was behind the bar, shining glasses.

"Hey there, Jackson, a bit early for a drink. Margarita or wine today?"

"Is Stan here? Tell me fast."

Declan set down the glass he was wiping and moved his head back, arching a confused brow. "No…"

Hayley proceeded to walk behind the bar, open her palm, and swing it at Declan's face. Kinsley ran through the door just in time to pull her away before she hit her intended target. Declan turned beet red with shock and anger.

"What the fuck is your problem?" he seethed.

She pointed an accusatory finger in his face. "Why can't you leave Gavin the hell alone?"

Declan walked from behind the bar to the door and motioned for the girls to follow him. Once they were outside, he got in Hayley's face, arms bowed up at his sides.

"Don't ever walk into my place of business and take a swing at me. I don't care who your family is, that was disrespectful."

That may have been the most hypocritical statement Hayley had ever heard. "Ha! You wanna talk about disrespect? You broke into my phone, captioned, and posted a picture of Gavin and me on social media because somehow, I don't know how, but somehow you found out about his past and knew what kind of shitstorm would follow. You're such a jealous piece of shit!"

"Pfft, *hell* no, I'm not jealous. You are way too high maintenance, city girl."

"Well why else would you do this to us? You've been swinging your dick around for the past month because you're threatened by him. And then you found out he played pro ball and it made you feel less than, so you pulled this shit?" A sob ripped from Hayley's chest. "Do you know what he has been through? His wife died, Declan. He lost his pitching career. I don't care if he wasn't born in Timber Creek and used to drink too much. He's a good guy who was dealt a shitty hand in life, and he didn't deserve this."

Declan dropped his head, scratched the back of his neck, and sighed. "Look, I admit I played a part in it. But I didn't actually do it, and it wasn't my idea."

Kinsley spoke up. "So, you admit that you had Jake offer us free shots at the bar to get me away from her phone?"

He held his hands up in front of him. "Yes, but that's all I did. I promise. He's not well-liked around here."

Hayley gasped. "Mallory."

"That bulldog-looking bitch," Kinsley added.

Declan's silence let her know she'd hit the nail on the head. Mallory had been creeping nearby and must have heard them talking. And overheard Kinsley say Hayley's password.

"Hey, he messed with her husband and her son. You know that doesn't fly around here. The boys and I didn't trust him, so we did a background check and looked into his past. But I swear to God, Hayley, once I saw what he'd been through I immediately backed off. That shit's messed up. But Beau and Mallory were out for blood. She wanted your phone to look for something to embarrass you guys, but she overheard you talking about how he didn't want anyone to know about his past."

Hayley covered her face with her hands. "Oh my God."

"I'll fix it, okay?"

"You'll fix it? Declan, the damage has been done, there's no fixing this!" Even in her livid state, Hayley took a second to register the fact that Declan offered to help.

Kinsley pulled on Hayley's arm. "Hayley, honey, let's go home and cool off."

"Oh my God, they're here." Hayley pointed to the line of cars along with a news Van headed right for them. Hayley ushered Kinsley and Declan back into the bar to wait until the coast was clear. Fortunately, Kinsley had already closed up shop, because the media was now surrounding the store, peeking through the windows.

Once the media had surmised that no one was there and left, Hayley and Kinsley left the bar without a word to Declan and made their way home, just before it started to rain. Hayley sat on a bar stool in the kitchen, fluctuating between crying and staring straight ahead in shock. Kinsley uncorked a bottle of wine and poured a generous amount of its contents into two wine glasses and slid one of them in front of Hayley, who immediately chugged the entire thing.

"He's totally overreacting," Kinsley said. "This will be old news in a day or so. When it quiets down, you'll talk to him then."

Hayley twirled her empty wine glass around by its stem. "Maybe I shouldn't. I'm to blame for a lot of this by opening my big mouth about his ball career, but I can't have him going to the same dark place every single time something bad happens. The fact that he actually thinks I would post that picture on social media hurts like hell." She gave a resigned shrug. "Maybe this is as far as we go."

"I can't tell you what to do. Just know that he's definitely gonna come crawling back to you on his hands and knees, because I'll go tell him myself that that bitch Mallory did it," Kinsley said, refilling Hayley's wine glass.

"No. Promise you'll let me handle this, Kinz."

She walked over to Hayley and wrapped an arm around her. "Or we could leave it alone and go on a rich-bitch World Tour and hit Cancun this winter."

Hayley sniffed, wiped her eyes, and held her glass high. "Here's to being a rich bitch wintering in Cancun."

FIFTEEN

Gavin

Gavin tossed another log into the brick fireplace and watched the fading flames come alive again as rain dinged furiously off the tin roof. Sitting down on his recliner, he poured himself a glass of bourbon. Old habits die hard, and the events of the past week had brought his whiskey habit back to life like a log to a flame.

It was Halloween. Trick-or-treating was a no go because of the weather, but June was taking Madison to a Halloween party at the town hall and then back to her place to stay the night. Things were tense between him and Madison, to say the least. A break from his daughter's sour countenance, which was butting heads with his brooding one, would be a welcome thing.

When Madison emerged from her room, Gavin was already two drinks in. She stood in front of him, and he blinked, slow to process the meaning behind her strange costume. But then his eyes narrowed in on Carly's Padres cap on her head. Fake blood covered Madison's entire face and was splattered across her t-shirt and jeans. Her blue eyes cast an icy cold glare. Gavin's heart stopped beating.

"I thought I'd go as mom. How do I look?" She rested her hands on her hips. "I'm sure at this point everyone will guess who I am."

Gavin stood up and gripped the arm of his chair for balance, dizzy with both alcohol and anger. "You think this is funny?" he roared.

"Oh, does this make you mad?" She looked down at the bottle of whiskey. "Maybe you should drink some more. See if that helps."

Gavin pointed in the direction of her bedroom with a trembling hand. "Go back to your room and change. *Now.*"

"Or else what?" She folded her arms in front of her, daring him to act.

"You're done with Hayley and the clothing line."

Madison screwed up her face. "Oh, I'm pretty sure you already killed that."

He knew she was right. When he had calmed down enough to try and talk things out with Hayley, she wanted nothing to do with him. He assumed the sentiment extended to his daughter as well.

"Do you hate me because I look like her?" Madison's voice caught in her throat. "Is that it?"

The question took him by surprise. He was quiet, unable to answer her. Not because the answer was yes; of course he didn't hate his daughter, but right now she looked so much like her mother, and he'd give anything to erase the images of that night. They had been a constant in his life for so long, projecting across his mind day after day and night after night, and he hated the man he had become because of them. Being with Hayley hadn't taken them away completely, but it had given him hope. When he was with her, they faded to the background, like ambient noise. For the first time, he'd thought that maybe he could find the peace he'd lost on that horrible night. He'd started to think that maybe they could build a life together, the three of them. But he'd gone and messed things up, once again, by getting angry and not listening to her side of the story or giving her the benefit of the doubt. She cared about him; he was sure of that, and she wouldn't have betrayed his trust like that. He sat back down in the recliner and squeezed his eyes closed. "Madison, I don't hate you. But I need you to wipe the makeup off your face and put your pajamas on. You won't be going anywhere tonight."

"I wish you had died and not her." A sob tore from her throat as she turned and walked back to her room, slamming the door behind her.

"So do I, Maddie," he whispered, pouring himself another drink.

A sharp crack of thunder shook the house. Gavin's eyes flew open. His heart pounded like a drum in his chest. He felt nauseated, remembering Madison's costume and the things they had said to each other. He brought his phone to life to check the time. Half an hour had passed since his altercation with Madison, but it felt like he'd been asleep on the recliner for hours. He scrubbed his hands over his face. The front door opened, and the Praters scurried in, hunkered down from the storm, and soaked to the bone carrying huge trays of food and a large tote bag.

"Oh my stars, this storm is shaping up to be a real doozy," June said, setting the trays of food and the bag on the kitchen table. She took Jim's rain-soaked coat from him and slipped out of her own, setting them both out on the porch. "I thought I'd bring you two over a tray of my famous lasagna, along with some garlic bread and double chocolate brownies," June said, when she walked back inside.

It was so like her to always think of them, Gavin mused, standing to stash the bottle of whisky in the cabinet underneath the TV.

"Six inches of rain expected," Jim said, pulling a coffee pod from its box in the cabinet. "It's a given that we'll see quite a bit of flooding. Turning out to be quite the lightning storm, too."

"Where's Madison?" June asked, lifting the tin foil off the trays. A mouthwatering cheesy, garlicy aroma filled the room. "I apologize in advance for the bags of candy I brought. That little candy monster will want to eat most of it tonight," she chuckled.

"She's in her room," Gavin said in a clipped tone, walking into the kitchen. He had called June before he fell asleep to let her know Madison wouldn't be going to the party, which had been cancelled anyway, due to the severity of the storm, but was too emotionally spent to give her any details. June knew how hostile things had been between the two of them, so he was sure she'd guessed that whatever happened wasn't good. He leaned a hip against the counter and raked a hand through his hair. "You're welcome to talk to her if you like. Obviously, things have been extra tense as of late. For all of us."

June pursed her lips and pulled a knife from a drawer. "Ah, yes. Well, at least everything is out in the open now," she said, cutting the lasagna into square portions. After wiping her hands off on a dish towel, she rested her hand on Gavin's back. "It's gonna take some time, but I have faith that everything will be okay," she said with a wink and a smile. "I'll go check on her and see if this deliciousness might tempt her to come out."

Gavin gave her a small, grateful smile. "Thanks, June."

He filled a glass with water from the sink and looked out the window. A brilliant flash of white lit up the kitchen, followed by a booming clap of thunder. "I hate thunderstorms," he muttered, "Zeus is probably scared shitless." Another bolt of lightning lit up the sky and he frowned, pressing his palms on the edge of the sink and narrowing his eyes at something moving in the distance.

"Jim, I thought we had everything buttoned down. The barn door is wide open."

Jim walked to stand beside him. "Dammit. Wind must have loosened it."

"Gavin!" The panic in June's voice punched him in the chest with a shock of adrenaline. He and Jim ran to Maddie's room. June was standing by herself with a worried look on her face, pointing at the open window. The curtains flew on a gust of wind. Rain showered the windowsill and the carpet below it.

"Where could she have gone?" June asked as she slid the window closed, concern laced through her words.

"I don't know," Gavin said, curling his hair into his fists as he paced the room. "I... I was asleep... I didn't hear anything."

He took a deep breath in an attempt to steady his nerves and think rationally. And then, the obvious answer came to him. He and Jim looked at each other knowingly. *Pegasus.* Racing to the back door, shoving their feet into rain boots and grabbing their heavy coats and flashlights along the way, they ran to the barn. Sure enough, Pegasus's stall was empty.

"Shit!" Gavin shouted, running to Zeus's stall. But he knew that his stallion was way too spooked to be of any use to him.

Running outside of the barn for clues with Prater fast at his heels, Gavin spotted puddled horse tracks leading towards the woods where the creek ran. The thick tree line would prove difficult to drive the side-by-side through. And then, as if by cosmic design, he looked up to see a white horse galloping towards them. Gavin was flooded with relief until he registered that Madison wasn't with her.

"I'll take Pegasus and follow the trail," Gavin shouted over a sharp smack of thunder.

Jim nodded. "I'll follow you in the side-by-side."

Gavin quickly mounted Pegasus. Lightning danced across the sky. Pegasus reared up, but he gripped the reins tightly. "Take me to Madison, girl," he yelled into her ear.

The rain fell in sheets now, cold and soaking through his clothes to his skin. It was slow going, almost zero visibility as they sloshed through brush and deep, mucky puddles. Every few feet he screamed Madison's name over the commotion of the storm.

And then there was a break from the noise, as if time stopped for a moment. He heard a small voice. Gavin urged Pegasus forward, past the fallen trees and branches that tore at his clothes, all the way down to the creek bank. He yelled Madison's name again. The driving rain lost some of its momentum, improving visibility, and he made out her tiny form, huddled against a nearby tree.

"Madison!"

Dismounting Pegasus, Gavin bit down on the end of the flashlight and was quick to find a sturdy branch to knot the mare's reins around. He ran to his daughter, flashlight in hand, and knelt in front of her, cupping her face in his hands. She was covered in mud and soaked through. Blood oozed from a deep cut on her forehead, mixing with drops of rain and fake blood that ran in streaks down her tiny face. Once again, his mind went back in time to seven years ago and he was frozen in place, staring at her. The image of Carly–bloody and broken, the image that haunted his dreams, flashed before him. He ripped off a portion of his drenched shirt and held it to his daughter's head. "You're going to be okay, Carly," he said. "I'm going to save you." A sob ripped from his chest as he scooped Madison up into his lap and cradled her.

"Dad?" Madison said weakly, staring up at him, her small hand resting on his arm. "It's me. Madison."

Looking down at his daughter, he separated memory from reality and squeezed her to him as if she were his lifeline. Because she was. She was all that he had left, and she meant everything to him. "Madison, are you okay?"

"My head hurts so bad. Pegasus got spooked and reared. Knocked me off. I passed out for a little while… didn't know where I was when I woke up. It was so scary." Her chin wobbled as she began to cry.

"Shh… you're going to be okay. I've got you." Gingerly, he picked her up. She winced and told him that her left arm was sore. She didn't have on a jacket, and he saw that there was a deep red scrape slashed across her forearm. Fortunately, he didn't see any evidence of broken bones. After placing her on Pegasus's saddle, he unleashed the reins and swung his tall frame behind her. With one arm wrapped securely around her waist, he directed the mare through the brush. Jim was nearby in the side-by-side,

196

the lights of the vehicle illuminating their way. When they reached the side-by-side, Gavin put Madison in the passenger seat. Jim drove her to the house, while Gavin followed behind on Pegasus.

After five hours in the emergency room, the doctor determined that Madison needed stitches on her head and arm and had suffered a minor concussion. He said she would be fine, but that they would need to monitor her for the next 24 hours.

When they arrived home in the early hours of the morning, June cleaned Madison up, put her in her pajamas, and tucked her into bed. Gavin laid beside his daughter, her head resting on his chest and her bandaged arm wrapped around his middle.

He watched her as she slept soundly, overcome with love for her–his precious gift. She was all he had left in this world. He couldn't go back in time and make different choices, erase the years of selfishness and neglect, but he could choose to be different now. Stroking her hair, he swore to himself that he would do whatever it took to make things right. There would be no more lies, no more omissions. He would be the man she needed him to be, and they would move forward and navigate life as a team.

Having his child in his arms filled him with a peace he didn't think he'd ever felt before. He let sleep pull him under, deep and dreamless. When he woke up hours later, Madison was still asleep. The midmorning sun slanted in through the bedroom window, the calm after the storm. He carefully brushed the hair from Madison's head, cringing when he saw her stitches. She stirred, burying her head in his chest. His heart swelled at the physical connection, the bond between parent and child. He gave in to it then, and he let himself sink into the feeling. Hot tears escaped his eyes and streamed down his face, but he didn't wipe them away. He wanted her to see his vulnerability, open and raw.

Her eyes fluttered open, and she looked up at him through long lashes. The sun cast an angelic glow on her face. "I'm sorry for running off," she said, her voice craggy with sleep. "That was really dumb of me."

He held her closer, not wanting to say anything more about it for now.

"You called me by her name," she said. "You called me Carly."

His body tensed. He knew Madison felt it as he watched her hopeful face fall.

It's time.

He took a deep breath, releasing the tension from his body. "I met your mom at a party when we were in high school. My entire baseball team was there." He laughed softly. "A bunch of stupid meathead jocks looking for babes." Madison's eyes lit up as if she were hanging on his every word. "I remember, I was tired that day and didn't want to go, but I was the star attraction, so I was expected to be there. I ended up hiding in the garage, playing pool by myself." He looked down at Madison and smiled. "And then, suddenly, as if from nowhere, there she was in the doorway. She walked into the garage and picked up a pool stick, challenging me to a game. She was so cool and sure of herself."

"And then what happened?" Madison asked. "You asked her out?"

Gavin chuckled. "No, she asked me out. Man, I was a goner. One date was all it took for me to fall head over heels in love with her. I knew she was the only girl I was ever going to want. We got married right after high school, and for the next few years I was traveling the world playing ball. But even during the times when we were apart, she was always with me. I'd see other guys cheat on their girls all the time, and I never understood it. It's extremely hard to maintain a marriage in sports, but we did it."

"Because you really loved each other."

Gavin nodded. "I loved her with every ounce of my being. When your mom died that night, it was like the best parts of me went with her. All of my confidence and joy. My mom left when I was five. My dad, your grandfather, basically abandoned me when I was seventeen. He put his military career above me and left me to sleep on whatever couch I could find. Your mom became my family. My rock. And then she was just… gone. She loved you so much and was so good with you. Better than I was. I've always felt like it should have been me, because she was without a doubt better for you."

Twin lines formed between Madison's brows. "I'm sorry I said that before, about wanting it to be you. I was just mad." He squeezed her closer.

"Tell me more," she said.

"We had such big plans for you. Wanted you to have a brother or a sister."

Madison gasped. "I would love to have a sister. A brother, meh."

Gavin chuckled softly.

"Do you think I will one day?"

A vision of a toddler with big honey brown eyes flashed through his mind and squeezed at his heart. "I don't know, Mads."

"So, how did we end up living here?"

"Your mom wanted to live on a ranch during the off season. She wanted you to ride horses and have acres of land to run around on. I wanted to honor her wishes, so after I knew my career was over, we moved here. Carly's parents… your grandparents…" he paused, not knowing how she would respond when he told her the truth, but knowing he had to. "They were vicious and blamed me for the accident. When I told them we were moving, they hired an attorney and lied to the media. Said that I had been drinking a lot and that I had been abusive toward you and your mom so that they could get custody of you. The irony was I didn't even drink until after the accident. The media was relentless, hounding me every day. Those vultures wrote lie after lie about me. I was eventually cleared, but they really did a number on my sanity. I can't even see a camera without experiencing PTSD. I'm so sorry, Mads. It was easier for me to say they were dead, but the easy way isn't always the right way. I'm learning that."

"They sound horrible, so I get it. I guess I also get why you drank so much."

"I always hoped that one day I'd wake up and everything would feel better. That I'd feel peace and hope. But that day never came, so all I wanted to do was numb the pain. That's why I drank so much, so I wouldn't have to feel my hurt and the hurt that I was inflicting on you."

"Maybe you should talk to someone."

"I think you might be right. But the first thing I need to do is make amends with the people I've hurt. None so more than you. I've been a terrible father, and I am sorry, Madison. For everything. For the lies and neglect, and just being an awful person in general. Even when I was dating Hayley and felt happier, I was neglecting you. I'm vowing to you now that you'll always be the most important person in my life. We can make all of our decisions together, as a team, and I promise I'll be here to support your dreams. Fashion, if that's what you want to pursue."

"What about your dreams? Are you gonna play baseball again?"

He drew his brows together. "No, Madison. I'm not going to play professional ball again. I want to build a relationship with you, not leave you."

"Are you good enough? If you wanted to play again, I mean?"

Gavin smiled down at her. "Yes. I think so."

"Well then, I think you should do it," she said resoundingly.

He cocked a brow and moved his head back to look her in the eyes. "You'd have to get used to sleeping in a hotel."

Sitting up taller, her eyes lit up with a flicker of excitement. "That would be so cool." She twisted up her face. "But maybe not all the time. Nana June and Papa Jim would miss me too much."

His smile grew wide, his heart flooded with excitement and relief. Suddenly, the impossible felt possible again.

"What about Hayley?"

Gavin's heart sank. "I think I burned that bridge."

"We both burned that bridge."

"What do you mean?"

She cringed. "Don't ask."

"I really, really like her, Mads. I think I may even love her. It's scary, feeling vulnerable like that again."

"I like her, too," Madison said. "I know posting all that stuff on social media caused a lot of problems, but maybe it was a good thing, because everything is out in the open now. A happy mistake."

Gavin tilted his head and gave her a hint of a smile. "Yeah. Maybe you're right." At the festival he'd told himself he never wanted to be responsible for hurting Hayley again. No matter what she did or didn't do, everything that had happened was ultimately his fault. Maybe one day she'd forgive him enough to listen to his groveling one last time.

SIXTEEN

Hayley

A little over a week had passed since Hayley left a seemingly remorseful Gavin standing alone on her front porch steps. Beyond *I'm sorry,* she hadn't let him get a word in edgewise as she faced him from the doorway with tear-stained cheeks, telling him all of the reasons why it wasn't going to work out between them and that they probably shouldn't see each other anymore. The pain of his accusation was far too fresh a wound to offer forgiveness and the chance to start again, if that's what he'd been after. She'd closed the door in his face before she had a chance to find out if the purpose of his visit went beyond apologizing for being a presumptuous ass.

Stupidly, she'd let herself get too close too soon, to both him and his daughter, so mourning the loss of them both cut deep. They had become genuinely important to her in such a short amount of time. But, although it hurt like hell, she even found it hard to breathe at times, Hayley knew that Gavin had a lot of mending and soul searching to do before he was ready for a serious relationship.

It was a lazy Sunday afternoon, and all Hayley wanted to do was spend the day in her pajamas, nursing a bottle of wine. She had just dozed off when the doorbell rang, jolting her awake like a defibrillator to the heart. The first thing Hayley noticed when she opened the front door was the stitched up, four inch cut on the right side of Madison's forehead. She felt a sense of motherly affection swell within her as tears welled up in Madison's eyes and she flung herself at Hayley, squeezing her tightly.

"I'm so sorry, Hayley," Madison sobbed. "I was so mean to you."

"Hey, hey," Hayley whispered, running her hand down Maddie's soft hair and kissing the top of her head. "You had every right to be upset. I'm not mad at you. *None* of this is your fault."

She pulled Madison back at arm's length with her head tilted, examining her forehead with knitted brows and a frown. "What in the world happened to you? Come in and sit down."

"It was a whole thing," Maddie replied, sniffing, and wiping her hands over her flushed cheeks as Hayley ushered her inside. Her tiny frame settled into the couch, just the toes of her pink fuzzy boots reaching the floor. Hayley handed her a tissue. "I was an idiot and ran away from home during the storm. Pegasus got scared of the thunder and threw me off. I fell and hit my head. Dad found me and I ended up in the hospital."

Hayley gasped. "Oh my God, that's awful! I wish someone would have called me." It made her heart hurt even more that Gavin hadn't thought to call her. But, considering she'd basically told him she wanted nothing more to do with him, she could understand why he didn't.

She sat down next to Madison and squeezed her hand. "But you're feeling better now?"

"Way better. And my dad and I talked *a lot*. He told me all about mom, how they met, and what it was like when he lost her. He's been in mourning all these years."

Hayley's heart ballooned with happiness at Gavin's breakthrough. She thought about what a rare quality it was in a man to love a woman as much as he'd loved Carly. In a world full of infidelity and betrayal, his faithfulness was what stood out to Hayley the most.

"About what happened, I hope you know I would never do that, Maddie."

Madison smiled. "We know," she said, an impish gleam in her ocean blue eyes.

"We?" Hayley's heart gave a hopeful beat, betraying her desire to stand firm in her pragmatism.

"Just give him a chance to explain. I really think he's ready to move on from his past and stop being such a dum-dum. I'm supposed to tell you he'll be waiting for you where you first kissed. But first of all, change out of that." Maddie curled her lip at Hayley's flannel snoopy pajamas. "Mama June and I will be waiting in the driveway to take you to the ranch. My dad said you could either take Pegasus or the side-by-side to wherever you guys went to play tonsil hockey."

Hayley tipped back her head and laughed. She loved the infectious, no-nonsense way Maddie had about her.

"Sweetie, I'm so glad that you and your dad talked. It makes my heart so happy for you both. I'm just not ready to see him quite yet. It would be too hard. I care about him so much, but you guys need time to heal without me distracting or interfering."

The determined look on Madison's face grew more resolute. "I don't see it that way. You make my dad happy, and I think he needs a lot of happiness in his life right now. I'm sure he'll still be a pain in the ass sometimes, but you and I can work together and keep him in line. We already know we make a great team." Madison stood up. "I'm gonna wait in the car with Nana June. You have five minutes." Before Hayley had a chance to respond, Maddie ran out the door.

Five minutes later, Hayley emerged on her front porch, dressed in jeans and a long-sleeved shirt. The rain had moved on, and the afternoon was bright, blue skied, and mild. Kinsley and Hunter were sitting on the porch swing, sipping from styrofoam cups.

Kinsley cringed and stuck out her tongue. "Damn, you southerners and your sugar. What this needs is some vodka."

"Ahhh…" Hunter said, taking a sip. "Ibrahim's sweet tea has a certain," he motioned with his hand, "je ne se quoi charm about it."

"By charm do you mean type two diabetes?" Kinsley teased.

"We southerners live in denial of the diabetes thing," Hunter replied. "I'll give up sweet tea when I become Parisian."

Kinsley nodded to June's sedan. "What's going on here?"

Inhaling a cleansing breath, Hayley shook out her hands. "Apparently Gavin's waiting for me at the spot where we first kissed."

Hunter smiled. "Home field advantage."

"Awww… Hales, that's seriously romantic!"

Hayley chewed on the tip of her thumb. "Am I doing the right thing by hearing him out?"

"If he wants to talk, talk," Kinsley said with a shrug. "What harm could it do?"

"I agree," Hunter chimed in, leaning back and stretching his arm across the back of the swing. "It's best to lay it all out there, especially when you live in a small town. These characters I'm writing in my book, all of their drama is self-made. Choose to be better than that. At least talk it through so there's no animosity."

Her eyes moved back and forth warily between the pair. "What's going on between you two?"

"Nothing serious," Hunter assured her, sliding his gaze over to Kinsley. "This gal's a good time, like too much dessert is a good time. A blast until you end up with a headache and massive amounts of regret," he said with a playful grin.

"Hey!" she said, smacking him on the arm and pointing a finger at him. "You better watch it. Remember, I've seen your penis. I can spread some rumors."

Hunter's face turned tomato red. "What the hell, Kinz?"

"Ew!" Hayley pressed her hands to her ears. "Aaaaand that's my cue. Wish me luck, guys."

"Luck!" they both yelled at the same time.

Thankfully, June didn't believe in awkward silence. The ride to the ranch was filled with laughter and pleasant small talk. She was one of those rare gems that didn't hold animosity, take sides, or think the worst of people. Once she loved you, she loved you for life, no matter what. And Hayley felt honored to be a part of that club.

Hayley rode Pegasus along the edge of the riverbank with the warm wind blowing through her unbound hair. She drank in the sight of Gavin sitting on the rock where they'd first kissed. He was wearing a Padres baseball cap, and there was a bouquet of sunflowers lying next to him. She couldn't help but smile. Inhaling a deep breath to center herself, she dismounted Pegasus and walked to stand in front of him with her arms crossed in front of her.

He pulled off his cap and ran a hand through his hair, one corner of his mouth pulled up into a sexy half smile that made the butterflies in Hayley's stomach turn into blue angel fighter jets doing aerial flips.

"Hey. Thank you for coming."

"No fair, using Madison to coerce me here."

Maybe it was because she hadn't seen him in a week, but she thought he'd never looked more handsome than he did then. The fitted t-shirt he was wearing stretched across his broad shoulders and accentuated the swell of his biceps. He had on light-washed jeans and his signature boots. The afternoon sun glinted off the flecks of blonde in his hair, and his eyes were warm and welcoming. He looked lighter, like a burden had been lifted. She knew it had to do with finally opening up to Maddie, and her heart filled with happiness for him.

"She wanted to apologize in person before I did, and I wanted to do my groveling at the place where my mouth met yours for the first time." He shrugged a shoulder. "I can't help it if my daughter's powers of persuasion are strong."

Hayley laughed softly; arms still crossed in front of her like a shield. "That they are."

"After our first kiss, I knew that your mouth was the only one I wanted to kiss for the rest of my life. I messed up that day, too, because I was scared, but I will always associate this place with finally turning the page to the next chapter of my life."

Hot tears burned the back of her eyes, and it felt like her throat was tied in a knot. "I didn't post that picture."

"I know you didn't," Gavin replied, "It was Mallory."

A tear slipped from Hayley's eye. "It really, really hurt that you would think I'd do something like that to you when I've only ever shown you support and compassion."

"It caught me off guard. I was upset." He held out his hand to her.

She sighed and dropped her arms before taking his hand and sitting down next to him. "I have to be honest with you," Hayley said, looking him in the eyes. "I am partially to blame. I told my friends about your ball career when we were at The Republic. Mallory overheard and took my phone from my purse when I was consoling Candy. She posted it to my social media accounts while Declan distracted everyone with free shots at the bar. I put two and two together and Declan confirmed it."

He brushed her hair behind her ear and smiled softly. "While I appreciate you telling me, none of that matters now."

"Who told you it was Mallory?"

"Believe it or not, it was Declan."

Hayley's eyes grew wide. Declan had shown remorse and told her he'd fix it, but she didn't think he'd actually do the right thing.

"He risked getting his ass kicked by Prater and me today by coming to us with his story, so I believe him."

She shook her head, disbelieving. "Never thought I'd see the day that Declan Reynolds grew a heart."

"I wouldn't go that far, but yeah, he surprised me."

Gavin pulled up his knees slightly and rested his elbows on his legs, pressed the tips of his steepled fingers between his eyes, and drew in a slow shaky breath. "I know I messed up. Again. And I know I've lived the last seven years as a horrible father and a waste of oxygen." He squeezed his eyes closed and shook his head. "Nope. I'm done with self-deprecation. I've been playing that tape in my head for too damn long, and all it's ever done is keep me down." He turned to face her again. "I have hope and faith in myself for the first time in a long time, and you are responsible for so much of that. You brought me to life again, Hayley Jackson. But I got so caught up in us that I didn't do what I should have done first, which was to have some important conversations with my daughter. I had planned to, the day she found out. And then the reporters came, and I was just so stressed out, knowing how much I'd hurt her yet again. I wasn't thinking rationally." His eyes glossed over with tears. "She had an accident. I could have lost her. That was all my fault." He grabbed her hand. "Please, hear me, Hayley. I'm not blaming you for my lack of communication with Maddie while you and I were together. That is on me. You have only brought us both encouragement, generosity, and light. And this, right here?" He motioned back and forth between them with his finger. "You and me? I believe in this. In us. I understand if you need some time, but I'm not giving up on us, Hayley."

"How do I know that tomorrow you're not going to freak out on me again? I care about you, Gavin. A lot. But I can't do the yo-yo thing with you. I have a career, people who count on me to not be lying in bed with a bottle of wine and a pint of Ben and Jerry's every time you decide it's too much, because that's what you'll do to me." She pulled her hand from his grasp. "Also, and please believe me when I say that I don't mean this disrespectfully, but from what you've told me about Carly, she was an all-around amazing woman. While she should be remembered and honored, I don't want to compete with her or live in her shadow."

A deep crease formed between his brows. "Hayley, no woman has caught my eye since Carly died, until I met you. How *weird* is that? It's almost as if she sent you to me." He brushed his fingers down her cheek. "Can we look at it that way? Instead of living in her shadow, we'll live in her light. I'm ready to honor her in a way that's healthy. The way she would have wanted. I will always love Carly, but I'm *in* love with you."

Hayley blinked, processing the words. "You're in love with me?"

He nodded slowly. Tears tracked down her face, all feelings of hurt swept away by the genuineness of his words and the look in his eyes.

"So, June recommended a therapist." He dropped his gaze. "She went for a while after her son died. I think I'm gonna start going, even if it's only for a few months to learn some coping skills. Help heal the underlying wounds and learn how to not live life white knuckling a bottle when things get tough. I had built things up so much in my mind over the years, thinking how awful it would be to have cameras in my face again and stories written about me. After what Carly's mom did, I had the right to feel that way, but I didn't do what she accused me of, and it was proven and made public. I was also in mourning, but I shouldn't have hidden away." He sighed. "I have a lot of work to do; a bridge to rebuild with Madison and with you as well, if you'll let me. I'm not expecting you to dive in headfirst, just give me a chance to prove myself."

She nodded, wiping her cheeks with her fingers, and then he leaned in and cupped her face, rubbing his thumbs over her cheeks and kissing her with as much passion as he did the first time.

Resting her forehead to his, she sighed contentedly before pulling her head back and frowning.

"What are we gonna do about Mallory? She's a brute of a woman, but I think I can take her. Channel the old Hayley Jackson who would wallop girls for messin' with Hunt."

Gavin let out a deeply timbered laugh, and she reveled in the sound of it.

"While that would be so incredibly hot, I think we should leave Mallory and Beau alone. What they did was wrong, but it helped me get my head out of my ass. I've already lived through the worst kind of pain, so there's nothing those two can do to hurt me now. I think we should take the high road and let it go."

Hayley arched a brow and smiled. "That's very noble of you."

He looked at her then for a long time, his gaze roaming over her face. "I missed you so damn much."

"I missed you, too. Hey, speaking of missing you, are you gonna play again?"

"I have to try out first." He held both of her hands between his. "But, Hayley, no matter how all of that pans out, trust me when I say that I've found my home in Timber Creek. With Madison, the Praters, Miguel, Alejandro, their families, and, I pray to God, *you*."

"Well, Mr. Taylor. You'd better say a prayer of thanks."

A wide smile bloomed across his face. "Really?"

She nodded, mirroring his smile. "Really. I'm so proud of you Gavin. And if finding home means Timber Creek, then I'm thankful too."

"If I make the team, I'll have to travel a lot, obviously, but I'll always come home. Sometimes Maddie will travel with me, sometimes she'll stay here with June and Jim. I don't expect you to neglect your career and leave the store behind for your crazy friend to run so you can hit the road with me."

Hayley laughed. "My Kinz is crazy, you've got that right. But she's also very capable. We're gonna hire a few people soon, so I'll be able to come to some of your games. Cheer you on. Kiss you big when you win, and make you feel better when you lose," she said with a naughty smile.

"First I have to make the club."

"You'll make it. If not for your ability, then for how hot you look in a baseball jersey."

Gavin blushed, and they both laughed. "Well, thank you for the compliment, but baseball is more than looking hot in a uniform. I'm twenty-nine, and all those damn twenty-one-year-olds are gonna be looking to constantly one-up me."

She ran her hand down his stubbled cheek. "I believe in you, Gavin Taylor. Even when you don't believe in yourself."

He kissed her softly, and she breathed in the smell of his skin, pressed her hand to his chest and felt his heart beat wildly, just for her.

"And I love you, too."

SEVENTEEN

Gavin

One month later

It was Christmas day at the Taylor Ranch, and everyone was decked out in festive pajamas. Miguel and Alejandro's kids were sitting around the tree, tearing open presents with Madison while the adults were gathered around them, snapping pictures and drinking Mexican hot chocolate.

"Dad, I love it so much!" Maddie had just opened the ornament he'd had made—a gold wreath frame with a picture of Carly holding her when she was two years old. Maddie stared at it for a long moment, her eyes pricked with tears, before standing to hang it front and center on the brightly lit tree. He also bought her a pair of vintage floral print Doc Martens that she went wild over. She'd squeezed him so tight his eyes nearly popped out of his head.

June had just brought out a tray of her famous cinnamon rolls when the doorbell rang. Everyone except for Gavin looked at each other with perplexed expressions, as they weren't expecting anyone else.

Gavin walked to answer the door with Hayley right behind him for moral support, just in case it was the press again. However, the last time they showed up, Gavin had openly kissed her for the cameras, told them he'd be at Spring Training, and wished them a Merry Christmas. He had been working out around the clock to get into competitive shape, and that included staying sober.

There was an older couple standing on the other side of the door that Hayley had never seen before. They were well dressed and formal looking.

"Merry Christmas, Mrs. Lawson. Mr. Lawson," Gavin said, motioning for them to come in.

"Merry Christmas, Gavin!" Mr. Lawson replied, stepping inside.

Hayley's jaw dropped to the floor.

"Thank you for inviting us," Madison's grandmother said stiffly, following behind her husband, brushing a fine layer of snow off the shoulders of her black pea coat. It was Maddie's first white Christmas, and Gavin was going to take her out to sled later, just the two of them.

"I'd like you to meet my girlfriend, Hayley Jackson."

"We're happy to have you in the family," exclaimed Steve, rather jovially, as he shook Hayley's hand.

Denise placed a hand on Gavin's arm. "I can't begin to tell you how sorry I am." Her large, pale-blue eyes filled with tears.

Her husband cleared his throat and nodded in agreement. "We want to make amends."

"I acknowledge and appreciate your words," Gavin said with a tight smile. "It will take some time, but I'm willing to work on it. For now, let's start with your granddaughter. Mads, I have another Christmas present for you!"

Madison ran to the entryway. "Madison, these are your grandparents," Gavin said, motioning to them.

Everyone was quiet, aside from Bing Crosby crooning *I'll be home for Christmas* softly in the background. Maddie stood stock still, and Hayley saw the wheels of her brain turning, trying to sort out how she should react. But then, Gavin and the Lawson's smiled at her reassuringly, and she ran to give them a hug. Hayley wrapped her arms around her boyfriend, the love of her life, and looked up at him, beaming with pride. "You're a good man, Gavin Taylor."

He kissed the top of her head and squeezed her closer. "Merry Christmas, baby."

EPILOGUE

Two months had passed since Gavin last walked into The Republic. Fried food and alcohol were poison for him now, but it wasn't pleasure that brought him there that day, it was business. *Maybe a bit of both*, he thought as he strolled into the bar with a smug smile on his freshly shaven face.

Hunter tagged along to make sure Gavin stayed on the wagon. Although they didn't have much in common besides their love for Hayley, the two of them had bonded in their own unique way.

They sat at the bar in front of Declan, who was yammering on about politics, trucks, and country music. Gavin hadn't realized just how much of a talker the man was, a good trait to have in the bar business, considering the fact that the extent of their conversations had been insults and dirty looks.

"You in for drinks?" he asked the boys, his mouth pulled up into a half smile. "Revenue hasn't been as solid since you started training."

"Very funny," Gavin said. "But yeah, your dad mentioned that profits have been down lately."

"I'll take whatever hair on your balls beer you've got on tap, man," Hunter said. Declan poured him a stout beer, ensuring just enough head, then slid the glass down to Hunter, who deftly caught it and took a swig.

A crease formed between Declan's brows. "You're talking to my dad now?" Ever since Declan owned up to the part he played in operation Take Gavin Down and outed Mallory and Beau, the two men had stopped

215

being complete dicks to each other. He had also apologized to Miguel and Alejandro for his racist comments. That didn't stop the verbal jousting and one-upmanship their testosterone egged on, but it was mostly in jest. Mostly.

"Better," Gavin beamed, sliding a stack of paperwork in front of Declan. "I bought your dad out this morning."

Declan flipped through the pages. It was a signed contract. He shook his head and narrowed his eyes at Gavin. "You motherfucker."

"Now hang on. I gave your dad a more than generous amount for this shit pit." Gavin grinned, letting him know he was teasing. "He's going to have a good retirement."

The bartender slid the papers back to Gavin. Grabbing a nice bottle of whiskey, he poured three shots and placed two of them in front of Gavin and Hunter.

"I'm not drinking," Gavin protested.

"Pfft. Bullshit, you're in the bar business now," Declan said, holding up his glass. "And for the record, I still don't like your ass."

"You should be kissing my ass. I'm the one who talked to your dad into making you an equal partner." Declan's eyebrows shot up his forehead. "I'll obviously need you to be in charge of the day to day."

Declan put down his glass and extended his arm to Gavin. "You've got yourself a deal."

"I just need one favor," Gavin said, lowering his voice.

"Of course," Declan mumbled, rolling his eyes as he lowered his arm.

"Your barmaid is screwing my future sister-in-law's husband. She needs to be shitcanned, like, yesterday."

Gathering glasses, Declan appeared to be choosing his words carefully. "Talia's a good waitress. What or who she does on her time is her business."

Gavin looked at him pointedly. "It's a matter of family."

"No offense, but Candace Jackson is a nutjob," Declan replied. "Her shady ass cop husband's been cheating on her for years, and their

216

relationship is toxic. He's pulled me aside more than once asking if I'd hire more hotties for the bar. I've talked to Talia and told her she was playing with fire, but I'm not letting her go." He grabbed Hunter's glass and poured him a refill. "She's a single mom in a shitty situation."

Not happy with his choice of words concerning Candace, but impressed with how Declan stood up for his employee, Gavin agreed not to press the issue. Things between him and Declan were cordial, and he wanted to keep it that way. He'd have to do some groveling with Hayley and her family, but, for now, he'd let it be. He and Declan shook hands and tossed back the shots.

With that taken care of, it was time to focus solely on Spring Training.

March 1

Facing the New York Yankees in the first game of the preseason meant the Cardinals' rookies were getting their asses handed to them. Three home runs had been given up in five innings, giving the Yankees a 7-0 lead.

Twenty minutes ago, Gavin's former teammate-turned-pitching-coach Joe Massey gave him the signal to start warming up. Don't overthrow, Massey told him. Stay focused and calm. *Easier said than done, and he knows it*, had been Gavin's thought as he took a series of cleansing breaths he'd learned in therapy.

Gavin had been guaranteed a spot with the Memphis Redbirds, but had impressed the powers that be enough during his workouts to throw with the big-league club during spring training. He signed a one year $75,000 contract with St. Louis shortly after. Now it was time to prove himself.

Tonight, Gavin was a regular relief pitcher. It wasn't his traditional closer role; he was there to throw some garbage innings to see what he was made of, and prove that he could be serviceable to the club. A stellar performance tonight would show that he was worthy of the chance he'd been given.

Thousands of Cardinals fans graciously stood and clapped as he made his way across the field, recognizing the long road he'd been on getting back to majors. He'd sat down with a journalist from ESPN to share his story candidly, and they aired his interview last week. His fan's support, as well as the support of the people of Timber Creek, was overwhelming. Even Beau had contacted him, expressing his remorse.

Gavin tipped his hat to the crowd, overcome with emotion.

When he got to the mound, he circled it, scuffed his cleats against the dirt and knelt down to run some dirt through the fingers of his left hand, just like he used to.

One of the Yankees most dangerous hitters was up to bat. Thrown with too much adrenaline, Gavin's first pitch sailed above the batter's head, causing him to fall on his ass to avoid being hit. His second pitch didn't fare much better, as it went wide and outside the strike zone. Seeking to correct, Gavin slowed his delivery, throwing an ill-advised fast ball to the inside corner of the plate. The batter ripped on it, sending it high into left field and just foul.

From the dugout, Xavier called "Time," to pay Gavin a visit on the mound.

Gavin blew out a hard breath. "Sorry, Xavy, I've got the jitters."

Xavier patted him on the shoulder. "Hey, it's okay. The fact that you're here speaks volumes. You're doing great, man. I just want two things from you."

Gavin nodded. "What are they?"

His manager and friend pointed to Madison, Hayley, and the Prater's, who were standing up in the stands, clapping and shouting their encouragement. They were dressed head to toe in Cardinals gear, aside from Maddie, who was wearing her mom's Padres cap. She was jumping up and down with her arms wrapped around his girlfriend's waist, and

Gavin's heart swelled with pride. Hayley and Madison made such a great team. They finished designing the *Sassy Chic* juniors' line a week ago, and he couldn't have been prouder of what they'd accomplished together.

Tonight he was going to ask Hayley Jackson to marry him. Madison and June had offered to help him plan the perfect proposal, but he decided that all he needed was a ring and the right words. But, because it was impossible to put into words just how much that woman meant to him, he'd have to show her as well, even if it took him all night. He'd booked a fancy suite just for the occasion.

"*Familia*. Take a look at your precious family, and soak in their enthusiasm, energy, and love. And then just be you on the mound. You know who you are, and you know what you can do. Now, show them." With that, his manager jogged back to the dugout.

Gavin inhaled a cleansing breath and reset into his stance. When the catcher flashed the signs, he was transported back in time, to those defining moments in the last game of his young career. It felt like a lifetime ago that he'd been that cocky twenty-two-year-old with everything in front of him, not knowing that his world was hours away from shattering to nothing. But he'd been so young then, so devastated over the loss of Carly and void of any parental love in his own life, he hadn't realized that the most important part of him was still alive. He looked up at his daughter, smiling with so much love and pride for him. Tonight he was playing for her.

Understanding the selection, Gavin nodded. He went into his wind-up and delivered. Surprised at the pitch location, the batter hit a weak pop up.

Feeling loose with one out behind him, Gavin felt adrenaline give way to confidence and command. He threw with laser sharp precision and accuracy. Each pitch improved his velocity and location. He made the next two batters look like rookies. When the umpire yelled strike three on the third out, Gavin pumped his fist in his glove and roared.

His family went wild in the stands. He fell to his knees and sobbed like a baby. They'd lost the game, but this particular game represented so much more than a simple win or loss. It was a real chance to start again, playing the game he was born to play. He kissed the tip of his index finger, touched it to his heart, pointed at his daughter, and then at the sky. Carly would always be with him, cheering him on. But those four remarkable people in the stands were his foundation, and this game his destiny, for a time. And no matter what happened tomorrow, he would never again give up on what was important to him.

ACKNOWLEDGMENTS

Gina Lynn Arivett:

I would like to thank my husband, Aaron Arivett, for his unconditional love and support throughout our twenty-three years together. Marrying you was the best decision I have ever made. My love and respect for you truly only grows stronger with each passing day. Thank you for providing such an amazing life for us and our children. Thank you for believing in me, encouraging me, and picking up the slack so that I could fulfill my dream. You are a kind, loving, selfless, hilarious, rare gem of a man. I'm so proud to call you mine.

Thank you to my amazing kids Caleb, Lainey, and Nathan for being your wonderfully unique selves, and putting up with your frazzled mom who walks around the house like a zombie after hours of writing. I'm so honored and proud to call you my children.

Thank you to Nicole Green and Leah Logan, my forever besties, for your love and friendship. Thank you to my mom, Patricia Gentile, for your precious heart, words of encouragement, and for always believing in me.

Thank you to our amazing editor, Amber Koontz, for your invaluable help. Thank you to my sweet sister-in-law, Stephanie Arivett, for being our last-minute beta reader.

Christopher. There are rare moments in life when things just click. Reconnecting with you a year ago felt serendipitous, and then meant be.

The timing was exactly right. For years I knew I wanted to author a novel more than I wanted to do anything beyond being a wife and mother. But not having a degree and not believing in myself cast so many doubts, realizing I had a tall mountain to climb in order to grow and learn enough to actually pull this off. Because of your amazing ability to tell a story and imagine characters in a way I never could, you make me want to dig in my heels and fight tooth and nail to bring your stories and characters to life. I couldn't have gotten this far without you. Your words of encouragement and belief in me were the reasons I was able to accomplish this. We've come a long way from our youth group days, haven't we? I'm so proud to call you my writing partner and my friend. Here's to the first of many more to come.

Christopher Huntingford:

I want to thank God, the architect and creator of life. You've transformed my life in ways I never thought possible. You have set my course on this river of life, and from it I hope to never stray.

To my wife Stacy. You have always believed in me. You've taught me to take risks and to be adventurous. You're the perfect partner on this river we're traveling, with destinations unknown. I acknowledge I wasn't living until I married you. I'm okay with that because now you're always by my side. We've been through so much. Even when we were separated by two thousand miles, you were always in my heart. I love you mostly.

For my kids Wyatt and Tori, it is my hope that you will be wildly successful beyond your dreams, but remember it stems from desire and passion. You can't create a life worth living without it. Also, video games and the internet aren't the real world. You need to touch, taste, smell, and feel everything.

Kristin, I want to acknowledge all the times you've been there for me. You're less a cousin, and more like a sister to me. Remember that you're an inspiration to so many people. I love ya!

I want to thank my parents for pushing me to do things I didn't want to do. I guess it worked out? True growth is found outside of your comfort zone, suffice to say you have all modeled that for me.

Gina. What the actual eff? It's been twenty-five years, but it definitely hasn't felt like it from the start of this adventure. You're a great writer. You take the skeletons of stories and ideas that I have, outlines and concepts, and weave brilliant threads into them, breathing the stories to life. You are a master painter with words. You are the yin to my creative yang. I appreciate your feedback, organization, patience, and dedication to this artistry. Here is to many more books between us.

Amber Koontz! Thank you, Ice Queen. And just like that, while I was wasting time playing a video game, you came along to save the day with your rock star editorial skills. Many thanks!

To all my friends and acquaintances, you are the inspiration behind my stories. They are yours.

88124794R00142